**"Leave me alone. Don't
you understand your
meddling's going to get
both of us killed?"**

"Four people have died already. You can't walk away from that."

"Yes, I can. And I will."

"Henry will be glad to hear you're alive," I said, trying a new tack.

"Don't talk to Henry."

I'd struck a nerve.

"Don't tell him I'm alive. Please. I beg of you. He's got nothing to do with any of this. I —I want to resolve this before I see Henry again."

"Then come with me. Talk to the police."

"That's exactly what will get me killed."

"They'll put you under protective custody if you cooperate."

She glanced over my shoulder again. "I can't explain now, but I'm working this out my own way. Please. If I promise to meet you, will you leave then?"

"I'm not leaving here without—"

I didn't see her fist come at me. I barely even felt its impact. All I remember is stumbling and falling backward, then seeing the sky go dark. After that everything around me turned to soft black velvet.

Also by Gloria White
Murder on the Run

MONEY
to
BURN

Gloria White

A DELL BOOK

Published by
Dell Publishing
a division of
Bantam Doubleday Dell Publishing Group, Inc.
1540 Broadway
New York, New York 10036

The trademark Dell® is registered in the U.S. Patent and Trademark
Office.

ISBN: 0-440-21612-5

Printed in the United States of America

Published simultaneously in Canada

September 1993

10 9 8 7 6 5 4 3 2 1

RAD

ACKNOWLEDGMENTS

I wish to thank Carlotta O'Brien, C.P.A., and Jim Stanker, C.P.A., for sharing their expertise. If there are any accounting discrepancies in this book, they are not the result of misinformation from either of them, but rather my own creative license. Thanks (and apologies for the deep cuts) also go to the enthusiastic Leila Dobscha. Finally, for their infinite patience and generous encouragement, I wish to issue a very special and heartfelt thank-you to Jackie Cantor, Vicky Bijur, and, always, Ramos K.

For Terry, John, and Carmen. Hey, guys.

1

IN MY DREAM somebody was tap-dancing in the next room. And whoever it was, was doing a damn poor job of it. No rhythm.

And the hissing sound. What was that? My dream turned vivid and the hissing became words. Short, terse words, or rather one word—my name—run together over and over again in a frantic whisper.

"Ronnie-Ronnie-Ronnie . . ."

My eyes blinked open to the neon light that streamed through my window from the sign on the bar downstairs. The light pulsed on then off, on then off, but not in sync with the tapping. Not at all. I sat up, glanced around the apartment, then at the clock by the sofa bed. Three-thirty A.M. Shit.

The rapping got louder. It was coming from behind me, from the other side of my apartment door.

I scrambled out of bed, grabbed the hammer from under the sink, and looked out through the peephole. Somebody—a man—was hunched over out there, his face alternately crammed up into the crevice where the door would open—if I was going to open it—and peeking over his shoulder down the hall. A textured, burgundy-colored muffler covered up the lower half of his face and an Indiana Jones–type hat hid the rest of it. He was wearing some kind of expensive, weird leather jacket —ostrich hide or something—dyed beige.

I gripped the hammer and tried to make my voice sound big. "Who is it?"

He started, then shoved his mouth up to the crevice and whispered, "Thank God—Ronnie? Is that you?" A gloved hand pawed at the door, but I still couldn't see his face.

"Who is it?"

"Shhh! They'll hear you." He glanced over his shoulder again, then mashed his face against the door. "It's David. Open the door."

"David?" I sorted my mind for Davids. The name didn't mean a thing to me. Unless . . . I still couldn't see his face, but hearing the voice, things started to click inside my head—not thoughts but connotations. Negative ones. "David who?"

"Open up, Ronnie! For Chrissake!"

"Step away from the door. Let me see your face."

He jerked his hat off and took one step back. In spite of the panicked grimace and the sweat streaming down both temples, staining his cashmere scarf, my ex-husband's best friend didn't look much different from the last time I'd seen him two years ago. He'd gotten me named codefendant in an insurance-fraud case that almost cost me my license, and I guess he figured he was off my A-list, because I hadn't seen him since. He didn't go by "David" back then.

"Bink?"

He gulped air, nodded, and for a minute looked about to crumble. Usually his blond coloring, sharp features, and droopy eyelids gave him the same careless look that made women flip over Robert Mitchum decades ago, but tonight his terrified face would scare off even a hooker. He'd seen trouble, and the terror showed in his white face and the agitated working of his lower lip. The man was scared.

I gripped the hammer and threw the dead bolt.

Bink Hanover shoved his way inside, cut the lights, and slammed the door back shut before I could even move. He was breathing hard, filling the small room that was my home with the scent of liquor and the sour smell of fear.

I backed off a couple of paces and raised the hammer. "Turn the lights on, Bink." I said it firmly.

He threw his hand over the switch. "No! They'll see us."

"Who?"

"The tankers out there. She's with them and she's going to make them kill me just like they did Artie. You've got to help me, Ronnie! You've *got* to!"

He scanned the apartment. There was just enough neon light from the curtainless window for him to see the junk stacked on the table I use for a desk, the single chair, and the sofa bed opened up to fill the little bit of space I have in my one-room studio. His gaze stopped at the door beside the little alcove that's my kitchen. He started to move toward it. "This the back way out?"

"It's the bathroom, Bink. Want to tell me what's going on?"

"Where's the back door?"

I pointed at the front window. "The fire escape."

"Damn!" He seemed to be dancing, shuffling his feet back and forth like he wanted to run but had no place to go.

"What's going on, Bink? Who's after you?"

He finally seemed to hear me. "Man, Ronnie," he gasped. "You won't believe—this is life or death!"

Back in college every little crisis was life or death for Bink. Getting a date for the big frat dance, passing business econ, borrowing money to buy a surfboard for a weekend in Santa Cruz. I guess he saw the doubt in my eyes.

"No, no. I'm serious. Out there. Look out the window. They should be there by now."

As he came toward me, my hand tightened automatically on the hammer, but all he wanted was to push me toward the open patch of neon.

"Look out there. Do you see them? Maybe I lost them."

I edged up to the window and glanced down at Grant Avenue. The sidewalks were deserted, and both curbs were lined with parked cars. Directly below, in front of the Quarter Moon Saloon, the bar that takes up the whole first floor of my apartment building, sat a red Corvette convertible, double-parked, its driver-side door yawning open in the damp night air.

"Your Corvette?"

"Yeah." Nothing moved. "See them?"

I started to shake my head, but just then a navy-blue Mercedes screamed around the corner and squealed to a stop behind the Corvette.

All four doors burst open, and four huge guys—I could see why Bink called them tankers—jumped out. A fifth person, a woman, stayed in the car while the others headed straight for the Corvette, trying to keep their Uzis inconspicuous as they ran. Through the closed window I could hear their low, rumbling voices, but I couldn't make out what they were saying. They sounded mad, though. Mad as hell.

I turned to face the skinny, smart-aleck jerk who had saved my ex-husband's life by accident one night when a freshman college prank backfired and who as a result had earned Mitch's eternal goodwill and tolerance and had become his best friend all through college, his frat brother and roommate, best man at our wedding. The guy Mitch wanted eventually to set up an accounting partnership with. The same guy who'd cheated through all his exams, found every easy way out he could, and smooth-talked his way through whatever was left. The

Eddie Haskell of Stanford. I'd seen him in a lot of tight and not-so-tight binds before, but I'd never seen him in anything quite like this.

"What the hell did you do, Bink?"

2

HIS PINCHED EYES scanned my face. "Are they . . . ?"

I nodded.

"Oh, God." He sort of slumped, then made a faint-hearted run for the door and stopped midway, turning circles like a spinning top. "Oh, God! Oh, God. What am I going to do? You've gotta help me, Ronnie. She's gonna kill me if you don't. She killed Artie Spenger and now she's gonna kill me. I'm begging you."

I crossed the room and picked up the phone.

Bink froze. "What are you doing?"

He'd never impressed me as a genius, but I was starting to think he'd left his brain out in the Corvette. "You want help, Bink; I'm calling for help."

"The police?"

"Right."

"No!" He lunged for my arm.

I didn't mean to hit him so hard, but the reaction was automatic. I'd gotten my arm and almost my jaw broken on a case four months ago, and I'd been edgy about violence ever since. The hammer struck him in the pit of his stomach and sent him backward onto the opened-up sofa bed with a gentle *Umph!*

I would have apologized, but he caught his breath

too soon. "Shit, are you crazy?" he demanded, sitting up and clutching his midsection.

I took a step toward him and raised the hammer. "Come near me again, Bink, and I'll beat your brains out. Now, are you going to let me make this call?"

He ran a hand across his damp face. "You don't understand, Ronnie. These guys, they'll only come back unless— Talk to them. Tell them you're the daughter of the famous Ventana cat burglars. Tell them you know people—people who'll hurt them if they hurt me."

I just stared. No way was I going to call in markers and invoke my dead parents' name for *Bink*.

"Do it, Ronnie. She made them kill Artie Spenger and she'll make them kill me if you don't— This"—he motioned toward the window with his hand—"this is just the symptom, not the cause. They'll only get me later if the police scare them away now. Come on, Ronnie, just tell them who you are, and they'll back off."

I reached for the phone again.

"Don't call the cops, Ronnie. *Please.*"

"What'd you do to get this woman mad at you? Is she somebody's wife? Did you try to blackmail her? What did you do, Bink? Just tell me."

"I—I can't. They'll—"

"Try."

He started to sweat all over again. "It's real complicated, Ronnie. It's a mess."

He reached into his jacket, and his hand came out clutching an alligator-skin wallet. "Look, I'll pay. I'll pay you anything you want as long as you get me out of this alive—without the cops."

Poor fool didn't know *I'd* pay *him* just to get him out of my apartment.

"What do you charge? One-fifty an hour? Two hundred?"

He'd gotten my attention. I actually get forty-five an hour. And I'd just wrapped up a mind-numbingly dull case for an insurance firm and had no prospects of anything else. My calendar, as they say, was open.

"How about two-fifty?" Bink asked. "Look, I'll pay you two-fifty an hour. Just pull me through without any cops."

"They've got Uzis, Bink. I don't even own a gun."

He sort of slumped onto the bed and didn't protest when I picked up the receiver again. The dial tone hummed like a generator in the silence between us. I moved the handset into the light so I could read the numbers and got as far as punching the nine and the one before the line went dead.

"Shit." My first thought was that Bink had pulled the cord, but one look told me it wasn't him. His eyes were bugged out and his jaw flopped open.

"They're here," he squealed as I dumped the phone back on the table and sidled back over to the window.

"They're going to kill me!" His voice was about an octave higher than it'd been a minute ago.

Two of the guys were shredding the Corvette's upholstery like a pair of mad Dobermans. Another one was shimmying down the telephone pole across the street. I was pretty sure I knew what he'd done to the phone lines, since I'd pulled the same thing a couple of times myself. No long-distance tonight. No local calls either.

Bink started chanting in the dark behind me just like he had outside my door earlier. "Please—please—please—Ronnie—Ronnie—Ronnie—"

I tuned him out and watched the tankers spread out in different directions. They were scouring the parked cars, looking under and inside them and trying the doors on each of them. Any minute they'd be branching out to the doorways nearby. I turned to Bink. He was huddled by the table, sort of swaying back and forth like some kind of wild, cornered animal. *Thank you, Mitchell.* If my ex weren't in Tahiti, I would have driven Bink over to

Mitch's house in Marin and dumped his quivering car-
cass on Mitch's redwood deck.

Downstairs a couple of thugs disappeared under my
building's entry arch.

"How'd you get past the front door, Bink? Did you
kick it in?"

I looked over my shoulder. More swaying. More
chanting.

"Bink!"

He stopped and fixed me with a terrified look. "If
we're going to die, Ronnie, at least get your gun out."

"I told you, I don't own one."

Bink moaned. "No gun! Oh, *no.*"

"What about the front door?" I insisted.

"It was open, okay?"

"Unlocked?"

"Yeah."

"Did you lock it behind you?"

"Yes. What kind of asshole do you—"

Heavy feet tromped up the steps and passed outside
in the hall. Bink froze, and for once in his life he did the
right thing. He didn't say a word.

The tankers were talking, low, but not too low. "It's
Ventura, ain't it?"

I gasped, then said a silent prayer of thanks that
paranoid old Mrs. Parducci had insisted on apartment
numbers instead of names on all our mailboxes.

"Fuck if I know," another voice said. "I'm not the
one lost the fax."

Bink's hand went to his breast pocket and came
back empty. He mouthed the word *shit* and didn't even
notice my glare.

". . . bust the doors . . . ? We could . . ."

". . . nuts? . . . the cops . . . cellular phones
aren't out . . . Better send Junior back for it."

"Nah . . . bust in the bar downstairs . . . gotta
have a phone book."

The voices got faint and the stairs squeaked. Seconds later they popped out onto the sidewalk. Three seconds after that I heard the clear, tinkling sound of broken glass.

3

IT WOULDN'T TAKE a physics degree to make the short leap from Ventura to Ventana, and Veronica Ventana, Private Investigations and Security, was definitely in the book. I even paid extra for the bold type.

I threw on a pair of jeans and a jacket over the sweatshirt I sleep in, then tossed Bink a big navy-blue sweatshirt my friend Blackie Coogan had left in my closet.

"Put it on," I said. "Hurry."

Bink stared at the shirt at his feet.

"Put it on, Bink. I'll get you out of this, but you're going under your own steam. I'm not going to carry you."

He snatched up the sweatshirt and slipped it over his head. It was too big for him, but it covered his pastel leather jacket and altered his silhouette, which was the idea.

"Leave the hat," I told him.

He set it on the table, then turned his frightened gaze on me like some trusting little boy. It was that fleeting, seemingly guileless and boyish look that usually gave Bink a lot of mileage with women. Not with me, though. Not anymore.

I grabbed my backpack, looped the strap over my shoulder, and headed for the door. "Come on, Bink."

"But—" His eyes shot toward the window. "Are they gone?"

"It doesn't matter. Just hurry up and you'll be fine."

He nodded and made some sort of gargling sound deep in his throat. *Brother.*

I unlocked the door and squinted out into the lighted hallway. From the draft of cold air up the steps, I knew the downstairs door was ajar. I pulled Bink out the door, told him to lock it, then dragged him down the hall toward the back of the building.

We made it down the hall, through a door, up the steps, and right up to the little hatch that lets out onto the roof. That's where we ran into problems.

I was already out, kneeling over the hatch, helping Bink up, when he went stiff. He stood on the top step, doubled up with his hands clutching the edge of the hatch, and started swaying. His eyes seemed to glaze over and turn opaque.

I pulled at his arm. "Come *on*, Bink."

"Uh-uh."

"What's the matter?"

"Uh-uh," was all he said.

"What do you mean, 'uh-uh'?" His hands were shaking worse than they'd been downstairs, and now he was sweating all over Blackie's pullover. I was starting to think the guy had a death wish that included taking me down with him. He opened his mouth.

"A—aa-aak—"

Shit. "Acrophobia? You're scared of heights?"

He nodded, looking mortified, and started to back down. I dug my knees into the gravel roof, tightened my grip on his arm, and tried to pull him back up. "Wait a sec, Bink. It's okay. I understand. I *understand.*"

I didn't, of course. I was ready to kill him myself. Instead I talked and talked—listening all the while in vain for the crunch of my door being smashed in—until finally he crawled through the hatch.

The minute he planted all fours on the gravel surface, I heard the front door of the building slam shut. I left Bink huddled in a quivering fetal crouch by the hatch and scurried to the edge of the roof.

Three of the tankers had piled back into the blue Mercedes. The fourth one hovered by Bink's Corvette, watching the others like he was waiting for a signal. He had a gas can—the kind you get at the service station when your car runs out of fuel—tucked sideways under his arm.

The blue car's brake lights flashed red. Its engine turned over. The tanker stepped back, struck a match, and tossed it into the Corvette. The whole thing burst into flames. He jumped into the moving Mercedes as it zoomed past the Corvette, then up the street. They vanished around the corner before I could even get a glimpse at the license plate.

"It's over!" I shouted to Bink, then ran for the roof hatch. There was a fire extinguisher in the trunk of my car, but the car was parked in the alley a couple of doors down. If I hurried, I might make it before the gas tank exploded.

Bink rose, stumbling, unintentionally blocking my path. "W-w-what?"

"Out of the way!"

I reached around him to lift the hatch cover while he turned in bewilderment toward the street. "What's that noise?"

The fire was building up to a solid little roar down below, and the first black wisps of smoke were just now reaching us at rooftop level. Bink must have figured something out, at least subconsciously, because he grabbed my arm just as I started down the hatch.

"What is it?" he shouted. "What's burning?"

I stared into his wild eyes and opened my mouth to answer, but the explosion drowned out my words.

4

T HE FIRST THING that went through my mind the
instant I opened the door to my studio was gratitude. Bink hadn't locked up like I'd told him, so
the goons had just walked in. That meant my door was
intact. And they hadn't trashed my apartment.

I felt not respect but at least a warm regard toward
them for their consideration. Then I smelled the gasoline
and saw the note next to an open book of matches on the
table I use for a desk.

Without turning on the lights I angled the note so
the neon from the window lit up the scrap of paper.
"Catch you next time," it read. The fumes were nauseat-
ing.

"Open the window, Bink."

He had followed me into the room and was staring
through the glass at his smoking car. A tiny moan es-
caped him. Without turning, his eyes still fixed on the
mess outside, he said, "I just bought that car, Ron. You
know how much one of those things costs? Sixty K. *Sixty
K.* And I only drove it a week."

"The window, Bink."

He didn't budge. He just stood there shaking his
head and making occasional small whimpering sounds
while I tried ineffectively to sop up the gas off my mattress with a roll of paper towels.

"Still want to call the cops?" he asked after a minute.

"They're probably on their way."

Bink moved mechanically to raise the window. I gave up on the bed and stepped into the bathroom to pop open the porthole that gave out to the air well between my building and the one beside it. When I came back out, Bink was gone.

"Bink!"

I ran out the door and hopped down the steps three at a time. When I hit the sidewalk, I stopped and looked first left, then right. He was gone. Vanished.

It was three forty-five Tuesday morning, and the only signs of David "Bink" Hanover III's lightning predawn visit were the smoldering remains of his car and the distinctly bad taste he'd left in my mouth.

5

I COULD HAVE waited for the cops. I guess I *should* have waited for them. But a hot trail is a hot trail. Besides, I knew exactly what I was looking for: Since Bink's car was a molten pile of plastic lava, he needed a set of wheels. Unless he'd picked up some skills I didn't know about over the last couple of years, I didn't think he'd try to steal one by hot-wiring it. No. Bink would take a cab.

Half a block down Broadway I pulled my old blue Toyota left onto Romolo Place. But Jonah, the midnight-to-dawn-shift cabbie who usually parks outside the nudie joints to kill time between fares, was gone.

I wanted to think that Bink was the fare that had taken him away from his darkened neon nipples and quiet chained-up doors, but there was no way Bink could have made it there before I did. Not on foot, anyway.

I crisscrossed the neighborhood, looking for a desperate man in a dark sweatshirt, keeping my eyes open the whole time for the four clunks and the woman in the blue Mercedes. I kept at it for over an hour, but Bink didn't show, and neither did Jonah or the tankers.

Finally I pulled into Jonah's spot on Romolo Place and glanced at the clock on my dash. It was five o'clock. The sky was still dark, and a cold September fog had floated off the Bay and onto the streets. Everything was wet.

I sat there a minute staring out at Broadway's glistening pavement and tried to psyche out where Bink might go.

Ordinarily he'd run to Mitchell, my ex-husband. But Mitch was three months into a six-month leave of absence in Tahiti.

A girlfriend would be next. That one was tough, since Bink went through women like most people go through underwear. I didn't know who his other friends might be, but if they were anything like the ones he'd had in college, they were very much into soccer and golf.

Then there was his sister. His poor, long-suffering sister in a wheelchair. Barbara. Bink had talked Barbara into dipping into her car-accident settlement at least twice that I'd heard of just to clear him out of his "troubles." He'd go to her, but only as a last resort. Even a jerk has some pride.

Where was I on the list? I thought about it. Normally I wouldn't even be on his list. Unless . . . Mitch must have told him to look me up.

I reached for the ignition, started the engine, and drove four blocks into the financial district to the nearest pay phone. I rummaged through my bag for my calling card and Mitch's number in Tahiti.

Thirty-seven numbers and ten rings later I got a lousy connection and a groggy Mitch on the phone.

"Wha? Huh?" *Crrrrrrrrishshshsh.* "Hello?"

"Mitch. It's me."

"Ron?"

"Yes." My voice echoed over the line, so I could hear myself speak a second after I'd finished.

"What time is it? Damn, Ron, it's three in the morning."

"Did you send Bink Hanover to see me?" I heard

my voice say, . . . *to see me?* Then there was a long pause.

"The Binkster? Yeah!" Mitchell's voice perked up. "I faxed him your address. I know he can be a pain in the neck sometimes, but I thought you could give him a hand. He got in touch, huh?"

"You could say that."

"I know he didn't save *your* life—"

"And I haven't saved his fifty million times like you have. When are you going to call it even, Mitch?"

"He's changed."

"Right. Listen, Mitch, what kind of trouble is he in? Why'd you give him my address?" . . . *my address?*

"You sound angry."

I was, but I wasn't about to admit it to Mitch. If I did, we'd have to talk about it until he was comfortable that we'd "cleared the air." At ten dollars a minute, or whatever the call was costing me, I didn't want to have another one-on-one, heart-to-heart open communication like he always insisted. "I'm not angry, Mitch. He's spouting off about some murder and he's disappeared. I need more information."

"Murder? Wow, it must be worse than I thought. Hang on, let me get the fax he sent me." Across the wire I heard papers rustling. "Here. Here it is. 'Mitch, old brother, I need your help. I'm in a jam but I can't leave town. I need a relationship liaison, a sweet-talker to help me clear things up. If I can get past this glitch, buddy, I'll have money to burn. Fax me back fast, my life's in the lurch. D.W.H. III.'"

"That's it?"

"Yeah. Who did he say was murdered?"

"Art Spenger. Know him?"

"Isn't he an attorney?"

"I don't know, Mitch. I never heard of him before tonight. Listen, did you actually talk to Bink?"

"Sure. But you know the Binkster, it all sounded

half-baked. I couldn't make much sense out of what he was saying. He sure didn't mention murder. It was something about somebody was after him."

"Did he say who?"

"All he said was some idiot was going to blow his one shot at making it big and that he couldn't leave town. I offered to come back and help him out, but he was real cool to that. I asked if it had to do with something at the office or if it was personal, but he wouldn't say what the deal was. He just wanted a name, so I gave him Georgie Sander."

"The P.R. guy?"

"Yeah. Bink said the whole thing'd probably be history in a couple of days."

"When was that?"

"Last night. I tried him later when I remembered Georgie was in Palm Springs for the month, but all I got was his answering machine. So, just in case he was into something dicey, I faxed him at the office and gave him your address. I thought you'd be happy for the referral."

Under any other circumstances I would have been. It was the first time Mitch had actually sent somebody to me, somebody who wasn't offering me a salaried job in some other field. Maybe he'd finally come to terms with the fact that I was going to be a P.I. no matter what he thought. Maybe eventually he'd even finally figure out we weren't married anymore. It was a small victory, but Bink sort of threw a bad light on it. "Thanks," I said.

"You're not happy, Ron. I can hear it in your voice."

"Forget it, Mitch. I'm fine, okay? Just tell me, do you know why Bink didn't go to the police?"

"No. And I don't think you're fine, Ronnie. I think we need to talk about this."

"Not now. What else did he say?"

"Why not now?"

"It's not a good time, Mitch."

"There's never a good time. Ronnie, we've got to

talk. We've got to keep channels of communication open."

"Why? We're not married anymore."

"We're friends, aren't we?"

"At this rate, not for long."

Mitch answered me with total silence. I knew the tactic. Mitch was good at it. Silent reproach. It took me only a couple of seconds to feel lousy for hurting his feelings. But I was angry too.

"Listen, Mitch, I'm sorry. It's just that there are four guys with automatic weapons and a woman chasing Bink through town. The last place they saw him go was my apartment. He's disappeared now, and as far as they're concerned, I'm the one who disappeared him. Bink says there's been a murder and they're going to come to me, Mitch. I don't know a damn thing about what's going on. I don't even know where Bink is. So, in the scheme of things, whether I'm happy about your referring him or not and whether we sit and talk about it for an hour at ten dollars a minute isn't real important right now. Now, what else did Bink say?"

"Nothing."

Great. He was pouting. I wouldn't get anything else out of him until I'd spilled my guts one more time about all the resentments and unmet expectations we set ourselves up for when we got married. We'd discussed it in person, over the phone, in private, and in front of a priest and a marriage counselor. Finally eight years ago we'd gone over it all again with lawyers before a judge. None of it worked, and I wasn't about to run through everything again at five-thirty in the morning long-distance to Tahiti.

"Bury it, Mitch," I said, and hung up.

THE COPS WERE GONE when I drove back to the apartment. So was Bink's car. I guess they hauled it off to clear the street for morning traffic.

Nobody had filled my slot under the No Parking sign in the alley, so I pulled the Toyota in and curbed my wheels.

When I hit the top of the steps, I noticed the light seeping out from under Mrs. Parducci's door across the hall. I wasn't about to knock, though. She'd moved in a month ago and pretty much wore out her welcome by day one. I guess the phony "borrow a cup of sugar" gambit was mostly what turned me off.

I'd done my best to avoid her, but she made it tough. Every time I opened my door, she'd whip hers open and try to lasso me into a discussion about her "bad-seed kids" and how they never call and never come by. But since she'd been the one who insisted we take our names off the mailboxes—the sole thing that saved my life this morning—I felt like I at least owed it to her to rethink my attitude.

I was surprised she hadn't come out when Bink was scratching at my door earlier, but I figured I'd find out why soon enough. And just like the palace guard, as soon as I topped the stairs, her door flew open. She cannoned into the hall, cornering me in front of my door.

"Ronnie, dear, I thought I heard you come in."

I'm not sure what kind of crap life had dealt Enid Parducci, but none of it had beaten her down. Her chest was caved in and her face looked caved in, too, but she kept on butting in wherever she could, whenever she could. She was a hefty, bottle-black-haired woman in her late sixties with a gold-toothed smile and a grating voice. I had no idea what her past was, but I had the distinct impression that she'd love to share it with me if only I'd give her half the chance.

I looked at her now and her tired old face had new life in it, like maybe the excitement of the last few hours had given her something besides her creepy kids to talk about. She wore a flannel nightgown under a green quilted robe, and shapeless furry things on her feet. I don't think she realized she wasn't dressed.

"The police want to talk to you, Ronnie. They asked me to call when you came home, dear, but I thought I should let you catch your breath first."

Catch my breath? Neither one of us believed that one. She was stalling so she could pump me first. Still, I appreciated the break. It was another point in her favor. Maybe she wasn't so bad after all.

"Thanks, Mrs. Parducci."

I pushed my door open and sort of backed into my apartment, trying to use body language to keep her out. It didn't work. She charged in after me, snuffling the air with her caved-in, bulbous red nose. I took in a deep breath. The place reeked like a gas station.

"Smells a lot better in here now," she said, and pointed to a purple bottle on the end table by the sofa bed. "I loaned you my AirStick Refresher. The police wanted to close the windows, but I wouldn't let them."

"The police were in here?"

"Well . . . yes. When I told them about that young man waking me up, they wanted to see where he'd been. The door wasn't locked," she added defensively.

If I stood next to the open window, the fumes weren't so bad.

"They think it's drugs, Ronnie. Is it?"

"Can't say." But if Mrs. Parducci was right, I'd be wasting my breath talking to the police. During the two years I'd worked as a parole officer, I'd heard more than one cop say drug killings save the taxpayers money: no trial, no jail, no city-issued bullets. If the cops thought Bink was involved in a drug dispute, they'd just bow out quietly and let bad nature take its course.

Mrs. Parducci was studying me closely, like maybe she was trying to figure out if I could be some kind of junkie or something. *Let her wonder*, I thought.

"Do *you* think it's drugs, dear?" she finally asked. "My son, Albert, got into that LSD when he was in high school thirty years ago, and I don't think he's been right since. Awful stuff, drugs. That young man *was* peculiar, you know. Worked up, I'd say. At first I thought he wanted to kidnap you, but then I saw you drag him out of here and I knew you had things under control. But why did you take him to the roof, dear? Why did they set fire to his car?"

"Don't worry about it, Mrs. Parducci."

She'd been clutching something in her pocket the whole time we'd been talking, and now she brought out her balled-up fist.

"I found this on the roof," she said, spreading her fingers to expose a crumpled newspaper clipping. "Your young man must have dropped it. Think it's important?"

I smoothed the yellowed scrap and held it up to the light. It was a death notice. Spring Haven Mortuary announced the death of one Arthur D. Spenger. Like all death notices, it was short on detail: "Mr. Spenger died suddenly in his home in San Francisco on June 13."

That was one way to describe a murder.

"Who's Arthur Spenger?" Mrs. Parducci asked.

"I don't know, but I think I'd better ask Bink."

"Bink? Is he your young man?"

"Look, Mrs. Parducci, can I talk you out of calling the cops right away? I'd like to clean up a little first. Get rid of this mattress so I can breathe again."

"Well, I . . ."

I knew I was asking her to give up the biggest thing that had happened to her since, I guess, her wedding, if she'd had one, but I promised myself I'd do penance by listening to her spiel on about her ratty kids for an hour. Maybe two. But not now. Tomorrow. Yes, *tomorrow*.

Mrs. Parducci lingered in the center of the room, an inappropriate grin on her wrinkled old face. "It must be so exciting to be a private investigator."

I sighed. Maybe I was just making up excuses, but after Bink's rude wake-up call and Mitchell's touchy-feely-let's-talk-things-over rap, I just wasn't in the mood.

I set my jacket down on the chair, made small, shepherding motions with my arms, and moved toward the door. Mrs. Parducci moved with me and looked surprised when she ended up in the hall.

"Thanks, again," I said, and closed the door in her face.

7

"**S**O WHY are you telling me this?"

Lieutenant Harold "Philly" Post leaned back in his chair, stretched his legs out, and hoisted his feet up to his desk. He looked incredibly bored.

I was starting to think that maybe the plan—the inspiration—I'd had in the shower to unload Bink on the SFPD Homicide Department was somehow flawed. The way the scene had played out in my head, Philly Post had sort of fallen at my feet in gratitude for the tip.

I blinked and stared into Post's unreadable eyes, trying to figure out what I'd said to make him act so hostile.

"I'm giving you a material witness to a homicide, Post. You still work Homicide, don't you?"

Post put his hands behind his head, exposing huge stains of sweat under his arms, and stared back. "Yeah?"

That's when it hit me. "You're still blaming me for the graveyard-shift thing, aren't you?" After the last case we'd worked together, Post got assigned permanent night watch by his sour-grapes boss. "I told you I was sorry."

I tried a conciliatory smile. "Besides, you're back on days again now, right?"

"No thanks to you. The Captain still thinks I'm shit."

"Well, here's your chance," I said brightly. I ignored his scowl and the deepening shade of his complexion. "If you're on the outs with the Captain, this'll fix it. Not only am I handing you a witness to a three-month-old murder, but how often do you get a chance to *prevent* a homicide? You're always there after the fact. Wouldn't it be nice, just once, to save a life?"

He eyed me sourly, but I could tell he was considering it. I pressed on. "Think of it this way: You could set a precedent for the department, start a trend—homicide prevention."

I wanted to throw in all the potential for medals and commendations but decided not to push it.

Philly Post's big barrel chest heaved. His rumpled clothes moved with him, frayed tie and frayed cuffs, shirt straining taut. He ran both hands through his thick, graying mane of hair, then let them drop onto the rat's nest of papers on his desk.

"You're not giving me anything special."

"It's the night-shift thing, isn't it? Can't you just forget that and listen to what I'm saying? If you've already arrested somebody for Arthur Spenger's murder, you've got the wrong person. If you haven't made an arrest, I'm giving you somebody who can tell you exactly who killed him. It's a win-win situation. Are you going to let a chance like this slip by?"

Post raised his thick eyebrows for an instant, and I managed to read something in his eyes, but whether it was anger or interest, I couldn't tell.

"It might just be your ticket off the shit list, Post."

He glanced at the crumpled death notice on his desk. "How reliable is your source?"

"A-one," I lied.

"So where is he?"

"He's scared, so he's hiding. We're going to have to find him."

"Huh-uh, Ventana. *You're* finding him."

"Come on, Post. He won't leave town. I can guarantee that."

"Then it'll be easy for you."

I tried every angle I could think of to get him to buy into finding Bink, but all I got back was a rehash of the night-shift thing.

The way we left it was Post would look into Bink's burned-up car in Police Impound, get his last-known address off the DMV, and send a patrolman out to see if he was home—in other words, nothing. I was supposed to do the rest.

STEPPING OUT onto the forty-second-floor offices of Ellis, Pogue & Lipscomb felt like I'd just arrived at the undertaker's. The lobby was hushed and deserted except for a console bleating softly, blinking on a desk in the corner. The woman who sat behind it kept repeating, "Ellis, Pogue and Lipscomb. Please hold," or, "Mr. Pogue is not in this morning. Would you like to leave a message?"

She looked like she was talking to herself until I noticed the headset with the little translucent plastic tube looped over her head and a tiny microphone in front of her face at about chin level.

I let her clear the lines, told her my name, then asked if Bink was in. When she said no, I asked to see his secretary.

"Marcella? Sure. Hold on." She pressed a button on the console, averted her eyes, and mumbled. Then she looked up at me. "She'll be right out."

Marcella Nilsson looked like she was about nineteen. She was plump, but she dressed well, and despite dark circles under her eyes, her face was pretty. She had an almost angelic look, with fine, chin-length, chestnut-colored hair and that rich, glowing, babylike complexion some heavy women have. When she opened her mouth, her voice was surprisingly deep and throaty.

"I'm sorry, Mr. Hanover's not in today. Did you have, like, an appointment?"

Before I could answer, a lanky, frazzle-haired man in his twenties burst out of the door behind her. "There you are, Marcella! What am I supposed to do about this afternoon?" he demanded angrily. "I haven't got a thing to work with. Where's his stuff? I looked in his office and—"

"I put everything you'll need on your desk, Chris."

"My desk?"

"Yes."

He slunk away quietly while Marcella turned back to me and asked me again if I had an appointment with Bink.

"No," I said. "It's you I came to see." I stepped in closer and lowered my voice. "It's about David Hanover. Is there someplace private we can talk?"

"Uh—I—" She looked desperately around the lobby. "Uh—"

"Why don't we try back here?" I suggested, taking her elbow and steering her through the door she'd just come through. I nodded and smiled at the preoccupied receptionist as we passed the console, and sort of hoped Marcella would autopilot us from there. She responded by walking straight past a huge work matrix board posted in the hall to right where I wanted to go: Bink's office.

It was down the hall from Mitchell's and not as nice, which made sense: Mitch was a partner and Bink was only a manager. Bink's window was smaller and it was covered with a set of closed blinds. I guess if he was acrophobic, he didn't really want to look out and see how high up he was.

Marcella shut the door, then stood in front of it, her round, pink hands behind her, like I was holding her prisoner or something. She knew where Bink was. I could tell just by looking at her.

I crossed over to the desk, circled it, and plopped

down in Bink's chair. The desk calendar was open, but a
little square of blank paper covered up the bulk of the
page. The only appointment I could read was the last
one: *M. Solis* was penciled in for six o'clock yesterday.

I flipped the page. Bink was scheduled to meet with
Donziger Associates at one o'clock today to start an audit, but he'd drawn a big *X* through the morning hours. I
flipped back to Monday.

"I don't think you should be doing that," Marcella
said timidly.

"Do you know who I am, Marcella?"

She nodded slowly, big doe eyes showing white like
a scared deer's.

"Bi—David told you he was going to come to me,
right?"

"He thought he could trust you. Your parents—"

"—My *parents*?" They'd been dead seventeen years.
Bink had never even met them.

"He thought since they were, like, ah—burglars, I
mean, jewel thieves, uh—I mean . . ." She flushed,
brought her hands around in front of her, clasped them,
then dropped them to her side and sort of shrugged.
"I'm sorry. I don't want to make it sound bad . . ."

"Then say 'alleged.' They were never convicted."
They'd died in a car accident during the trial, so their
record was clean. A lot of people overlook that fact, but
it's important to me.

"Bink's in pretty big trouble, Marcella. You know
that, don't you?"

Marcella looked stricken.

"Listen, Marcella. I can see that you care a lot for
David. And that's important right now. He needs your
help. But what he's asked you to do isn't in his best
interest. He's so panicked, he doesn't know what he's
doing."

She kept her gaze on the blinds covering the window and didn't move, but her eyes teared up.

"You know where he is, don't you?"

Slowly, with her eyes still averted, she nodded.

"Do you want to help him?"

"You'll make him go to the police. If I tell you where he is, will you promise you won't go to the police?"

"I can help him," I coaxed. "You know where he is. Just tell me."

"I—" She eyed me like I was trying to trick her.

"Is he at your house?"

She bit her lip some more, then finally nodded.

"Will you take me there?" I could probably find the place by myself, but I didn't want to risk having her call ahead to warn him.

"But I—I just got here." She wanted to go, though. I could see it in her troubled face.

"Tell them you forgot a doctor's appointment or something."

"You mean lie?"

"Right, Marcella. Lie."

9

"I'D BETTER come up," Marcella said. We'd both parked our cars in the open parking lot in front of her tacky Pacifica apartment complex. "He won't answer the door, and I've got a key."

That was fine with me. It'd be harder for Bink to knock down and run away from two of us.

Marcella huffed and puffed up the stairs to the second floor, then led me down the carpeted hall to number 233. She fumbled through her bag while she caught her breath. There were tiny droplets of sweat on her upper lip and along her temples, and I guess her body heat had set off her perfume, because all of a sudden she smelled of gardenias.

She tapped on the door. "David? It's Marcella. Are you decent?"

When he didn't answer, I slipped in front of her and used the key.

"Wait here," I whispered, easing the door open.

The apartment was sunny and bright, with a big picture window in the living room and a long hall down one side. It was done up with overstuffed furniture covered in floral pinks and yellows, and it had the distinct smell of used kitty litter.

I stood in the middle of the living room and looked around, then checked behind the front door. No Bink.

I motioned to Marcella that I was going to the back and that she should stay where she was. She nodded.

I padded along the carpet down the narrow hall and peeked into the first doorway. The kitchen. It was a small brown room with a tiny table, two chairs in the corner, and no place to hide.

Next was the bathroom. Beige tiles, towels, and furry toilet-seat cover. Framed sketches of beige plants on the walls. The cat box was under the sink, and so was the cat, hunkered down, adding to the pile that was already there. I held my breath while I stood with one foot in the hall, reached over, and pulled the shower curtain back. Still no Bink.

I stepped out of the bathroom, breathed again, then caught Marcella's eye down the hall at the front door and shook my head. She was starting to look worried.

There was one more door and it was closed. I tapped on it gently. "Bink? You in there, Bink? It's Ronnie."

I put my hand on the knob and turned it slowly. It gave, so I threw the door open and stepped into the room. More pink again, softer this time, and the room was darker, but there was no sign of Bink. I checked out the closet and under the bed, but he just wasn't there.

"Think somebody kidnapped him?" Marcella asked, clutching the buff-colored cat while she stood at the bedroom door.

I hadn't seen any signs of a struggle. "Why would anybody kidnap him?"

"Well, he wouldn't just leave like that." Marcella sounded betrayed. "I told him he'd be safe here. He knows I'd never tell anybody where he was."

I didn't want to point out that I was the first person to come around asking for Bink and she'd led me right to him.

We walked from the bedroom back to the living room, where I talked Marcella into opening one of her windows so I wouldn't have to smell the cat box while we talked. Now she was on the couch with the cat in her lap. Every time she stroked it, big tufts of yellow hair flew through her fingers into the air. The same fine hair was on everything—tables, chairs, even her coffee-table book on cats. If I was allergic to cat hair, I'd probably be dead.

"Listen, Marcella, I'd like you to tell me everything you know about Bink's situation."

She seemed willing but confused. "Well, like what?"

"Tell me about this morning."

"He rang the bell just after, like, four-thirty and said he was in trouble and could he hide here."

"Did he say what kind of trouble he was in?"

She hesitated. "Well, that's the part that's weird. It's like he's in some kind of bad movie or something, you know?" She set the cat down and stood. "I'm so nervous, I've gotta have something to munch. Can I get you some coffee?"

Since I hadn't had breakfast, coffee sounded great. But I would have accepted anyway. Rule number fifty-two of private investigating is never turn down whatever your host offers you. It's sort of like those tribes in Africa that get insulted if you don't drink their goat blood. If you accept something out of somebody's kitchen, you're one of them. So, even if she'd offered me catnip coffee, I'd drink a sip or two, just to keep her talking.

"Tell me about this morning," I prompted when she came back with a tray piled high with cookies and, almost as an afterthought, a coffee mug crammed in at each end.

"Here." She set the tray down, handed me a cup, picked up the second one, and grabbed a cookie. After she bit into the cookie, she rolled her eyes like she'd just tasted heaven. "I *love* shortbread, don't you?"

"Yeah." I forced myself to take one, blew a cat hair off of it, and took a bite. "About David?"

"Oh, right." She took another bite and swallowed. "Somebody's trying to kill him."

"A woman and four men."

Her mouth was full again, so she nodded. "I don't know about the guys, but"—she reached for another cookie—"but the woman, I think they used to, like, date or something."

"Date?"

"Um-hm." She swallowed. "And, like, he tried to break things off and she didn't want to."

"This whole thing is about a *soured romance*?" I asked incredulously.

"I guess so."

"What about Art Spenger?"

Marcella's angel face went blank.

"Didn't Bink mention Art Spenger?"

"Oh, right, the lawyer. Sure. But you know Art's, like, dead, you know. He committed suicide about three months ago."

"Suicide?" The specter of Philly Post's angry face filled my eyes. "Did you say *suicide*?"

"Yeah. He, like, killed himself," she explained unnecessarily. "I remember 'cause it happened on my birthday—June thirteenth." She eased up on the cookies and focused on stroking the cat.

"You're sure it was suicide?"

"I guess it could have been an accident, but I doubt it. I mean, like, how many people accidentally lock themselves in their own refrigerator with a tank of laughing gas?"

"That's how he died?"

"Isn't it awful?"

"Bink thinks Art Spenger was murdered."

Marcella's little cupid's-bow mouth formed an O. It was obvious the thought had never occurred to her.

"That would be a terrible thing," she said. "Why does he think that?"

"I wish I knew, Marcella. I only wish I knew."

I was trying to convince myself that Bink hadn't just made up Art Spenger's murder and that I hadn't blown my entire credibility with Post, when Marcella cleared her throat.

"Mary," she said. "I think her name's Mary."

I knew it was too much to hope for a last name, but I asked anyway. Marcella stuffed another cookie into her mouth and shook her head.

"Did he mention her appearance? Where they met? Where she works or lives? Her car maybe?"

She brightened. "Oh, yeah. He was really excited because she drove a big blue Mercedes." She munched and swallowed again. "As far as what she looks like, he didn't tell me. But I know his type: blond, skinny, big teeth. Cheerleaders."

I thought back to the series of girlfriends Bink had had over the years I'd known him. She was right.

"Where do you think Bink went? Would he keep his afternoon appointment, the one on his calendar?"

"Donziger? Uh-uh. I asked him this morning what I should do about it and he told me to let Chris Mullin handle it."

"The frazzle-haired guy at the office?"

"Yeah. He's the senior on David's audit team. He's supposed to handle it automatically anyway."

"How about his sister? Would Bink go to her place?"

"Barbara wouldn't let him put his Corvette in her name, so he's not speaking to her."

I ticked off everybody I could think of, and for every name I mentioned, Marcella gave a reason why Bink wouldn't seek help from that individual. Mostly he was angry at people who protested his abuse of their friendship.

Marcella couldn't think of anybody else, so we went over the apartment a second time, searching not for Bink but for clues. After sweeping through every room, looking under all the furniture, and sifting past acres of cat hair, I thought of the phone.

"Where is it?" I asked.

Marcella took me to a small pink trimline set next to her bed. I picked it up and pressed Redial.

Dissonant notes beeped rapidly in the silence between us, then softened into a purring ring. Someone at the other end picked up before the second ring. The voice was nasal and definitely masculine.

"The Saint George Club," it said. "May I help you?"

10

I'D NEVER BEEN to a private men's club before, so I couldn't tell if the man at the front desk of the Saint George Club on Franklin Street was trying to make my life difficult or if he just got paid extra to be a jerk.

He refused to say whether Bink was there or not, refused to call or let me call upstairs to find out, and didn't seem impressed when I showed him my P.I. license. If Bink had phoned the club, he couldn't say whether he'd handled the call or not.

I was getting the stone-wall treatment, and the old creep was pretty good at it. As things stood, I was positive I'd never get past the velvet-and-mahogany lobby. Five minutes of being polite hadn't bought me a thing.

"Okay," I finally told the effete little weasel behind the desk. "See those doors?" I pointed at the double front doors. "I'm going out those doors just like you want me to, but I'm not going far. I'm going to stand out there on the sidewalk—on city property—and I'm going to stop every single person that comes out of this place. I'm going to ask if they've seen Mr. Hanover this morning. If they say no, I'm going to ask them to come back in here and check for me."

The weasel's mouth gaped open. He stammered something about police and harassment and private property.

"The sidewalk belongs to everybody, mister. Go ahead. Call the police and ask them. In the meantime . . ."

The elevator door had just opened and two thirtyish, captain-of-industry types plowed into the lobby. Their expensive-looking suits and freshly barbered Kennedyesque haircuts told me I was in the right place. These were the kind of people Bink thrived on. Young elites, handsome young Turks, the kind who keep up an image. *Christ,* I thought.

The two were intent on their own conversation and didn't seem to notice me, but the clerk behind the desk practically choked when I pushed myself off the counter and started off behind them.

"I'll be right outside," I called out over my shoulder.

"Wait! Miss—er—*Miss*! *Please.*"

The two guys paused midway across the lobby and turned their heads toward the desk. The cute one grinned at me. He was closer to twenty than thirty.

"Miss, I found it," the weasel announced. He waved an envelope in the air and kept a tight but determined smile on his face. "My apologies, madam. I have what you need right here."

I smiled at the cute suit, winked, then went reluctantly back to the desk. The blank, empty envelope lay on the counter in front of the desk clerk. He was angry but ready to talk.

"Mr. Hanover hasn't been here in over a week," he whispered angrily.

I heard the front doors close. "Could he have come in without your knowing?"

The skinny old man shook his head. "Impossible."

"Is there a back door?"

"It's reserved for staff."

"Do me a favor. Just in case he snuck in the back, call upstairs for me."

He made savage little noises under his breath, but

he called. The upstairs people checked to see if Bink had signed into a room or if he was in the restaurant or the gym or the squash courts or the sauna. No Bink.

"Anyplace else he could be? On the premises, I mean."

The little guy's eyes sort of bulged. He said in a barely controlled voice, "Mr. Hanover is not here. Mr. Hanover has not been seen at this club in more than a week. I've already explained this to you once, miss. I don't know of a more direct way of putting it: Mr. Hanover *is not here.*"

People were suddenly milling around the lobby now, waiting for, or having spewed out of, the elevator. But the desk clerk wasn't paying any attention to them. He was fingering a white file card with Bink's name at the top. I leaned over the counter, my eye on the card. "Is that his record? Does it say who sponsored him?" Nobody got into these clubs without a recommendation from a member.

The little weasel gave me a hostile look and said, "Will you vacate the premises if I tell you?"

"Sure."

He leaned in close and signaled for me to do the same. I took advantage of my position to scope out the card. It was tricky reading upside down, but only three lines had been filled in. The first line said Bink had joined three months ago. His monthly dues were a thousand dollars and he was already two months behind. There were a couple more entries on the card, but by that time the desk clerk had cleared his throat and whispered in my ear.

"Felix Ashton," he said.

My jaw dropped. I jerked my head away and stared into his little, black weasel eyes. "Felix Ashton? The mayor's son?"

The creep's thin, dry lips twisted into a wry little smile. "Precisely."

11

PROBABLY THE ONLY REASON the old geezer told me about Felix Ashton was because he figured I'd back off once I knew somebody big was involved. Not likely.

My head was reeling with implications as I stepped out of the subdued mahogany and velvet into the sunlight and traffic outside. Bink must have done some mighty maneuvering to get Felix Ashton to sponsor him. If Felix Ashton knew Bink at all, he knew Bink could never afford the dues on a club like this. And if he didn't know him that well, why would he recommend, and risk his own reputation on, a stranger?

Either way the old weasel's tactic had backfired. I decided Felix Ashton was my next stop.

I had started down the street, trying to remember where I'd parked my car, when I felt a sudden pressure on my shoulder.

"Excuse me," a man's voice said.

I jerked forward and wheeled around, heart in my throat, then realized no thug would ask me to excuse him before bopping me on the head.

The cute guy I'd seen leave the club a few minutes earlier stared back at me, startled, I guess, by the violence of my reaction.

"Sorry," he said. "Didn't mean to scare you." His

smile seemed a little bashful now that we were face-to-face, but my God, he was beautiful. Curly black hair, green eyes, square jaw, and those just barely bowed legs I love in a man. If anything came of this, I'd call it lust at first sight.

"Hi," I said, wondering if my grin reflected my lecherous thoughts.

He offered me the hand that had been on my shoulder. "I'm Mike Neal."

"Hi, Mike Neal." I wanted to pinch his cheeks.

"This is kind of embarrassing," he began. "I overheard Binkster Hanover's name inside. Are you a friend of his?"

"Only in the loosest sense."

He chuckled. "Wish I could say that. God, that guy's a rip, isn't he?" He paused, meeting my gaze and smiling with just a bare hint of reservation. He was trying to make up his mind about me and being very transparent about it. "Are you looking for him?" he finally asked.

"Have you seen him?"

He snorted. "Have I? He got me out of bed this morning. Wanted to borrow my Callaway graphites."

"Your what?"

"Callaway graphites. Clubs."

"Clubs?"

"Yeah, you know, woods and irons, Arnold Palmer, eighteen holes." He put his hands together, arms flexed, legs apart and slightly bent, and executed a perfect imaginary swing. "Golf clubs."

"Golf clubs?" I repeated. Bink must have lost it entirely.

Mike Neal looked at me like he was starting to have doubts about me, like maybe he thought I was slow.

"Golf clubs," I said again.

"Yeah. The Binkman wanted the Callaways, some clothes, and my golf shoes. What's with him? He's really been maxed out lately."

"What time this morning?"

"Eight, eight-thirty. I didn't want to let him have the clubs, but you know how Bink is. You sort of hate to say no because it makes you look like a jerk. You feel sorry for him. Then you hate yourself later for letting him talk you into whatever it was he talked you into."

I nodded. I knew exactly what he meant.

"He said it was life or death. If I didn't give him the clubs, I'd be responsible for ruining the rest of his life."

"Golf clubs?" I was still having a tough time processing this. "You don't think he was going to play golf?"

"What else is he going to do in my best golf outfit with the Callaways? He took off for a nine-o'clock tee at Mount Vesuvio. Jesus, he was really psyched for this game. He kept saying it was going to seal his fate."

"Sounds ominous."

Mike Neal's expression made me think that maybe he didn't know what *ominous* meant. Maybe he wasn't my type after all.

I said good-bye, took a step toward my car, then stopped. "Any idea who he'd call here at the club this morning?" I asked.

Mike grinned. "That's easy. Harry—that's the guy that came out of the elevator with me. Harry keeps a room here. He said the Binkster rang him up at seven. Wanted to borrow *his* clubs. But Harry had the good sense to say no."

12

AS I NEARED the Mount Vesuvio Club's golf course and its big white-brick portals, I hesitated and checked the clock on the dash. It was almost noon.

I steered the car down a narrow frontage road, turned left onto a dirt road that paralleled the golf course, then drove a few yards and parked where I had a clear shot at the rolling green expanse. The binoculars were in my glove box.

I rolled the window down and spotted a group of golfers. With the field glasses I could make out four of them, all sixtyish except for one in his forties, all dressed in pastel plaids with white golf shoes, driving golf carts the size of my Toyota. Old boys taking a break from their CEO slots probably. Tightening up the old network.

I looked closer at the younger one and was surprised to see Chuck Vardigan, a government investigator who'd crossed my path when I worked as a parole officer. He'd been an ambitious climber back then and was probably head of the regional office by now, able to take Tuesday afternoons off to golf with the big boys.

Another group popped out from behind a clump of trees, younger, smiling, joking, but still looking very important. No Bink, though. I was about to give up when he crested the horizon riding passenger in one of those huge golf carts.

Damn you, Bink. He had to be nuts playing golf when a murderess and her four thugs were out to kill him.

I trained the binoculars on Bink's golf partner and recognized him instantly: Edwin Elliot Pogue. If anybody was important enough to outrank a death squad in Bink's eyes, it was Pogue. His picture graced the business and society sections of the *Chronicle* on a weekly basis. He was on half a dozen corporate boards and he headed Ellis, Pogue & Lipscomb—the accounting firm where Mitch and Bink both worked.

Looking rich and self-satisfied, old enough to be Bink's father, Pogue dwarfed squirrely little Bink with broad shoulders, a thick torso, and a bare massive bald head. His bright red V-neck sweater and tan trousers looked expensive and, in spite of the relaxed expression on the old man's face, he gave the impression of somebody who didn't suffer fools.

I shifted the lens a little to the left. Bink looked like he was sweating bullets.

The older man stopped the cart, said something to Bink, then reached back for a club. Bink laughed mirthlessly, sat immobile in the cart for a moment, then grabbed a club and hurried to catch up with the older man. Vardigan's group of four drove by, waved a hearty hello to Pogue, and sped on while Bink practically cowered at the edge of the green. *Christ,* I thought, *what is he doing here?*

Bink played lousy on the sixteenth and seventeenth holes. When the two vanished over a hill for the eighteenth, I pulled the car around to the front portals and waited, wondering what kind of story Bink had fed Pogue to get him out here to play golf in the middle of the week while poor, frazzle-haired Chris Mullin was going through hoops back at the office.

After about fifteen minutes a cab pulled in and disappeared down the long drive to the clubhouse. Ten minutes later it curved its way back with a passenger slouched down so low in the backseat that I knew it had to be Bink.

13

I ROUNDED THE CORNER in Saint Francis Wood just as Bink's cab pulled up in front of a huge Tara-style house surrounded by tall oaks.

Bink left the cab waiting out front. He dragged the golf clubs out of the car and went, not to the front door, but down the drive to the back. I parked behind the cab, jumped out, and followed.

The surface of the driveway was moist from water that had drained from sprinklers watering the lawn out front. I hurried past the house and into the backyard, then stopped and looked around.

The long drive ended a few yards in front of me at the massive double doors of a brick garage. To my right a tiny walk curved through a well-shaded lawn to the back door of the house. Birds twittered and a dog barked in the distance. I looked around for Bink, but he'd simply vanished, again.

I started toward the mansion's back door, then heard tapping from up above behind me.

"Mike! Mike Neal! You home, Mike?"

I followed the sound to a set of stairs built along the side of the garage, obscured from the front by a huge wisteria vine.

I started up the steps as the door rattled above me and Bink called out again.

"Mike!"

I stopped at the top of the steps. He still hadn't seen me. "Bink."

He pivoted, eyes wide. "Ronnie!"

I could tell that for a split second he considered throwing the golf clubs at me.

"Don't even think it," I said. And that's when he tossed them on top of me.

I stumbled backward, grabbed the banister for support, and shoved the bag off of me just as Bink pushed his way past. I reached for the bag, yanked a club out, then hopped down a couple of steps and hurled it like a harpoon between his ankles.

Bink tripped and slid down the last few steps in a spin and landed on his back. I pulled another club from the bag, jumped down the rest of the stairs three at a time, and stopped, panting, eight iron raised over Bink's head.

Bink took one look at the raised club, wrapped his head in his arms, and curled into a fetal position. "Don't, Ronnie! Please don't hit me! I'm sorry, okay? Don't bend the club—it's not mine."

"Are you going to try to run again?"

"No." Bink peeked out from behind his elbow, then slowly dropped his arms.

I lowered the golf club and motioned for him to get up. "Are you out of your mind? What are you doing playing golf? These monsters are trying to kill you, Bink."

He flushed and rose. "I can explain," he said, gathering the spilled clubs one by one and stuffing them into the bag. I followed him, and we ended up back upstairs outside Mike Neal's door. "It was important," he finally said.

"Important enough to risk your life?"

"I can explain."

I waited.

Bink cast a worried glance down the driveway, then propped the clubs up beside the door. "Okay, that guy I was playing golf with? He's got a daughter, and I'm this close"—he held up two fingers a quarter of an inch apart —"I'm this close to being engaged to her. If I can convince the old man, maybe he'll give us his blessing."

I narrowed my eyes and studied Bink's coolly handsome face. "Something tells me you're after more than a blessing, Bink. Edwin Pogue is a millionaire. Is this what you were talking about when you told Mitch you'd have money to burn?"

Bink flushed and stared at his shoes.

"Bink, that's wrong. You don't marry somebody for financial gain."

"But I love her, Ronnie. She just happens to be rich. It's a coincidence."

"Sure."

"You've got it all wrong. I'm crazy about her, and she loves me. We're great together. And the money—it's like a bonus. It's true love this time."

With dollar signs for hearts. As far as I was concerned, Bink hadn't learned a thing in the two years since I'd last seen him. Mitch might think he was salvageable, but I was ready to write Bink off—as soon as we cleared up the mess he'd brought to my doorstep.

"Are you ready to talk to me? Or are you going to run again the minute I turn my back?"

He glanced nervously over my shoulder to the driveway. "Not here, Ronnie. For Chrissake. I mean, what if they followed you?"

The lock on Mike Neal's door caught my eye. It was a new one Hammersmith Security had come out with last year, supposedly pick-proof.

"They could be here any minute, Ronnie. And we'd be cornered. We wouldn't have a chance."

Bink took my arm and tried to steer me back the way we'd come. I dug in my heels and stared straight into his wild eyes. Through clenched teeth I said, "Let. Go. Of. Me."

In the sudden quiet I noticed he was panting. He was close, so close I could smell his breath, and his breath smelled of onions. *Onions.* My apartment was swimming in gas vapors, he'd brought murderous thugs to my door, ruined my apartment, possibly blown what little credibility I had with Philly Post, then had the nerve to have an appetite, to have lunch. With a wave of indignation I jerked my arm away.

"You creep," I said.

Bink dropped his hand to his side and gave me an injured look. "Jeez, Ronnie. What'd I do? *I'm* the one they're trying to kill. Don't be angry with me."

Telling him off would have made me feel better, but past experience had taught me it wouldn't do any good beyond that.

"Forget it, Bink. Nobody followed me—I promise. Look, let's just go inside and talk this thing through."

"But—the door's locked."

I smiled. "So it is, Bink. So it is."

14

PICKING MIKE NEAL'S Hammersmith pick-proof lock was the first fun I'd had all day. Too bad it couldn't have lasted longer. Two seconds into the operation I'd sprung the door open. I sighed.

"All right, Bink." I pointed to the clubs. "Bring those inside. Let's talk."

He moved automatically, then hesitated, golf bag in midair. "You're not going to make me talk to the cops, are you? 'Cause I don't think we need to bring them in, you know. It's not that big a deal." He smiled tentatively.

I motioned him inside, shut the door, took a couple of steps into Mike Neal's richly furnished living room, and said in a barely modulated voice, "It *is* a big deal, Bink. Believe me, when people with Uzis hunt you down in the middle of the night and torch your car, that's a pretty good sign somebody's upset about something. Come on, put the clubs away and sit down. I want you to explain why you think Art Spenger was murdered and why these people are after you."

"No cops?"

"Not yet. First you're going to tell me what the hell you've gotten me into."

Just as he propped the golf bag in the corner of the living room, somebody knocked at the door.

Bink spun around and turned accusing eyes on me.

"They followed you!" he squawked. "They're here! Oh, God, they're going to kill me! Oh, no . . ."

I tried to block him out and deal with my own fear. For some reason I couldn't catch my breath. Everything seemed to slow down.

"Stay here," I whispered to Bink, then tiptoed across the carpet to the front door. The face I saw through the peephole wasn't one of the goons. It wasn't even a woman. The man outside was a short, unshaven Filipino dressed in denim. I glanced over my shoulder at Bink. He was cowering in the corner just like he'd done at my place earlier. Useless.

"Who is it?" I shouted from behind the closed door.

"I want fare," he shouted back.

"What?"

"You pay taxi."

Every muscle in my body sagged with relief. "It's your cabdriver, Bink. Pay the man."

Bink stopped his manic swaying and reached into his breast pocket all in one motion. I had to give it to the guy, he could segue with the best of them.

I opened the door, handed the cabbie his money, and told him he could go. He stood there and counted it, then looked up at me. "Waddabout tip?"

"Bink, did you promise this guy a tip?"

"No."

"He promise twenty-five percent if I wait," the driver shouted. "I want twenty-five percent!"

Bink sneered. "No way."

"Pay him, Bink. Or I'm calling the cops."

The driver looked startled at the idea, then seemed to like it. He nodded vigorously. "I call cop too."

"What! Jeez, Ronnie, you'd believe this stupid—"

"Pay him, Bink."

"Pay me!" the cabdriver demanded. He turned to me. "He pay twenty-five percent."

Bink reluctantly rummaged through his alligator-skin wallet and pulled out a couple of small bills. "Here," he said, and tossed them at the little man. "Now, beat it, you squirt. Next time I'll report you for gouging your customers."

After I'd closed the door, Bink slumped into a leather armchair and tried to bargain for my silence with the cops.

"Forget it, Bink. There's nothing I can do about it."

For once he seemed to accept what I said. He sat back and stretched his arm out along the top of the chair. His whole demeanor changed. No more sniveling terror. Now he was back to the Eddie Haskell–type guy I'd met in college. "You know, Ronnie, I'm trying to get people to stop calling me that. Can you call me David? Or Dave?"

I hadn't eaten anything since Marcella's shortbread cookies and coffee. No breakfast and no lunch lowered my tolerance for Bink by about two notches. I counted to ten, shifted in my seat, and tried to tell myself he wasn't quite so bad. What came out was a testy "Do you want me to help you or not?"

"Sure, Ronnie. Absolutely. I'm putting myself in your hands. I'm giving you all my trust. My life depends on you from now on."

"Don't tempt me."

"Hey, I'm serious."

"Then tell me why these people want to kill you."

He rubbed the back of his neck, then fixed me with a puzzled frown. "Jeez, Ronnie, I don't know where to start."

I heard a smothered snarl, saw Bink's startled look, and realized I'd made the sound myself. Bink got the message.

"Okay, okay. I ride in to work on this car-pool dealy, right?"

"What car-pool 'dealy'?"

"You know, in the East Bay, where you line up at

the bus stop and people pick you up so they can use the free car-pool lane to get across the bridge? You know about it."

I'd heard of it, but somehow, Bink had never struck me as the environmentally sensitive type. There had to be an angle. "So?"

"So Artie Spenger told me it's a great way to meet the babes."

"The dead Artie Spenger?"

"Yeah. He'd been getting dates off of it for a year, he said. Artie said it's better to hitch than to give the ride in case you get a dog. She can't trace your license plate and do a Glenn Close on you, know what I mean?"

Bink being who he was, I could see how he'd worry about something like that. "Get to the point, Bink."

He looked annoyed at hearing his nickname, but he went on anyway. "So this chick gives me a ride a few times and we hit it off pretty good."

"You started dating?"

"Nah, not really. I've seen her a couple of times, let's just say. I thought she said she had a boyfriend. And like I said, I got somebody special, too, but we hit it off. So she asked me for my phone number and picked me up at my house a couple of times and dropped me off at work. I didn't push her to break up with the guy—hell, I didn't want her to. Then yesterday I'm supposed to meet her after work. There she was standing outside my building with those four linebackers. I waved and started to walk over to her when she shouts, 'That's him!' and these guys came for me."

"So you ran."

"Sure I ran. You saw those guys. Yow! They're death in the flesh, Ronnie. Grim reapers."

I wasn't going to argue. "When I talked to your secretary—"

"You saw Marcella?"

"Yes. Marcella said the woman's name is Mary."

"Yeah, yeah, that's right. Mary Solis."

"Okay. Tell me about how Mary Solis ties in with your friend Artie."

"Oh, man, Artie." He rolled his eyes and shuddered. "Are you ready for this? On our third date she hands me this death notice off the *Chron*. I had it so I could show you, but I lost it someplace. But anyway, she hands this to me, right? It's the guy she dated off and on for a year and he's dead, right? Is she cryin'? Is she torn up? What she says is, this is what happens to guys who break up with me."

"But Art committed suicide."

"No, he didn't. Do you know how he died? In a box, man. Artie wouldn't kill himself like that. Not in a million years. Never."

"How can you be so sure?"

"Because he's like me, Ronnie. I've got a thing with heights, and Artie, he's got a thing for tight places."

"He's claustrophobic?"

Bink nodded his head up and down. "Certifiable."

Philly Post would never buy it. Or would he? "Why didn't this come out at the inquest?"

"Not too many people knew. The only reason I found out was I tried to get him to hide in a closet at Don Coulter's surprise party last year, and he tried to get me to hide out on the fire escape."

Maybe I could locate some medical records to prove what Bink was saying. But that still wouldn't point a finger at Mary. So far the worst she was guilty of was a sadistic sense of humor.

"Let me get this straight. You're telling me Artie broke up with this Mary—what's her last name again?"

"Solis."

"And Mary Solis murdered him in the most cruel way she could, and now that you're trying to dump her, she's trying to kill you too?"

"Right!"

I knew I hadn't heard the whole story. "What'd you do to her, Bink?"

He threw up his hands and assumed an offended air. "Why's everything always my fault? I didn't do anything, Ron. Nothing. I swear! What do you think Artie Spenger did, huh?"

"I don't know. Did you and Art run a scam on her?"

"A scam! Jeez, Ronnie, cut me some air, will you? What do you think I am?"

I let the question hang. He squirmed and finally said, "I didn't scam her out, okay? Nothing like that. All we did was date."

"So what am I missing here, Bink? Where do the Uzis come in?"

He slumped against the back of his chair. "I swear to you I don't know. We went out a couple of times, okay? After she picked me up that first time on the carpool dealy out on Park, she told me Artie put her onto me. He's done that before. He gets tired of a chick and puts her onto me." He shrugged. "But that's it! I swear, she's a nut case. There wasn't even anything going between us."

"Did she know that?"

He glanced at the floor and shrugged again.

"Is she pregnant? Is that why you tried to break it off?"

Bink looked pained. "There was nothing to break off. I keep telling you that. This is a deal like in that movie, like I said, where the girl goes psycho, boils the rabbit, and comes after the guy. Only this chick's got heavy artillery to back her up. I went out with her, okay? What's the crime in that?"

"You tell me."

We sat there a few minutes in silence, then Bink spoke, this time without the whine or the bravado.

"Things have been going good for me since Mitch got me the job at Ellis Pogue. Then I got the promotion, and I'm about to get engaged. Everything's finally falling into place for me. I wouldn't mess up now, Ronnie. Not on purpose. Not *now*."

Against my better judgment I found myself being swayed by his sincerity and his logic. I'd probably regret it later, but for now I believed him.

Bink rose from the chair and paced the room a couple of times, rubbing the back of his neck. Then he stopped and looked at me. "You want a beer?"

I followed him in case Mike Neal's kitchen had a back door, and watched him fish a pair of Coronas out of the fridge. Mike Neal's last, I noticed. We went back to the living room, and this time I sat down opposite Bink's lanky frame.

"Have you got a way to get in touch with her? A phone number? An address?"

Bink, in the middle of a long slug of beer, brought the bottle down on his leg with a sputtering cough. "I'm not phoning her, if that's what you want," he said after he'd stopped choking. "The bitch is trying to kill me."

"You want her to call these guys off, don't you?"

He hesitated, reluctant to agree.

"How are we going to know what her problem is unless we talk to her?"

Bink stared at the floor and fingered the neck of the Corona.

"Look, call her," I said. "Set something up. You don't even have to come if you don't want. We'll work with the police, and they'll be there to arrest her."

"No police."

"Yes police. There's no way around it."

"What do I say to her?"

"Tell her that you want to straighten things out. Tell her you want to meet her at—at the Marina Green, by the east viewing scope. Ten o'clock tomorrow."

"But—"

"It's public and it's open, so we'll know if she's setting you up. Have you got the number?"

He fumbled in his breast pocket and came out with a small alligator-skin address book that matched his wallet.

"Great." I looked around for a phone and hauled him across the room to an imitation Louis XV desk. I shoved him into the chair, handed him the receiver, and said, "Okay, go."

But he hadn't even found the number yet. His hand was shaking so much, he couldn't even turn the pages in the little black book.

"Here, give me that." I took it from his trembling fingers and turned to *S.* Silvio. Susan. Sackert. Seven Square Rest. Sal's Salon. No Solis and no Mary.

I looked down at Bink. He was sweating, staring at the door like he thought the thugs were coming to get him right here in Mike Neal's apartment. If sheer will could have put him in Tahiti with Mitch, I was positive he'd be there right now.

"Bink?"

He started, then followed my gaze to the open page in my hand. "Oh, right. She's under *C.*"

"C?"

"Car pool."

Poor woman didn't even rate enough to get listed under her own name. No wonder she set the goons after Bink. I found the entry, read the number, and felt my spirits sag. "It's a phone booth, Bink. Did you ever try to call her?"

"What?"

"See this nine? All numbers on public telephones have a nine for the fourth digit. Did you ever call her?"

Bink shook his head. "She always phoned me at work or picked me up in the car-pool dealy."

"Let's try it anyway."

He dialed and let it ring ten times, but nobody

picked up at the other end. When he replaced the receiver, I said, "I don't suppose you got an address?"

"Uh-uh."

I set the phone back where it'd been on the desk and said, "Come on, Bink. Let's get out of here. It's time to go to the cops."

He didn't move.

"Come on. It's where you should have gone in the first place."

"Look, Ronnie, it's real important to me that we don't. My engagement—it's—look—what if I hire you?"

"I don't do Uzis. Besides, we've already done this, remember? You offered me two-fifty an hour up in my apartment."

He rose from the chair and reached for his alligator-skin billfold. "What if I pay you up front? Here's three hundred dollars."

I stared at the money in his hands, mostly because I was surprised to see Bink with that kind of cash. Usually he was asking to borrow money to pay his phone bill and the PG&E. He misunderstood my silence.

"Will you do it for four hundred? Listen, five hundred's my top." He pulled out another pair of bills and returned the billfold to his back pocket. "I gotta live, you know."

I thought of his men's-club dues and his sixty-thousand-dollar car. "Where'd you get that much money, Bink?"

He flushed. "I pulled it out of savings—"

"Savings?"

"Yeah, to run and hide from these guys. Look, Ronnie, I'm begging you."

"I know a lieutenant you can talk to."

Bink scowled.

"Look, Bink. You brought this mess to my door and I'm telling you how to deal with it. It'll be clean and simple: You're coming forward as a witness in a homicide. You give them a statement about Artie Spenger, they pick up Mary Solis, and that's the end of it. Murder's a capital offense, so she probably won't get bail. It's pretty cut-and-dried."

Bink looked skeptical.

"Talk to him, Bink. It's your only chance of getting me to take the case."

Bink brightened. "Yeah?"

"Right. If he won't help—"

"You'll go to work for me?"

"I'll consider it."

I plucked a bill from the five he held in his hand. "Why don't you change out of those golf clothes? We'll talk money later if we need to. But for now this will take care of the new mattress you're buying me."

15

"**Y**OU DON'T WANT ME, Ventana," Philly said as soon as Bink and I sat down in his office. "You want Night Ministry."

Bink turned to me, confused. "What's that?"

"It's a suicide hot line," I answered. "Cute, Post."

He wasn't even trying. It was three o'clock, and Bink and I had waited an hour outside his office before he'd even see us. Now he was being snide.

"Okay," I said. "So it looks like Art Spenger committed suicide. Sure, that's what his killers want everybody to think. But Art Spenger was murdered and Bi— David Hanover here can prove it."

Post focused his gaze on Bink. "Yeah? What's your friend got to say?"

Bink was busy tracing scuff marks on the linoleum floor with the toe of his lizard-skin boot. I nudged him with my elbow. "Tell him, Bink."

He jumped, then turned caged-animal eyes on me. "Tell him what?"

It was like he'd dropped his brain outside the building and left it there. "Explain about Art Spenger."

"Oh, that. Uh . . ." He glanced over at Post, then back at me. "You mean about him being claustropho-bic?"

"Right," I said through clenched teeth.

Bink twisted his old fraternity ring and stared at the floor. Post made some sort of disgusted guttural sound that made us both look at him.

"Get this kook outta here, Ventana. Quit wasting my time. This isn't a homicide."

Bink started to rise, but I grabbed his arm and yanked him back down. My eyes locked in on his.

"Tell Lieutenant Post what the deal is, Bink. Tell him, or I'm cutting you loose right now."

"Walk, Ventana," Post said, flipping a sheaf of papers into his Out box and digging a six-inch stack from his In box. "What you're selling I'm not buying."

I stared at Bink, and Bink just stared at the floor. Post picked up a pencil and made some marks on a page in the folder in front of him.

"Terrific," I said, then stood. "You're on your own, Bink."

"Wait! I'll tell him, okay?"

"The truth?"

"Yeah. Right."

I slumped back into my chair. Bink swallowed hard, then looked at me while Post raised his eyes and frowned at both of us. Bink swallowed again, then said, "I don't really know how to start."

"Forget *how*, just tell him *what*."

Bink focused on the sagging Pirates pennant dangling on the wall behind Post's desk, just above his head. He gave the class ring one final twist and launched into a monotonous description of the car-pool pickup line. A couple of sentences into it, Post exploded.

"Christ, Ventana! Are we talking Oakland? I've got no jurisdiction in Oakland. You must be—"

"Sit down. Will you just listen?" I said. "He's not done yet."

"Is this my jurisdiction or not?" Post demanded.

"Yes."

His eyebrows twitched. He settled into his chair and frowned at Bink. "Get to the point, Mr. Hanover."

Bink went through the whole thing and finished up with "So when Artie died, she says, 'That's what happens to guys who dump me.' I thought she was making a joke, you know, a raw joke. Only she wasn't laughing. She didn't even smile, man."

"Why didn't you come forward then?"

"She wasn't trying to kill me back then."

Post glanced significantly at me, then turned back to Bink. "What makes you think she wants to kill you?"

"She set me up. I was supposed to meet her last night at six, and when I show up, she sends these big tankers after me. Tell him, Ronnie, you saw them. You saw their guns."

Post scowled. "That's it?"

Bink glared at me, then nodded.

"You spell your name with one *n*, Mr. Hanover, or two?"

"One."

Post came around his desk and opened the door. The chatter and hum of the detectives working outside his office flooded into the room.

"Wait outside, will you? Over there." He pointed to a bench against the far wall of the squad room. "You, too, Ventana."

Bink and I sat wordlessly and watched Post's obsequious assistant, Kendall, go in and out of Post's office. Kendall came back about five minutes later clutching a white sheet of paper. Through the glass we could see Post study it, then shake his head. He picked up the phone, talked for a while, then, when he hung up, looked across the room through the glass and motioned us to come over.

"Wait outside a minute, Mr. Hanover. Thanks."

As soon as Bink closed the door, Post was out of his chair, standing beside me. He touched my elbow solicitously and lowered his voice. "Where'd you dig up this crackpot?"

I was so surprised by the sudden lack of antagonism, by the actual suggestion of gentleness in his voice and on his face, that I gaped. "What?"

"How'd you run across this dandy?"

"It's a long story." I slouched into one of the hard wooden chairs in front of his desk and stifled a yawn. Bink's three A.M. wake-up was finally starting to hit me.

Post hitched one buttock onto the edge of his desk and leaned forward, his forearms propped on his thigh. "My advice? Lose the guy, Ventana. He's bad news."

"Bad news with a problem."

He turned and picked up the paper Kendall had brought him. "I checked him out. He's got no convictions, but it's not because he hasn't tried. This guy's chased every fast buck there is. He's a con man, and nothing I've seen or heard so far tells me he's not running a con on you."

"A con? On me? What have I got that he'd want?"

Post shrugged. "You come into any money lately?"

"Come on, Post. There's no money in this. He's just trying to get a psychotic woman off his back. What about Spenger? What does Bink get out of solving his murder?"

"I checked out Spenger. He was a wreck. He was so tanked up most of the time that he'd messed up on the job. Things were so bad, his firm asked him to resign. And his girlfriend had just left him. He was pushing overtime for a gold medal in suicide."

Bink hadn't mentioned any of that. But then if Spenger had been plagued with a vengeful "black widow," he *would* be falling apart. I tuned back in to what Post was saying in time to hear, "Look, this Hanover's a loser. I don't know what his game is, but from what I see, it's not good. Maybe he likes it rough. Maybe

Mary Solis didn't like him as much as he liked her but he wouldn't pick up the signals. Maybe *she's* the one ought to be in here filing charges."

"You just told me Bink's never been convicted of anything. Now all of a sudden you think he's a rapist?"

"He ever get rough with you?"

"Me? And Bink?" I laughed. "Give me a little more credit than that. He's not really even my friend; he's Mitchell's friend, my ex's. And whatever you see in Bink's past, he's on the straight and narrow now. He hasn't been in any trouble in a year, not since Mitch got him the job at Ellis Pogue."

Post snorted. "What do you call this?"

"Are you going to help him or not?"

Post exhaled dramatically, rounded his desk, then stood rubbing the back of his neck. "What is this guy to you, Ventana? What do you owe him?"

"A lot less than you do. Post, I'm just asking you to do your job."

"You want to follow up, talk to Property Crimes."

I stood. "That's how you're going to play it?"

He sat down without answering, picked up his pencil, and reached for the next folder from his In basket.

"You can say 'I told you so' if you're right." It was as close as I'd come to begging.

"Property Crimes."

"Fine." I turned on my heel.

"Oh, and Ventana, return Spenger's autopsy report today and I won't bust you for stealing it."

"His autopsy report?"

Post pinned his unfathomable eyes on me and studied my face hard. Then he frowned. "You didn't take it, did you?"

"Of course not. How long has it been missing?"

Post hesitated. "Coroner's office said some woman asked to see it this morning and walked out with it when nobody was looking. Sounded like your M.O."

"I don't have an M.O., Post. *Criminals* have M.O.'s," I said, and stalked out of his office.

"Ronnie? Hey, Ronnie!" Bink caught up with me in the hall outside the squad room.

"What happened? What'd he say?"

I stopped in front of the bank of elevators and punched the Down button with my clenched fist. "Philly Post is a jerk."

"Does this mean you're gonna help me out?"

I thought of all the times Bink had screwed me over and left me holding the bag. Then I thought about what Post had said. "Did you rape Mary Solis?"

Bink recoiled like I'd slapped him. *"Rape?* Good God! Is that what—"

"Yes or no, Bink. No bullshit."

He stopped sputtering, raised his left hand, palm out, and placed the other one over his heart. "I swear to you, Ronnie—I swear to *God,* I never forced her to do anything."

I stared into his face, trying to discern the truth. "So help me, Bink, if you're lying, I'll make sure you burn for this."

16

BINK FIDGETED on the stoop beside me. "Who'd you say this guy is?"

"A P.I.—one of the best. He's really sharp, you'll see. You'll be safe with him."

The door rattled, then opened. Blackie Coogan stood framed in the doorway, his perfect, sixty-five-year-old ex-boxer's physique filling the small space. He wore faded green sweatpants, an immaculate white T-shirt, and flip-flops on his bare feet. Gray stubble covered his cheeks, and his heaven-blue eyes, which he shaded from the light with a gnarled hand, sparkled with their usual I-don't-give-a-shit-about-the-world slant.

If anybody was ever tough and seedy and cool and all those neat things P.I.'s are supposed to be, it's Blackie. Not bad for somebody I met in a bar five years ago.

Blackie glanced with mild interest at Bink, then turned his sexy blue eyes to meet mine.

"What's up, doll?"

"Can we come in?"

Blackie stepped aside to let us pass, and that's when Bink spotted the three-quarters-empty fifth of Jim Beam in Blackie's left hand. He balked, so I grabbed his arm and yanked him inside.

"Blackie, I want you to meet Bi—David Hanover.

David, Blackhand Coogan. David needs a safe house," I explained.

"Yeah?" Blackie set the bottle on the floor beside the littered coffee table, sat down, and reached for a cigarette. "What's the beef?"

I started to answer, but happened to notice Bink's face. He was staring openmouthed at the mess around us, the mess I'd somehow grown used to overlooking. The disassembled motorcycle engine and sound equipment Blackie's son had brought over and left ten years ago was like part of the furniture as far as I was concerned. And I'd stop noticing the overflowing ashtrays, crumpled fast-food containers, and empty beer bottles a long time ago.

"Give us a minute, Blackie." I hustled Bink down the hall into Blackie's bathroom, then shut the door.

That was a mistake. When I turned around to yell at him, all Bink could do was stare at the black mildew coating the ceiling and walls around the tub, at the deep rust stains in the basin, and the dozens of empty liquor bottles in the wastebasket under the sink. He shook his head sadly, like a doctor watching a dying patient.

"This is a real bad joke, Ronnie. Real bad."

"What's the problem?"

"The old guy's a lush, Ron. I need a bodyguard."

"You need a baby-sitter."

Even with a gallon of Scotch under his belt, Blackie could outwit, outmaneuver, and outfight most thugs. I told Bink as much, but he looked skeptical. "Listen, Bink, he can protect you. That's what you want, isn't it?"

He glanced pointedly at the bottle-filled wastebasket. "Unless somebody offers him a drink."

I was too exhausted to be diplomatic. "Just shut up and treat him with respect. He'll take your head off if you don't. And believe me, he will. Now, give me a hundred dollars."

"What? Are you crazy?"

"Hand it over, or I walk," I said, hating the way Bink was making me behave.

I left Bink grumbling in the bathroom and went back to the living room. Blackie was sitting on the couch, elbows on his knees. A Navajo blanket was thrown carelessly on the floor at his feet and the quarter-filled bottle of bourbon sat on the table in front of him.

He offered me a drink, then reached for another cigarette while I cleared a chair and sat down.

"So what's the story?" he asked.

I gave him an abbreviated version of Bink's morning call, his golf game, and his trouble with Mary Solis.

Blackie listened, then stubbed out his cigarette and asked, "Where'd you find this guy?"

"Remember I told you about a guy who accidentally saved Mitch's life?"

Blackie frowned, then shook his head.

"Okay, maybe I didn't. Mitch and Bink were in the same fraternity at Stanford, but Mitch wouldn't ever have noticed Bink if they hadn't both screwed up. It was some kind of prank. They took an enemy frat house's limo and were going to park it in front of a butcher shop for some reason—I can't remember why it was supposed to have been so funny.

"Mitch was too crocked to know what he was doing, so when the car stalled on the railroad tracks, he sort of passed out. Bink was sitting in the middle of the front seat with four kegs of beer between him and the passenger door. The only way Bink wasn't going to get smashed up when the train came was if he pushed Mitch out first. But Mitch doesn't see it that way. He says Bink could have gotten out the other side if he'd wanted to. And ever since, Mitch has felt indebted to Bink."

Blackie's eyes narrowed. "Hanover. Isn't he the one left you holding the bag on that insurance scam a couple years back?"

"He's in trouble, Blackie."

"If I remember right, he was in trouble back then, too, doll."

"Not like this. He just needs a place to stay tonight, maybe tomorrow. Can you keep an eye on him? He's too scared to stay by himself. I told him it'd cost him, and he said he'd pay."

Blackie shrugged. "Is he good for the money?"

I set the hundred on the pile of rubble on the table in front of him. Blackie nodded and inhaled another long toke off the cigarette. Then he took a deep slug from his bottle, swished the Scotch around in his mouth, and swallowed.

"Go ahead," he said. "I'll watch the little fuck."

17

WEDNESDAY MORNING DAWNED as one of those spectacular blue-skied days that make you want to spend the rest of your life hiking Marin or sailing the Bay. But since I'd spent most of the night putting the word out on the street and checking the usual sources for Mary Solis without results, then sleeping on the floor propped up by the open window so I wouldn't succumb to the gas fumes in my apartment, I woke up feeling cranky and with the nagging sensation that I was supposed to be somewhere.

Even an hour-long run didn't help. When I got home, just past nine o'clock, I was so intent on trying to figure out what else I could do to track down Mary Solis that I didn't even notice the shadow at the top of the landing.

As I approached my apartment door, the shadow moved. I jumped back, heart in my throat, ready to run, but a small-boned woman stepped into the light and said my name.

I recognized her instantly. "Edna!"

Her eyes were full of reproach. "You forgot, didn't you?"

I checked her for visual clues about what I might have forgotten. She wore not the modest suit and pumps she usually wore when we'd worked together as parole officers, but jeans, a sweater, and jacket over sneakers. Something casual. We were going to do something casual. "What?"

"Gabriél's softball kickoff. For the kids."

"I thought that was Wednesday."

"It *is* Wednesday, Ronnie." Edna checked her watch and clucked. "Hurry. You'd better change. The speeches start at nine-thirty."

We hit the park just as the ceremony ended. Even though I'd been the one who slept late and forgot about the event, I blamed Bink. But it was hard to stay surly on such a beautiful day.

Sun streamed down on the crowd of kids from the Mission as they lined up for their free softball gloves, uniforms, and It's-Its ice creams. Next week, when the school year started, their respective softball teams would begin playing in earnest.

Gabriél Juarez, the philanthropist who had made it all possible, stood casually on the dais, about ten feet behind a vacant podium, talking to the mayor and a state representative. He was a swarthy and compactly handsome man who exuded goodwill and charm. His black hair tied in a ponytail at his nape, his high cheekbones, and his regal bearing harkened back to his Aztec forebears, but the kindness in his eyes and the gentleness of his full-lipped smile were strictly his own.

He spotted us the instant we saw him.

"There they are!" He opened his arms expansively. "So glad you both could come." He hugged Edna, then me. Keeping his arm around me, he said, "You remember this woman, Mayor, don't you? This is Ronnie Ventana, the one I thanked in my speech. She recommended probation for me when you were my judge."

The mayor nodded, smiling at me. "Of course, of course. Excellent report," he muttered. Mayor Ashton had been the judge on Gabriél's case, and I'd been the probation officer.

Gabriél went on speaking to Mayor Ashton. "Ronnie—like you, Mayor—is responsible for everything you see here. If it weren't for you and Ronnie, I'd probably be in jail. And a lot of these boys and girls might eventually end up there too."

"The credit's all yours, Gabriél," I said. "I couldn't have written the glowing report or convinced Judge Ashton to grant you probation if you hadn't provided the material."

"She's right, you know," the mayor said.

"Ah." Gabriél kissed my cheek.

"What about me? Don't I get any credit? Ms. Ventana there wouldn't have written a probation report if I hadn't caught you in the first place."

We all turned to find a thick-necked bulldog of a man in a business suit: Chuck Vardigan—the guy I'd seen out on the golf course yesterday. Gabriél grinned and clapped him on the back.

"Ah, Chuck. You *pendejo*! Didn't you hear my speech? I thanked you too." He winked at me, then gazed around the circle. "You know everybody here, don't you? Mayor Ashton? Ronnie? Do you know Edna? No? This fellow, Edna, was the best bloodhound who ever graced the SEC."

At Edna's puzzled look Vardigan explained. "The Securities and Exchange Commission, the federal agency that oversees the stock markets. I happened to stumble onto Gabriél's stock scheme. It was so brilliant, I told Judge Ashton Gabriél was too smart to put in jail. And look, I was right, wasn't I?"

Everybody agreed. Mayor Ashton made a couple of bland remarks calculated not to offend anybody, then let the state representative say something else just as bland.

Vardigan waited for an opening, then said, "Say, Gabriél, there's a reporter over there who needs to know how many zeroes to add to the figure this team concept cost you. Can I borrow you for just a second to straighten this guy out?"

Gabriél begged us not to go away, then vanished into the throng with Vardigan.

"He's quite a philanthropist, wouldn't you say?" The mayor beamed after them like a proud uncle.

"He's wonderful," Edna agreed.

I was too busy trying to figure out how I was going to ask Mayor Ashton about his son, Felix, to pay much attention, but then I noticed the state rep. Her brown hair fit her like a helmet. She was fifty, an ex-supervisor for the city who'd managed to get elected in spite of being conservative. And she was staring at me and frowning.

"Are you related to those burglars?" she finally asked.

The mayor stopped in mid-sentence and dropped his smile. Everybody was quiet.

" 'Cisco Ventana," the mayor said. " 'Cisco and Olivia Ventana. They stole a necklace from my wife. Years ago. We were living in a high rise at Green and Leavenworth."

"How do you know it was my parents?" I asked, trying my best to sound like I was making pleasant conversation.

"Why, the police—"

"The police don't decide guilt, Mr. Mayor. Judges and juries do that, remember? My parents were never convicted of a crime. Never."

"It was a necklace," the mayor said, staring at my throat like he thought I'd be wearing the damn pearls or whatever they were. "Rubies and gold."

"Can't help you there, sir, but maybe you can help me. Can we talk about your son?"

He took a step back in retreat and frowned. "Felix?"

"Right. Can you tell me why he'd sponsor a petty

scam artist with no money and no pedigree to the Saint George Club?"

His frown deepened. "Felix would never do such a thing."

"Don't bet the ranch on it, Mayor."

I felt a tug on my arm. It was Edna. "Ronnie, look!" She pointed into the crowd behind the mayor's back. "There's Gabriél's wife. We'd better go say hello."

She pulled me away and didn't release my arm until we were deep into the crowd and out of hearing range of the mayor.

"Whew!" she said. "I hate confrontations."

"Me too."

Edna laughed. "No, you don't. You thrive on them."

"It's just that every time somebody mentions my parents, I lose it."

"You never did at the parole office."

"Those guys thought my parents were heroes. They put them on a pedestal." I looked around. "Where's Juana? Did you just say you saw her to get me out of there?"

"No, I did see her." Edna searched the crowd. "She was over there a minute ago. There! Look! Over there."

Juana Juarez was kneeling near third base, talking to two little girls. Both were brown-skinned like Juana, like my own father, and like Gabriél. Each clutched her free glove and uniform in one hand and ice cream in the other.

"Hi," I said when we finally reached them.

Juana looked up, hesitated, then smiled, showing her dimples. Short, curly black hair framed a coarse-featured oval face that she softened with makeup. "Ronnie! Edna! Your timing's perfect. If these girls don't get their picture taken with Gabriél, their mothers will never forgive me. He's over there." She took each girl by the wrist and knelt again. "Go with them, *niñas*. You'll have your pictures taken, then you can play, all right?"

The smaller of the two tucked her glove under her skinny arm and trustingly offered me her hand.

"Hurry," Juana said, then sort of shooed us in the direction of the photographer.

I glanced back over my shoulder once and saw a beaming Chuck Vardigan approach Juana and embrace her. She pushed him away quickly and looked in Gabriél's direction. When she saw me staring, she turned guiltily away and left Chuck standing alone looking angry and confused.

"Hurry, Ronnie," Edna called from ahead of me.

The little girl tugged at my hand, and we plunged into the crowd, trying to catch up with Edna and her charge.

We got the girls there in time, watched as Gabriél told jokes and made them smile for the camera, then listened as the photographer asked each girl her name. The small one, the one I'd brought over, smiled up at me when she answered.

"Ana Solis."

I dropped to one knee between her and the photographer and took the child's hands in both of mine.

"Did you say Solis?"

She nodded.

"What's your mother's name, Ana?"

"María," she said sweetly. "María Elena Solis."

18

I T TURNED OUT the girl's uncle had brought her, not
her mother. "Uncle" could mean anything from uncle to her mother's boyfriend. I didn't have the heart
to ask the girl to explain which she meant.

"Do you know *mi mamá*?" Ana Solis asked.

"I might know a friend of hers. Where do you live?"

"Ronnie!" Edna touched my arm reprovingly.

"It's okay, Edna," I said, then turned back to Ana.
"Where do you live?"

"With my *abuela*."

"Does your *mamá* live with your grandmother too?"

"No, she lives with my uncle. I see her a lot, though.
She brings me *pastillas* and *muñecas*."

"Where's your uncle?"

The tiny girl looked around. "I don't know. Can I go
play now?"

Gabriél said something, and when I turned back,
Ana Solis had taken her little friend and vanished into
the crowd.

"Where'd they go?"

Edna and Gabriél stared at me.

"I've got to find that kid," I said.

There had to be at least two hundred children and a
hundred adults milling around the park. I dove into the
throng, and Edna followed on my heels. We worked the

crowd for about twenty minutes before Edna grabbed my wrist.

"There." She pointed at two figures crossing the street half a block down from the park. A man walking with a tiny girl in a blue dress and a baseball cap.

"Get the car and meet me at the corner," I shouted, then hurried after them.

19

WE TAILED THEM to a house a few blocks away and watched while Ana Solis skipped down the walk from the car to a green-and-white house off Mission. I jotted down the address, then fell in behind her "uncle's" white Ford Pinto.

The Colma trailer park where Ana Solis's "uncle" led us wasn't exactly in the kind of neighborhood you'd think a Mercedes-driving upscale woman would hang her suit, but maybe she liked to keep a low profile.

When we drove up, there was no sign of the navy-blue Mercedes, but the dusty white Ford Pinto was parked on a slab of concrete next to the trailer.

"What are you going to do?" Edna asked.

"I'll give him a minute, then I'll go in and talk."

Music suddenly blasted from the trailer. It was so loud, I could even make out the lyrics of the song—something in heavy rock about it shouldn't be like this.

"If I'm not back in twenty minutes, use that pay phone we passed at the entrance to call the cops."

Edna nodded solemnly and watched me leave the car.

The curtain fluttered at the window to the left when I pounded on the trailer's rusted door. Seconds later the music died and the door squeaked wide open.

The kid in the doorway was about seventeen, barefoot and bare-chested, in blue jeans, clutching twenty-pound barbells in either hand.

"It's the music, huh?" His smile was good-natured. He bent both elbows toward him to bring the weights up to his shoulders, then down again. His biceps, abdominals, and pectorals all rippled, but he had a long way to go before he'd beat out Arnold Schwarzenegger.

Ana's "uncle" was attractive, with thick black hair, tousled and uncombed, and teeth that flashed white against his olive skin. His wide, sensuous lips formed a perfect, soft cupid's bow that made you wonder what it'd be like to kiss them. The cocky way he held his head and sort of posed in the open doorway made it clear that he knew he was good-looking.

I told him the music was fine. "Actually I'm looking for Mary Solis. Know where I can find her?"

He kept working his arms rhythmically. "Haven't seen her in a week."

"She lives here, doesn't she?"

"Sometimes."

"Are you her boyfriend?"

"Ha! Don't make me puke." Another wide grin. "I'm her brother."

He didn't seem dangerous. In fact he seemed almost wholesome, with an awkward, goofy kind of bravado. "Is there someplace else I can find her? Does she ever visit her daughter?"

"Ana? Sometimes, not often. Ana said she came yesterday, so she won't see her for another couple of weeks."

"Look, it's really important that I talk to her. Maybe I can reach her at work?"

His brows narrowed. "You a cop?"

I showed him my I.D. He frowned, and his lips moved as he read the small print. Then he looked at me and grinned again.

"Ha! I never seen a lady P.I. before. Show me your gun."

He looked disappointed when I told him I don't own one. "Mind if I come in?"

He tilted his head to one side, then shrugged. "Okay, sure. Why not?"

The living room was probably eight by ten feet. It was crammed with the cheapest model of every sort of electronic gadget ever advertised: wide-screen TV, CD player, VCR, stereo, reel-to-reel tape machine, tuners, receivers, and a set of gigantic speakers in two corners.

Knotty-wood paneling and tiny windows with flowery-chintz curtains adorned the walls. There was a toreador and charging bull painted on black velvet in a gilt frame over a shabby red sofa, two armchairs, and a tiny coffee table. The carpet was an orange shag that wasn't very shaggy anymore, or very orange either.

"My name's Henry, by the way. You want to sit? Here. Sit right here." He switched the weights to his left hand and cleared some dirty clothes off an armchair by throwing them on the floor behind it. Then he resumed his arm curls.

"I got about a hundred more to go," he explained.

"Sure." I watched his arms move up and down, up and down, then cleared my throat. "About Mary?"

"Ah, *sí*, mon. I can tell you she's not at work, 'cause she don't really work. I mean, not really. She in some kind of trouble?" He seemed more curious than worried.

"She could be. I'll know more after I talk to her." I watched his arms and chest pump rhythmically.

"What's your sister do for a living?"

"This and that."

"Any idea why she'd sic four Uzi-toting thugs after a client of mine?"

His arms stopped moving. He grinned. "She did that?"

"Yes."

"Ha! That María! She's a crazy one." He shook his head, laughed again, and resumed the curls.

"You don't seem too surprised."

"Nothing María does surprises me." He kept moving his arms. His breathing was coming harder now. "I told you, she's crazy."

"Has she done this sort of thing before?"

"Well . . ." He grinned. "Not with Uzis, man."

"Tell me about it."

"Some punk rear-ended her Mercedes and jerked her around about paying for it, so she asked me and a friend to beat him up. It was easy. We didn't use no Uzis, though." He sounded disappointed that he hadn't.

"Could she be upset because my friend doesn't want to go out with her anymore?"

His grin widened. "You never met my sister, heh?"

"No."

"No. You'd know how silly that was if you had. Not María. She's turned down so many proposals of marriage, I lost track. Men forget themselves and their girlfriends and wives when they meet María. She makes men crazy. It's not the other way around. No, María wouldn't do such a thing, because she always gets her way."

"What if she were pregnant?"

"That's not possible."

"Oh?"

"María had a surgery a long time ago, after Ana. When she was fifteen, I think." His hands stopped. Slowly he lowered the weights until his arms dangled at his sides. His dark eyes held mine. "María can take care of herself."

"Did she ever mention a Bink or David Hanover to you?"

"Bink?" He wrinkled his nose. *"¿Qué es eso?"*

"It's his nickname?"

"No, she never said Hanover. What's he look like?"

I described Bink, but he was shaking his head before I'd even finished. "No."

"How about Art Spenger?"

"Uh-uh."

"What about the heavyweights?" I told him what I could about the goons, but he seemed genuinely without a clue. "Does she have any other brothers or sisters besides you?"

"Nope."

I asked if he had a picture of her, and he vanished down the hall and came back a minute later with a snapshot of the two of them on a beach. "She took me to Hawaii for my birthday in January."

I studied the laughing woman in the picture. She looked about twenty-two, with a knockout figure, a stunning tan, and thick, sable-black hair that just brushed the tip of her bare shoulders. Her toothy smile reminded me of a couple of Bink's former girlfriends. "Who took the picture?"

He scowled. "Her boyfriend came with us."

"Got a picture of him?"

He disappeared again and came back with a second photograph: a glowing, suntanned Mary Solis in an emerald-colored evening gown and an equally tanned fellow at her arm in a tuxedo.

I bent closer, lifting the image up to the light from the tiny window in order to see her companion's face. Dark hair, cleft chin, and blue eyes set wide beneath a high, broad forehead. I'd seen the face in the papers often, usually in the company of his father, the mayor.

"Felix Ashton?"

"You know him, eh?"

"I know of him. He's Mary's boyfriend?"

"Not anymore. He's a son of a dog, you know? He makes me puke."

"Why?"

"The way he is. He thinks he's better than me. Better than María. He was always asking us to do things for him, you know, pick up his laundry, get him a beer, wash his car, shit like that, like we were his servants. María did it, but not me. I told him to fuck himself. Just like that: 'Go fuck yourself,' I said."

I studied Mary Solis's image, searching for the secret behind her sadistic behavior, but the only thing I noticed was the emerald ring on her right hand—a huge stone set in a filigree of deep-yellow gold. It was beautiful, and if it was real, it could have paid for fifty house trailers like the one I was standing in.

"Why'd they break up?"

Henry Solis shrugged. "When something good happens, you don't ask why."

But breaking up hadn't been good for Art Spenger or for Bink. Why was Felix Ashton still alive?

I set the picture of Henry and his sister on the table and held up the other one. "Mind if I hold on to this? I'll return it when I'm finished."

"Keep it," he said. "What do I want a picture of that *pendejo* for?"

He stretched out on the floor and started doing sit-ups.

"Give Mary a message from me, will you? Tell her that the guy she's looking for wants to work things out, okay? Tell her to phone me, day or night. My number's on this card. We can explain everything, but she's got to call off the Uzis. Got that?"

He grunted, murmured "twenty-two" under his breath, then asked me to write it down. I did, on the back of my business card, and left him counting and puffing on the floor, almost to fifty-eight.

20

MRS. PARDUCCI CAREENED out of her door the instant my foot hit the top step.

"Ronnie, dear," she said. "I've been waiting for you to come home."

It was seven P.M., and even though it wasn't her fault my afternoon-long stakeout of Felix Ashton's condo hadn't produced Felix, I really wasn't in the mood. I glanced pointedly at my watch and gave her a faint-hearted smile.

"I'm kind of in a hurry," I said, slipping my key into the lock and remembering with a sinking feeling that I'd forgotten to buy a replacement mattress again today.

"But I've got something for you. Something for the case."

"The *case*?"

She beckoned me gleefully into her apartment. I realized as I crossed the threshold that I'd never been inside her place before. The furniture was all second-hand, flea-market stuff except for a huge brown corduroy BarcaLounger centered in front of a nine-inch television. A tiny cot in the corner was where she slept.

Mrs. Parducci crossed the room to a nicked-up dresser, picked up a manila folder, and grinned. The result was hideous: bulbous nose and long, yellowed teeth shining at me under the glare of the bare bulb overhead. "Here," she said. "Here's what I got."

I took the folder and read the name on the tab: Arthur D. Spenger. June 13, 19—.

"What is this?"

Mrs. Parducci moved her hands in urgent circles, like a child encouraging another to unwrap a present.

"Open it! Look inside!"

The heading at the top of the first page read, "Autopsy Report." I ran my hand over the paper and felt the indentation of typewritten letters.

"Mrs. P., this is the original."

Mrs. Parducci beamed. "It's part of the case, isn't it? You need it for the case, don't you?"

"Well, sure, but . . ." I glanced at the page and couldn't help myself—I started reading.

I skimmed the page for a list of injuries, but the report said Art Spenger's hands showed no signs of abrasion. He hadn't tried to claw his way out of the refrigerator he'd died in.

Maybe he'd been knocked out first, then put inside. I read on. His head and skull weren't injured in any way. I was about to give up when I turned the page and saw the results of the blood tests.

"Bingo!" I said. Arthur Spenger had had enough alcohol in his system to drown a horse.

"What's it mean?" Mrs. Parducci demanded. "Why did he kill himself?"

"He didn't. They got him drunk, then stuffed him inside the fridge with the tank."

Mrs. Parducci crossed herself and muttered something in Italian.

"He suffocated before he came to. That's how he died." But why? Why, if she was a "black widow," like Bink claimed, would Mary Solis kill Spenger and not Ashton?

I slapped the cover of the folder shut and handed it to Mrs. Parducci.

"Wipe the fingerprints off this and mail it back to them," I said. "And don't"—I paused at the door—"don't ever do anything like that again."

I could hear her cackle even after I was downstairs and had closed the front door.

I slipped the Styrofoam hamburger box into the white bag and dumped it onto the backseat. I'd decided to go back to Felix Ashton's, figuring that I'd rather sleep in my car than suck gas fumes all night again.

I'd been there for half an hour, but it was still early. Eight o'clock. And maybe . . . I glanced up and held my breath as the front door to the brown-shingled Victorian opened. Felix Ashton—in the flesh—with a tall, horse-faced woman on his arm. I guessed them both to be about twenty-five. She wasn't Mary Solis.

They were both pretty dressed up, like they were going someplace important, but the woman looked like she'd been crying.

Ashton guided her gently by the elbow to a red BMW parked in the drive. I rolled my window down and tried to be inconspicuous while I strained to hear what they were saying.

Their lips were moving, their expressions deep and serious, hers almost mournful and his angry, but all I could hear was the faint whine of her voice and his urgent, low tone.

It didn't seem like the kind of scene to interrupt, so I stayed in my car and waited. When they got in the BMW and drove off, I hesitated for only a second, cranked the engine, and followed.

A few turns put us on outer Broadway, the monied core of Pacific Heights everybody calls the Gold Coast. Power and wealth are the norm here. The mansions and their owners are all worth millions and, from what I remember of my mother's stories when I was a kid, most of the people who live in the neighborhood spend the greatest part of their time hosting or going to parties.

The house Ashton pulled up to had about three or four white-coated parking valets running from the sidewalk out to the humming Ferraris and Jaguars that kept pulling up on the street and disgorging well-dressed couples. I double-parked the Toyota about five doors down, near the start of the block, cut the engine, and watched.

When it was Ashton's red BMW's turn, one of the attendants ran out to take his keys. But Ashton didn't get out. He and the woman sat there a good minute or two, talking heatedly to each other, before waving the attendant away and driving off.

I didn't know if or what Felix Ashton could tell me about Mary Solis, but I was intrigued, and followed. They stopped by a pay phone at a corner market on Pacific. The woman got out, made a call, then joined Ashton again, and they sped off toward the freeway and Oakland.

Half an hour later I tailed them up Park Boulevard, where they turned left and veered up into Piedmont. They stopped at a darkened house on Eastview, and both of them went to the door. Nobody answered.

After circling around to the rear of the house, they returned to their car and drove back across the Bay Bridge to the party on outer Broadway. I watched from my car as they disappeared inside.

21

I'D NEVER BEEN to a Gold Coast party before and I was starting to wonder if I ever would. The guy at the door turned down the five different reasons I'd given him for letting me in. I was sulking out on the sidewalk, trying to come up with alternative plan B when the cute guy I'd met at the Saint George Club strolled up in a tux, a blond deb clinging to his arm.

"Ronnie! Hi! How are you?" He seemed as pleased to see me as I was to see him. "Mike Neal, remember? Bink's friend with the golf clubs?"

I practically lunged at him. "Do me a favor, will you? Can you get me inside?"

"Sure." He didn't even give a second glance to my jeans and backpack. Instead he turned to his date. "Would you mind, Chotsie?"

Chotsie fluttered her lashes at him and acted sporting, but the jerk at the door flagged us anyway. He was better than a German shepherd.

"I'm sorry, sir. I cannot permit . . ." He launched into a five-minute flack spiel that left me marveling at how somebody could take so long to say no and make it sound like he was doing you a favor.

Nice guy that he was, Mike Neal just sort of shrugged and backed off.

"Look," I said, scribbling a note on a pad from my backpack. "Do you know Felix Ashton?"

He nodded.

"Great. Can you find him and give him this for me?"

Mike Neal took the note, winked at me, and disappeared inside with his date.

Half an hour later Ashton appeared in the doorway. The troll pointed at me, and Ashton walked toward me with a mixture of alarm and curiosity on his handsome young face.

"Yes?" He stopped a few feet away from me, by the front gates, and tried to read my face with his anxious, wide-set blue eyes. We were out of earshot of the door weasel and of the valets behind us. "Your note said it was urgent. Who are you?"

"I'm a private investigator. My name's Ronnie Ventana and I'm trying to find Mary Solis."

"Mary? Why? Is she in trouble?"

For an ex-boyfriend he seemed pretty concerned.

"She might be. I need to talk to her. Do you know where I can find her?"

"No." He said it too quickly. "We don't see each other anymore. I don't know where she lives. She moved after we broke up."

"Can you give me her old address?"

"What's this about?"

"It's a long story, Mr. Ashton, but it's possible you might be able to save a man's life if you help me find Mary."

"*Save a man's life?* I don't get it. What's this got to do with her?"

"She's involved with some people." I told him briefly about the goons and sort of hinted at Bink's black-widow theory.

"That's crazy. Mary's in real estate. She doesn't

know any gangsters. Besides, we broke up six weeks ago and I'm still alive. She's not trying to kill me."

"Did you break it off or did she?"

"What difference does that make? Oh, I see. She did. And I'd take her back in a minute," he said fiercely. "I don't know who you've been talking to, but you've got the wrong Mary Solis."

I showed him the picture Henry had given me, and it seemed to anger him.

"I don't know what you're trying to do, but if you hurt Mary, I'll—I'll make sure you pay. I wouldn't give you her address even if I had it!" He turned on his heel and marched into the house.

The phone booth at Vallejo and Laguna smelled of urine, so I left the door open. Blackie didn't pick up until after the seventh ring.

"Yeah?" he growled. I could almost smell the alcohol and cigarette smoke through the wires.

"How's it going?" They'd been together over twenty-four hours.

He exhaled loudly. "Fuck, doll. This guy's like livin' with mosquitoes."

I laughed.

"What's it gonna hurt to throw him to the dogs? Say the word and I cut him loose. Do the world a favor."

"It's tempting, isn't it? Want me to say something to him?"

Blackie chuckled quietly. "Nah. He's not goin' anywhere. Any luck?"

"Not much." I told him about Mary Solis's brother, Art Spenger's autopsy report, and Felix Ashton's rudeness. "Need anything from the outside world? Food? Beer?"

"How about a grenade to shove down this creep's throat?"

"Listen, can you put him on? I need to ask him something."

"He's kind of tied up right now. Let me ask him for you."

As he spoke, a voice in the background, faint and desperate, shouted, *"RONNIE!* Is that Ronnie on the phone, you prick?"

Bink's voice sounded far, far away. "Help, Ronnie! Get me out of here. He—"

Blackie muttered a curse, covered the phone, and shouted something, then came back on to the sound of more screaming in the background. I couldn't make out Bink's words, but his tone was desperate.

"What's going on there, Blackie?"

"Later, doll," Blackie said. "I'd better shut this little fuck down."

"Don't—Blackie? *Blackie!*"

22

WHEN I GOT to Blackie's, his front door was unlocked and he was propped up on the couch, a can of beer in one hand and a cigarette in the other. The television was tuned to a boxing match with the sound turned off. In the background a radio played soft jazz.

"They call this shit boxing," Blackie said, shaking his grizzled head in disgust. "Fuck, a cripple could do better. Look—look there. Ever see a worse right hook?" He pointed at the screen with his can of beer. "Pitiful."

I looked around the room. "Where's Bink?"

Blackie jerked his thumb toward the back of the house. "Try the head."

The bathroom door was closed, so I rapped on it gently.

"Bink?" I tapped again and waited, then turned the knob and pushed. "Bink? Are you—"

He was slumped on the floor between the wall and the toilet, his head and one arm draped over the toilet seat, eyes closed, one leg resting straight out on the floor toward me. The other leg was crumpled up beneath him.

I rushed in, knelt down, and shook his knee. "Bink! Are you all right? *Bink?*"

His head jerked up and slammed into the tank hardware. "Ouch!"

He looked terrible. Dark circles beneath bloodshot eyes. Two days' worth of blond stubble on his cheeks. I backed away so he'd have room to stand, but he stayed where he was, muttering a string of groggy curses and eventually lifting his unfocused eyes to my face. The light of intelligence came slowly, but he finally recognized me.

"Ronnie!" he rasped with a voice so hoarse I barely recognized it. "Thank God, you're back. He's crazy, Ron. I thought he was going to kill me."

He moved his arm, and something clinked—metal against metal. I peered in close. Bink's right wrist was handcuffed to the toilet.

"What'd you do?" I asked.

"Me? Dammit, Ronnie! Why's everything always my fault?" His voice was gaining strength, but it was still hoarse. "This crazy chick sends tankers with guns after me, and it's because *I* did something to *her*. This lunatic handcuffs me to the plumbing, and you're worried about what *I* did. What about them? Why can't somebody else do anything bad? Look at me! I can barely move. You call this right? Shit."

"Did you try to leave? Is that why he put you here?"

"The old geezer's nuts, Ronnie. Nuts. And so are you for bringing me here."

"Are you all right?" I asked.

He raised his handcuffed wrist and half croaked, half snarled, "What's it look like?"

Apart from exhaustion and a bad temper, he seemed to be okay. Nothing freedom, throat lozenges, and a shave wouldn't fix.

I sat down on the edge of the tub. "We need to talk."

"Talk! Are you crazy?" He raised his hand and rattled the cuffs. "Get me out of here, Ron. I'm paying you to protect me, not turn me over to some maniac. For Chrissake, Ron, GET ME OUT OF HERE!"

I put a finger to my lips. "Shhh. You're going to get out of here when I say so. Not a minute before."

He stopped his pitiful, raspy shouting and stared.

"Now," I said, "did Art Spenger have a drinking problem?"

Bink's scowl deepened. "Who cares? Will you just get me out of here? Forget I ever said anything. Forget you ever saw me."

"Answer the question, Bink. Did he?"

Bink sighed and rubbed his free hand wearily across his eyes. "I heard a rumor he'd been through detox a couple of times in high school and college. Why? What difference does it make?"

"The autopsy report says he was drunk when he died."

"Sure, that makes sense. Mary can drink anybody under the table. She got him drunk and the goons shoved him in the box."

"Or he could have been so drunk he didn't know what he was doing. That's what Philly Post is going to say."

Bink swore. "Come on, Ronnie. Is that it? Will you get the key and unlock these things now?"

"Tell me about Felix Ashton."

"Felix? *Felix?* Felix Ashton's got nothing to do with this idiot bitch who's trying to kill me."

"Want to bet?" I unzipped my backpack, pulled out the picture Henry Solis had given me, and tossed it onto the toilet seat. Bink took one look at it and his face drained of all color.

"Good God! Where did you get that?"

"Doesn't matter. Tell me about Ashton."

"Felix knows Mary? Jesus! This could blow my deal with Carolina. Shit. They're cousins, you know."

"Who?"

"Felix Ashton and Carolina Pogue. If he tells Carolina about me and Mary, I'm dead meat. She'll drop me so fast, I won't even get a chance to explain. There goes the sweetest woman I ever had." He glanced forlornly at the photo. "When is this from?"

"Last January."

"Shit, how do they know each other? How'd you get this picture? Is she threatening him too?"

"No."

"Man, oh, man," he muttered, then blanched. "Damn! You talked to Felix? Did you mention my name?"

"I didn't blow your engagement, Bink, if that's what you're asking."

He managed a weak but relieved smile. "Good. You've got to get me out of this, Ronnie, and I mean fast. And don't talk to him anymore. I mean, not if you're gonna drag my name into it. This gets back to Carolina, and I'm out in the cold."

"Did Ashton ever mention Mary Solis to you?"

"Why would he?"

"They broke up, Bink. They used to date and they broke up six weeks ago."

"So?"

"So that sort of disproves your black-widow theory, doesn't it?"

Bink slid his legs out from beneath him until they lay flat on the floor. His back was propped awkwardly against the toilet tank and the wall. He couldn't have looked more miserable. When he spoke, his voice cracked. "Why is she doing this to me?"

I glanced across the mildewed tile at Bink. "That's something we're just going to have to find out. Come on, tell me more about Ashton."

"What's there to tell? I barely know the guy. Carolina introduced us so Felix could get me into the club. She thought her dad would like me more if I belonged. That's the only reason I met the guy. He's a real asshole, but I didn't care as long as he got me into the club."

"What's so important about the club?"

"Status, Ron. You ought to know about this shit. Wasn't your mom a big society name? You're nobody unless you belong to the right club. You know that. The golf game this morning? I wouldn't have been out there if I wasn't on the Saint George roster. Everybody accepts you if you're in. It's like the fraternity. Once you're in, you've got a bunch of blood brothers that'll help you make it for the rest of your life."

"Like Felix Ashton?"

"Forget Felix. You've got to check out the car-pool pickup line. Fifty bucks says she'll turn up there. Look for the blue Mercedes. I mean it, Ronnie. That's the only steady place I can think where you'll find her." He raised his wrist and rattled the handcuffs. "Now will you get the key off that old prick in there and get me out of here?"

23

ORNING ON WIDE, tree-lined Park Boulevard was pleasant in a suburban sort of way. The houses were all spread out and had yards and lawns, something only the priciest places in the city could boast.

I'd gotten up early, gone for a run, then showered, dug out my dark plaid suit and heels, and headed across the Bay to Oakland.

I stood in a line of seven business-suited hitchhikers near the corner of Park Boulevard and Avenida, watching a parade of BMWs and Peugeots and an occasional not-navy-blue Mercedes-Benz roll down from the elite heights of Piedmont and Montclair. Most of the cars zoomed past, their drivers intent on rushing into the city to bring home another bucket of cash. But the occasional one would stop and offer one of us a ride.

I was last in line for about three minutes, until a stocky, short-haired blonde with a gym bag and a briefcase queued up behind me. She smelled of soap and nodded hello when I glanced her way, so I made small talk with her and quickly steered the conversation to Mary Solis. I showed her the picture, casually keeping my thumb over Felix Ashton's face.

"Oh, her," she said, twisting her thin lips into a disparaging frown. "I don't know her by name, but I've seen her around. She's into men in a big way. I think she uses

this line as her personal dating service. See down there?"
She pointed to a spot a block and a half away. "She'll
wait down there until it's a man's turn, then she'll zoom
up and smile like it's a big coincidence. Can you believe
it?" A sudden wariness crept into her expression. "She's
not a friend of yours, is she?"

"Never met her."

"Good. I rode with her once. She didn't have the
woman who usually rides with her that day, so she
needed two people. The guy in front of me was that
squirrely idiot who thinks he's Casanova. You've probably seen him here, Dave something."

"Hanover?"

"I don't know his last name. I just heard her call
him Dave."

I described Bink, and she said, "Yeah, that's him.
Anyway, she made a date with him before we were
across the bridge. I couldn't believe it. I was sitting in
back, which is okay with me, watching these two. She
asked him a whole bunch of questions about himself, but
she wasn't nosy about it. She came across like a big flirt,
and this Casanova just lapped it up. I felt like a voyeur."

"What kind of questions did she ask him?"

"Personal stuff. Stuff you want to know before you
go out with somebody but never have the nerve to ask,
like where do you live? Where do you work? Do you
own or rent? Hobbies? Interests? Do you travel? She
gave him the works, which was fine with me. I don't care
if she uses the car pool to enrich her dating life. What
upset me was I was late for work that day because she
drove him straight to the Embarcaderos—that's where
he works—instead of the Transbay Terminal like she's
supposed to. I work south of Market, so I had to walk
five extra blocks that day. Can you believe the nerve?"

A blue BMW stopped and two people got in. We
moved up a couple of steps, and a bottom-heavy man in
a checkered shirt and a plaid sport coat ambled up the

sidewalk and got in line behind us. He looked about thirty-two and was prematurely bald, with a golden aura of fuzzy down at the top of his head where his hair should have been.

The blonde smiled at him, called him Bob when she said hello, then asked if he'd ever ridden with the vamp in the blue Mercedes. He sort of perked up.

"Yeah, once," he drawled in an accent that put him from somewhere in the Deep South. He smiled at me, friendly, automatically including me in the conversation.

"You know how sometimes the drivers ignore you and sometimes they talk your ear off. Well, she didn't do either. She was real chummy at first, asking me this and asking me that, drawing me out and making me feel like I was the most interesting fella she'd ever run across. And that friend of hers didn't say a word. Just sat up there quiet, like she was at church or something. Then she asks me where I work, and that's where I lost her. Happens every time."

"Where do you work?"

"The IRS, ma'am." His eyes twinkled. "See, I jus' lost you, too, didn't I?"

"It was probably for the best, Bob," the blonde said. Then she turned to me. "I think she's a gold digger."

"Why, Lucy, how can you say that? She drives a Mercedes-Benz," Bob said.

"It's an old one."

"What did she tell you about herself? Did she happen to mention where she lives, maybe? Or where she works?" I asked Bob.

"Now, that's a real good question, 'cause I thought about her afterwards, and to tell you the truth, she didn't give me enough to even dream about."

We moved up another spot, then two more in quick succession. The guy in front of me cleared his throat. "I rode with her once," he said.

He was young, probably twenty-five, with a goatee,

eyeglasses, and a nervous air, like he was afraid something bad was going to happen to him before he'd have a chance to worry about it first.

Bob chuckled. "Izzat so? She cut you, too, son?"

"No."

"No?" Bob eyed the officious little guy and looked skeptical.

"In fact," the little guy added, "she offered to fix me dinner."

"Must not work for the IRS," Bob muttered enviously.

"Bentley Stearns," the little guy announced like it meant he worked at the White House. I'd never heard of the company, but that didn't mean they weren't big or important. "Of course, I turned her down."

"Why 'of course'?" I asked.

He raised his left hand and wiggled his ring finger. The flat, hammered gold wedding band twinkled in the morning light.

"She was an odd person," he went on. "Asked me a lot of questions while being coy about herself. I was very uncomfortable with the whole scenario. I found out later an associate at my firm had been involved with her. Broke up his marriage, ruined his career."

I forced myself to sound casual. "When was this?"

"About a year ago."

I told him I'd like to talk to the guy and asked if he knew how I could reach him.

"Rob Yost? I'm afraid I can't help you there. He left under a cloud. I haven't kept in touch. You know how it is." He studied me a bit more closely. "I suppose I could ask around at the office."

He fished out a card of his own and handed it to me. "Why don't you call me this afternoon?"

Before I could ask him anything else, a gray Peugeot appeared with a driver and one passenger. The officious-looking squirt jumped in and sped away.

I grilled the rest of the people left in the car-pool line, but nobody could tell me anything else about Mary Solis. I hung around a little bit longer, turning down three rides after everybody else had left, then finally gave up around nine-thirty.

I killed some time eating breakfast in a little café on Park, then checked my phone messages. Edna's was the only call, so I dropped in another pair of dimes and called her back.

"Ronnie, hi! I checked my records for Mary Solis, María Solis, and María E. Solis. I got nothing."

It had been a long shot anyway. "What about the brother?"

"Henry Solis was arrested last year for roughing up a guy. Assault and battery. He got community service and hasn't been heard from since. Does that help you?"

"Sort of. Thanks, Edna."

I called Juana Juarez next.

"So good to hear from you, Ronnie. Thank you for coming Wednesday. It meant so much to Gabriél to see you there. We tried to find you later so you could come out to lunch with us, but you were gone by then."

"Something came up. Listen, Juana, I'd like to meet Ana Solis's mother. Can you arrange it?"

"Ana Solis?" She sounded surprised.

"The little girl, you said you know her mother."

"Actually Ana lives with her grandmother, Ronnie. Would you like to meet her?"

"You don't know where Ana's mother lives?"

"I can ask Guadalupe."

"The grandmother?"

"Yes. Shall I?"

"That'd be great, Juana. Thanks. If you find something out, just leave a message on my answering machine, will you?"

"Of course. Ronnie?"

"Yes?"

"This does not mean there will be trouble for Ana, does it?"

"Trouble?"

"Yes. Are you working on a case that involves Ana's mother?"

"No." The lie was out before I knew it. "I just want to talk to her about the kid. She's a heart stopper, isn't she?"

"Preciosa."

An awkward silence filled the line, then Juana spoke. "About Chuck Vardigan, what you saw the other night," she said. "I can explain."

A forgotten memory popped into my mind: Gabriél at lunch a year ago making a passing remark that since he was straight and honest now, he couldn't hold Juana's attention anymore. I thought he'd been joking when he said she liked him more as a bad boy than a rich boy. "You don't have to explain anything, Juana. It's none of my business."

She seemed relieved not to have to talk about it, but insisted. "Chuck's wife is an alcoholic," she said. "I listened to his problems, I was sympathetic, and he misunderstood. There's nothing between us. He is Gabriél's friend as much as he is mine."

I didn't comment, so she changed the subject and got off the line the first chance she got.

My watch said it was ten-thirty when I hung up, so I figured the guy at Bentley Stearns had had enough time to get settled in. I fished out his card and dialed.

"Oh, it's you," he said, not making any effort to disguise his annoyance. "I've only just arrived. Hold on."

I fed the phone coins until he finally came back on.

"You're lucky my secretary hasn't cleaned out my Rolodex," he said. "Try 1185 Meadow Lane. Piedmont."

24

THE YOUNG WOMAN unloading the green Volvo wagon in the drive had short, frizzy brown hair, a harried expression, and a baby on each hip. Her designer sweatshirt and sweatpants looked new and sort of hung off her narrow shoulders, giving her thin body a sporty look that her haggard face didn't live up to. She managed a weary smile when I waved at her and hurried across the lawn. "Mrs. Yost?"

"Sorry, she won't be back until late tonight."

I followed her to the front door. "Maybe you can help me."

"I don't know. I'm just the baby-sitter."

I kept smiling and asked her name, which was Suzanne, then told her mine. "I'm really looking for Mr. Yost, Suzanne, the Rob Yost who used to work at Bentley Stearns. Does he live here?"

She narrowed her eyes, jiggled one baby, then the other. "Uh—not anymore. Look, I've got to change this baby." She dipped her chin toward the one on her right hip. "Why don't you come inside and we can talk?"

I followed her through the foyer, down a hall to a carpeted room with a table, a blaring television she'd obviously left on, and stacked boxes of disposable diapers. She set one baby on the floor to crawl and the other on the table. She seemed glad to have an adult around.

While she took the kid's clothes off and wiped him down, she babbled and smiled at him—to keep him from crying, I guess.

I thought of all the creeps I'd met in my life. They'd all started out like this, helpless and innocent.

"They're twins," she said to me. "Nine-month-old twins."

I made noises like I thought they were cute, then watched her strap on the diaper and swing the kid to the carpet to join his brother. They crawled around making goo-goo sounds and sucking on every toy they ran across. They looked a lot happier than Suzanne.

"So," I said, "do you have an address for Mr. Yost?"

"Well, I don't know how much it's going to help you. Maybe we should sit down," she said, leading me to a breakfast bar that separated the room we were in from the kitchen. I pulled up a stool, sat down next to her, our backs to the bar so we could watch the twins.

One of the babies sat up, carpet fuzz stuck to the drool on his chin. She hopped off the stool, wiped the kid's face with her hand, then swabbed her fingers off on a moistened cloth on the bar. As she did, she gave me a curious sidelong glance. "Exactly who are you? Why are you looking for Rob?"

"I'm a private investigator. I'm not really looking for Yost; I'm trying to locate somebody he knows. Her name is Solis, Mary Solis."

"Uh—I think I'd better call Ellie—Mrs. Yost."

Suzanne hung up, checked the babies, then sat down next to me again.

"Ellie said it's okay to talk to you. I'm sorry, but I had to check with her first."

"Sure, I understand."

"I don't think so. You see, you can't talk to Rob

Yost." She smoothed the knitted fabric of her sweatpants, then raised her eyes to meet mine. "Mr. Yost passed away a year ago."

My heart quickened. "He's dead? How?"

"Car accident. He drove through a guardrail off Highway One."

I stared at the floor and I guess Suzanne thought I was looking at the babies and feeling sorry for them.

"Yeah," she said. "It's pretty sad for the boys. They'll never know their father. And poor Ellie, God, what she's been through. First she finds out her husband's having an affair when she's four months pregnant with twins. Then he gets fired. She files for divorce, and the next thing we know, the CHP's on the phone telling her about the accident."

"What can you tell me about Mary Solis?"

Suzanne winced. "The other woman," she said, then spread her hands out on her thighs and looked down at them. They were red and chafed. "I'm sorry. I can't help you there. I never met her."

"Did Rob Yost leave any personal papers behind?" I was thinking of an address book or credit-card statements that might show where he and Mary spent his money.

"There are a couple of boxes in the basement."

We got Ellie's permission to go through them and spent the next hour combing through the paperwork that stood for Rob Yost's life.

I found a medical bill for a hernia operation, a pile of ticket stubs from season tickets to A's games, and a diploma from Golden Gate University. Nothing showed anything even remotely pointing to another woman. I set the last stack of canceled checks back in the box and stood.

Suzanne, busy with a twin in each of the two high chairs in the kitchen, glanced across the counter at me. "Nothing?"

"No."

She spooned some mush into one kid's mouth.

"Did Rob ever talk to you about her?"

"Um—once. He told me what she looks like and said if she ever showed up here at the house, to call the police. He said she was dangerous and I shouldn't open the door or even talk to her. I was just supposed to call the police. That was near the end—right before he died."

"Did you tell the police?"

"Uh, no. I didn't think of it."

"Did she ever show?"

"No, thank God. She sounds like a maniac."

Suzanne spooned more stuff into one of the twins. "She wants to talk to you—Ellie, I mean. Did I tell you that?"

Suzanne gave me the name and address of a real estate office on Union Street in the city.

"She's got some houses to show this afternoon," she said. "But she'll be in the office all evening. She said to stop in anytime after five."

25

I T WAS CLOSE to one o'clock when I climbed into my blue Toyota and left Ellie Yost's house. Suzanne had plied me with Ding Dongs, Oreos, and Diet Coke, so I counted that as lunch.

In a burst of charity I decided to stop by Bink's place to get him a change of clothes. The address he'd given Philly Post yesterday was in Piedmont. It had to be close by.

When I pulled up, I realized I'd been there before—last night. The house Bink said he was house-sitting was the same place I'd followed Ashton and his date to last night.

In daylight the place looked a lot bigger and a lot more elegant. It was a modern house with a ton of glass and six skylights on a slanted roof, deeply stained redwood siding, and beautiful landscaping. It was set back off the street, with a drive that looped around a massive cypress.

I parked up the block for a few minutes and watched the neighborhood. Nothing moved. The houses all seemed to be empty and locked up.

I pulled into the drive, retrieved my lock picks from their secret compartment in the trunk, and walked up to the front door like I was the Avon lady looking to make a sale. I rang the doorbell, waited, then worked the lock and slipped inside. The instant I shut the door, I knew I'd made a mistake.

26

ASOFT, WHIMPERING SOUND came from somewhere in the back of the house. It sounded just like a child crying. And the air—the air in the house was strange in a way I couldn't identify—not stuffy, not cold, but charged with a faintly pungent scent that made the little hairs at the back of my neck stand on end.

I stood frozen to the spot, unable to move while I listened, holding my breath and tilting one ear toward the sound. It stopped, then started up again. *My God.*

I noticed a leather valise on the floor just inside the door. On a glass table against the foyer wall was a stack of mail. *What was that horrible sound?*

I slipped off my pumps, then picked them up, heels pointing outward, and started forward.

The gray marble floor felt like ice to my feet. With every step the house seemed to get darker and darker. I passed the living room and a couple of doors, but I didn't even bother to look in because the sound, the crying, was getting louder now, and whoever or whatever it was, was definitely ahead of me, in the room at the end of the hall.

Just as I crossed the threshold into a huge, three-story family room—an open atrium—the smell hit me full force: urine and feces and blood. The acrid smell of

death. I'd smelled it nine months ago when I'd found a
suicide in Genoa. I'd thrown up then and I was wondering why I wasn't throwing up now. Maybe I was too
scared or too shocked by what I saw.

On the floor, fifteen paces from where I stood, in
the harsh, unforgiving daylight that filtered down from
skylights above, was the body of a woman, splayed
facedown into an impossible position.

She was still, so still and so contorted, I knew there
was nothing I could do for her. The crushed remains of a
glass-and-metal table lay beneath her, and a dark splotch
had spread like a red shadow onto the floor beside her
head.

Beyond her extended right arm, beyond her delicate
fingers, was a small clutch purse, its contents scattered
across the floor like tiny treasures just beyond her grasp.

I glanced up. The protective rail along the edge of
the third story gaped open, showing raw, splintered
wood where she'd fallen.

Without thinking, I slipped on my shoes, crossed the
room, and touched her body. She felt weird: cool and
stiff.

I started to lift her shoulder, realized her face was
smashed in, and let go. That's when I noticed the gold-
and-emerald ring on her hand. It was the same ring Mary
Solis had worn in the picture with Felix Ashton.

A wave of sadness washed over me. It suddenly
didn't matter what Mary Solis had done to me, my apartment, or to Bink, or even to Rob Yost or Art Spenger.
The havoc, the mess, the *inconvenience,* for God's sake,
that she'd brought down on me didn't matter anymore.
All I saw was another female victim. Another woman
whose life had ended by violence.

I stared at her for what could have been a full minute or maybe even ten. Then the keening sound broke
back into my consciousness. Had it been there all along?
I couldn't remember.

I scanned the room. Two stories of loft above, with the broken railing on the top floor. Huge canvasses smeared with globs of red and black oils on the walls. A fireplace. French doors, slightly open. A brick patio outside. A beige sectional sofa. *There.* Behind the sofa. The noise was coming from behind the sofa. And now the whimpers were punctuated with a soft *thud, thud.*

"Who's there?" I asked, and cursed the timidity in my voice.

I waited, and when nobody came forward, I skirted the corpse and slipped my shoes off again. Gripping my high heels in both hands, too scared to feel foolish, I took a deep breath and rounded the sofa. The whimpering got louder. I dropped my eyes to the floor.

In a heap, huddled against the back of the couch, was Bink. His hands were clutched into tight fists. His eyes were squeezed shut, and he was sort of rocking back and forth on his heels, pounding his thighs. Tears were streaming down his cheeks.

"Bink?"

He opened his eyes but didn't seem to focus until I leaned down and touched his shoulder. Slowly he pulled himself to his feet, reached for my arm, and held on like I was life itself.

"R-uh-uh-uh-onnie," he stuttered. "D-d-did you see her, Ronnie? Did you? You've got to help me. You've *got* to."

I struggled to work my arm free, but he held on with some kind of manic strength. That's when I noticed the dark stains all over his shirt sleeves. He followed my gaze to the stains, then flicked his eyes up to meet mine without changing expression—no surprise, no shock, just a cold, disconnected stare. The look sent chills up my spine.

"Why'd you do it, Bink? You didn't have to kill her."

His face crumpled and he started sobbing again. "I

duh-d-duh-didn't do it, Ronnie! I swear t-t-to you. I didn't touch her. She was like that when I got here."

He shook my shoulders like a parent scolding a child. "You believe me, don't you, Ronnie? Say you do. *Please* say you do. *Please.*"

"Sure, Bink, sure. I believe you." I didn't think I sounded sincere enough, but he stopped blubbering abruptly.

"You do?"

"I do."

The corners of his slack mouth lifted into a pathetic smile. "You do. You *believe* me."

He took my hand and started kissing it like I was a Mafia godfather who'd just spared his life. "Thank you, Ronnie. Thank you—thank you—thank you."

All of a sudden the place seemed suffocatingly hot. With Bink clinging to me, with the smell of death filtering back into my consciousness, and with the fear that he'd stop kissing my hand just long enough to pull a knife and slit my throat, I felt like I was going to pass out.

The room started to swirl. I didn't care anymore if he knifed me or not, I just needed to get outside.

I tugged, pulling him with me toward the open French doors. "Air," I sputtered. "Gotta have air."

27

SUCKING HUGE LUNGFULS of cool oxygen, I managed to pry Bink's fingers from my arm and collapse onto an ornate metal bench at the side of the little brick patio. I dropped my head between my knees and closed my eyes. The world stopped spinning after the second deep breath. One more and I felt solid enough to open my eyes and sit up.

I turned to the whimpering figure cowering on the bench beside me. He didn't look like a murderer; he looked pitiful—unshaven, stained, wrinkled shirt and slacks, the same clothes he'd worn the night he brought Mary Solis to my door. Huge dark circles under his eyes turned his face sallow.

He must have felt my gaze on him, because he looked up. "I could never do anything like that. It's the truth, Ronnie, I swear. You *know* I couldn't, don't you? *Don't you?*"

I thought about what he was saying. Bink's game had always been petty scams and deceptions, not murder. In the thirteen years I'd known him, he'd always talked tough, but when it came to action, Bink had always shied away from violence. Had he changed enough in the two years I hadn't seen him to kill?

"What happened?" I said.

Bink splayed his fingers out on his narrow thighs

and stared down at them. He opened his mouth twice and tried to speak, but nothing came out. Slowly he shook his head.

"That *is* Mary Solis in there, isn't it?" I finally asked.

He cleared his throat. "Yeah."

I asked him how long he'd been there.

"I—I don't know." He sounded better. His voice was stronger. Color was returning to his face.

I was starting to feel better myself, so I looked around and noticed the back door we'd just come through. Deep gouge marks scarred its splintered frame. It had been crowbarred open.

"Did you do that?"

"What?"

"The door."

He stared at the broken wood for a full minute.

"Bink?"

He turned to me with a puzzled frown. "I've got a key. Why would I break into my own place?"

"We're going to have to call the police, Bink."

His shoulders slumped, and he went back to staring at his hands.

"First tell me what happened. Where's Blackie?"

"I don't know." Bink rubbed his hands back and forth over his thighs like he was cold. "I couldn't stay there with him anymore, Ronnie. He's a crazy old coot."

"Did you hurt him?"

Bink winced. "No," he said softly. "And I didn't kill Mary. You've got to believe me."

"When did you leave Blackie's?"

"This morning."

I glanced at my watch. It was just after one o'clock. "Okay, you snuck out from Blackie's. Then what?"

"I ran down the hill, caught a cab to the B.A.R.T. station, then got off at Twelfth Street and took a bus the rest of the way. I figured the tankers wouldn't look for me here. They already checked the place out, you know."

He swallowed before continuing. "I unlocked the front door and went to my room to pack a couple of things. It's the first door on the right. I dumped my bag at the door and went into the kitchen for a beer. I—I—" He took a deep, jagged breath and shook his head again. "She was like that when I saw her."

"Did you touch her?"

He straightened his arms and stared at the brownish stains on his sleeves. "I musta. Yeah, I guess I did. I knew she was dead the minute I touched her. She was kind of stiff, you know? She didn't feel right. I don't know what I did next. I can't remember. The next thing I see, you're standing there in front of me."

"Okay, Bink." I took a deep breath. "We're going to have to go back in there."

His eyes grew wide and he started shivering. "I can't."

"We've got to call the police."

"Uh, Ronnie . . . please . . . I don't think I can."

Since I wasn't real hot on going back in, either, I let him talk me into using the pay phone down at the super-market on Park.

"But I gotta change first. People are gonna think I'm some kind of maniac if I don't. Please?"

We circled around to the front of the house, and I waited while he reached inside the front door for the valise. Standing in the shadow of the huge cypress on the front lawn, he changed into a fresh shirt. Then he stuffed the dirty one into the bag and tossed it onto the floor by the front seat.

At the supermarket I left him in the car and only turned my back on him once. But that's all it took. When I turned back around, he was gone. Again.

28

IT TOOK ME three hours to convince the Oakland P.D. that I didn't kill Mary Solis. I might have done it in one, but some old sergeant connected me with my parents, and it took him two hours to run me through all their computer data bases in a futile check for outstanding burglary warrants.

About halfway through the inquisition they shifted their focus to Bink and tried to get me to say I saw him kill Mary Solis. When I refused, they kept me there an extra hour just out of spite, then warned me against taking any long-distance trips, and set me free.

The first thing I did was phone Bink's sister, Barbara, from the pay phone in the lobby. Things were desperate enough for Bink to run to her now, and Barbara was the kind of earnest person who hated to lie. Sometimes I wondered if she was the way she was because she was trying to make up for her con-artist brother.

I let the phone ring a long time, because it usually takes Barbara a while to negotiate her wheelchair to the phone. When she answered, I said, "This is Ronnie, Barbara. Let me talk to Bink."

There was a long pause before she said, "Bink?"

"I know he's there, Barbara. Let me talk to him."

"Is he in trouble?"

"He's wanted for murder, Barbara. And I know he's

there. If he's not, just tell me. Say, 'He's not here.' " She wouldn't lie.

"He's not here."

"He's *not*?" The tremor in her voice could have been because she was upset about Bink.

"Will this be in the news, Ronnie?"

"Probably."

"Oh, no. My parents . . ."

Bink's parents should have been used to Bink messing up by now. "If you hear from him, Barbara, call me. I'm on his side, okay?"

"Of course."

I hung up, fished out another pair of dimes, and phoned Blackie. He picked up with his customary snarl.

"Are you all right, Blackie?"

I heard the rasp of a match being struck, silence, then a soft exhalation. "Don't worry about me, doll. You run across the little fuck?"

"I guess you could say that." I told him about Mary Solis's murder.

"Tough break, doll."

To his credit Blackie didn't mention that I'd been the one who insisted he take the handcuffs off Bink. Instead he said, "You keep your lunch down?"

"What?"

"When you saw the stiff, doll, didja—"

"I didn't throw up, Blackie, no. Can we talk about something else?"

"Think he did her?"

My three hours of interrogation hadn't been wasted. I'd gone over the crime scene in my head so many times, I'd finally figured out why the whole thing had struck me as odd. "He couldn't have, Blackie. Bink's scared of heights. And Mary Solis was shoved through a banister three flights up."

"Somebody set him up?"

"That's what it looks like."

"Somebody like him's got to have a truckload of enemies."

"Of course. But whoever did this had to know Bink's connection to Solis." An accomplice, maybe? But an accomplice to what?

"Cops got a warrant?"

"Yes. Bink's fingerprints are all over the place. They didn't seem to think it mattered that he's lived there the past six months."

Blackie chuckled. "What do you expect, doll? They're cops. We workin' it?"

"That depends. Can you get a scanner for tonight?"

"Give me a couple of hours."

"Great. Meet me at the Quarter Moon at nine o'clock. Oh, and Blackie? Don't forget to wear black."

29

I SWUNG BY THE Paradise Realtors office on my way home, saw a light on even though it was past six, and went in to ask for Ellie Yost.

Somebody pointed to a thin, energetic woman in a coffee-colored designer dress. Her wispy ash-blond hair was cropped at the shoulder, with bangs, and she must have been wearing five pounds of ethnic-type jewelry around her neck—beads and tiny gourds and a couple of tiger teeth, thrown in for excitement, I guess.

The other two late nighters wore high fashion–type clothes, but nothing as eye-catching as Ellie Yost's.

She was busy on the phone, talking in a soothing voice that managed to be both businesslike and seductive. While she talked, she absently fingered one of the big round things hanging off her neck.

Her eyes flickered in my direction when I walked over. She held up a finger and pointed at the chair beside her desk, then kept talking.

"Yes, darling, I *promise* you'll *adore* this place. Three bedrooms, skylights, and a master suite. . . . Parking? Of course. It's *très très*, darling, so you'll have to be nimble. . . . No, I'm afraid we'll have to wait until tomorrow. I'm not even supposed to know about it, but the listing broker used to be my associate. He's having a *very* select viewing at ten tomorrow. . . . Wonderful! I'll see you then. Marvelous!"

She replaced the receiver and turned to me, taking in my nondesigner clothes and cheap pumps and probably calculating what size condo I could afford. With a practiced smile she arched her eyebrows and offered me a manicured hand. "Ellie Yost," she announced. "How may I help you?"

"I'm Ronnie Ventana. I talked to your baby-sitter earlier."

Her reserve melted. "Wonderful. I'm so glad you stopped by. Let me call Suzanne quickly, then we can go someplace and talk."

The someplace she had in mind was a chi-chi bar and restaurant down the street. The young, rich, and restless of the city all seemed to be crowded into the tiny anteroom that housed the restaurant's bar. We managed to snag a small table in the corner by a window and miraculously were served drinks within minutes.

When Ellie Yost's white wine and my beer arrived, she raised her glass and said, "Here's to dead husbands."

Clearly she'd gotten past the grieving stage. She savored the wine, then fixed enormous brown eyes on me. Ellie Yost was a woman primed to discuss her hurts.

"Suzanne said you're trying to find that slut," she began.

"Actually I found her."

"Oh?"

"Yes. She was murdered this morning in Oakland."

"Murdered?" She said it like it was too good to be true. "She's dead?"

I nodded, and she let out a sort of amazed snorting sound, half ironical, half triumphant.

"How?"

"Somebody pushed her down three stories."

"Maybe there *is* a God." She raised her glass. "To God."

"I still need your help, Ms. Yost."

"Why?"

"My client was involved with the same woman. The police think he killed her."

"Did he?"

"No."

Ellie Yost took a long, slow drink of wine. "That woman is like the plague. Is your client married?"

I could have told her he was on the verge of getting engaged, but I didn't think it'd help. I told her instead that I'd be interested in hearing anything she could tell me about Rob Yost's affair.

"Do I have to?"

"You don't even have to talk to me," I said.

"Then I will. What do you want to know?"

"An ex-boyfriend of Mary Solis told me she worked in real estate."

"That's impossible. I know everybody in this business. She's no more in real estate than I'm in the circus."

"Could you check for me?"

"Certainly." She flipped open her day planner and jotted a reminder. "I'll call you tomorrow. What else would you like to know?"

"Tell me about your husband."

She took a deep breath. "Sure you want to hear this?"

I nodded.

"All right. Before he met her, Rob was wonderful. The best husband a woman could ask for. He was constant and faithful. He worked hard at the office, but he devoted every minute of time off to our relationship. He respected my career, was planning to take a month of paternity leave when the twins were born. He was marvelous, a prince.

"Then he met that slut and regressed to third grade. He lied and snuck around behind my back. He spent thousands of dollars on her, and near the end I rarely saw him. He never lived to take his paternity leave or see the twins. Here I was pregnant with twins, juggling the house and my work, and Rob was awful. Awful. My schedule's always been unpredictable—that's the nature of real estate—but I couldn't count on him for anything. I finally asked Suzanne to move in. She'd been coming in days, but I couldn't depend on Rob anymore. The man he was when he died was not the man I married. I did all my grieving before he died, Ms. Ventana. The accident was, for me, anticlimax."

"How did you learn about the affair?"

She ordered another glass of wine before she answered.

"A woman knows. If she's the least bit perceptive, she knows. Something in the way his eyes don't quite meet yours when he speaks to you, something in his voice, something about the way he touches you changes, and you know."

I remembered how it had been between me and Mitch. I'd known the instant he'd been unfaithful. And even though I'd already decided the marriage was doomed, the hurt was something I'll never forget. I practically had to flaunt my retaliatory lovers under his nose before he noticed. And that pretty much cinched the end for both of us.

I looked across the table at Ellie Yost's wine-flushed face. She was still hurting.

"Suzanne said he had some problems at work too."

"Of course. He couldn't function. He was completely infatuated and couldn't hold a thought longer than a minute. Especially after I threw him out. The twins weren't born yet, but the tension between us was unbearable. He was never home, and when he was, we fought and fought. I decided he wasn't going to ruin the twins' lives, too, so I asked him to leave."

There was still venom in her voice. Venom and pain.

"Then he lost his job. That's when he finally realized what he'd done. He phoned me and begged to come home. He admitted he was wrong and said he'd ended his relationship with—her. He promised he'd never do it again.

"Do you know what I told him? I said he certainly wouldn't because I wasn't going to give him the opportunity. When I told him he couldn't come home, he cried. He *cried*. I hung up on him. The next night they called to tell me he was dead."

I asked her about Bentley Stearns.

"It's a bank, you know. Rob? Rob was in corporate lending."

"Do you remember his boss's name?"

"Eleanor Hightower. Lovely woman. I sold her a house on Telegraph Hill—before Rob went crazy. Four bedrooms, marbled foyer. The view out the back was splendid. Do you own or rent, Ms. Ventana?"

I swigged down the last of my beer and set the glass on the table between us. "I rent. Happily, thank you."

She pressed her card into my hand and managed a slightly skewed version of the practiced smile I'd seen back at her office. "In case you change your mind."

30

MRS. PARDUCCI BURST out of her door the instant my foot hit the top step.

"Ronnie, dear, I've been waiting for you."

I still hadn't done my Parducci penance, but I knew tonight was not the night for it. I had to meet Blackie in an hour. I kept walking toward my door. Mrs. Parducci followed.

"There was a young man here for you," she said.

I stopped. "Where? Here?"

"Yes. I ran into him downstairs and he asked for you."

"What'd he look like?"

"Handsome," she said approvingly.

"Was he the guy from the other night?"

"Oh, no. He was heavier, but not much." She described an average-sized, average-looking guy. I didn't have a clue who he was until I went inside and played back my answering-machine messages.

"Hi, Ronnie. It's Aldo. Sorry you weren't home when I came by. Please call me. It's urgent."

As a police connection Aldo Stivick wasn't much better than Lieutenant Philly Post, but he was crummy in a different way. Post doesn't like me enough, Aldo likes me too much. Every time I ask him for a favor, he asks me for one back. Usually I'm supposed to let him buy me lunch. A lot of people would say that's a fair trade, but that's always before they meet Aldo.

I steeled myself for the invitation to lunch while I let his phone ring.

"I'm so glad you called, Ronnie. Did you get my message?"

"It said to phone."

"I've got a fax for you."

"A what?"

"A fax. It's from Mitchell."

"Mitch?" We'd all gone to high school together, but Mitch had never kept up much with Aldo. "What's it say?"

"I don't know."

"Well, read it."

"I can't."

"Why not?"

"It's marked 'personal and confidential.' I'd hate to betray Mitch's confidence by reading the rest of the page without his permission."

"Never mind that. Just read it to me."

"Sorry, Ronnie. It's Mitch who has to say it's okay. He's the one who sent it, and he's the person who can best judge how confidential it really is."

Terrific. Aldo's ethics somehow always managed to get in *my* way. "Why didn't you leave it when you came by?"

"Something important like this? I couldn't. I know it's kind of short notice," he said, "but are you free for dinner?"

"I can't do dinner, Aldo. I—"

"How about lunch tomorrow?"

"Just stick it in the mail, Aldo."

"I can't. It says it's urgent too."

I silently cursed Mitch for doing this to me. "All right. Okay. Are you at the Hall of Justice? I'll come by for it."

"Ronnie, it's almost eight o'clock. I'm at home."

I sighed. I could leave a message with Marcus downstairs so Blackie'd know I might be late. "All right, Aldo. I'm on my way."

31

ALDO'S ADDRESS was in the Excelsior, a blue-collar Irish part of town that had about as much appeal as living in a Studebaker. His house was a tiny one, one of those 1906 earthquake shacks built to last a few months and now worth over a hundred thousand. The front door opened into a living/dining room, where Aldo had meticulously set a romantic table for two with candles and china, crystal stemware, and mood music.

"Sorry, I didn't mean to interrupt anything," I said, and started to back out of the room.

"You're not. This is for us." He smiled expectantly.

"I can't stay, Aldo. Really."

"But look." He raised the cover of a serving dish. The savory scent of garlic and cheese wafted out into the room. "I fixed veal parmigiana."

It smelled terrific, but I wasn't about to set a precedent with Aldo. My paybacks so far had always been limited to the midday meal. "No thanks, Aldo."

"Have you had dinner?"

I ignored my churning stomach and refused to try to remember when I'd last eaten. "Sorry, Aldo. I can't do this. Where's the fax?"

He looked crestfallen but went to a closet by the front door and pulled out a briefcase. With Aldo it's a place for everything and everything in its place. "It's right here."

I followed him over to the couch and watched him click open first one snap, then the other. He raised the top of the briefcase, pulled out a file folder, and handed me the single sheet of paper inside.

The top line, typed all in caps, read, "PERSONAL AND CONFIDENTIAL. FOR THE EYES ONLY OF OFFICER ALDO STIVICK. URGENT." The text dropped down a few lines before it began. "Aldo: Please don't read any farther. Give this to Ronnie. It's urgent. Thanks. Mitchell."

A few lines farther down was one sentence addressed to me: "Ask Bink about Teknikker Enterprises, Basystems, and Kopar Corp. M."

I flipped the sheet over. It was blank. I glanced up at Aldo. "Is this it?"

Aldo looked like he would have loved to produce another page if it'd mean I'd stay and eat his veal parmigiana. "We could go back to the office and check," he offered.

I stared at the fax. This was obviously all Mitch was going to give me, damn him. Did he know something, or was he just trying to—to what?

"Can I use your phone?"

I followed Aldo to a little desk in the corner of the room, fished out my calling card and Mitch's phone number, and started dialing. After about twenty rings the system cut me off and played a recording saying I should try again later. I dialed the overseas operator, told her nobody was picking up at the number I was calling, that it was an emergency and would she check the line for me and try it again.

I sat and waited, listening to the distant, hollow white noise on the line while Aldo squirmed in a chair across from mine.

"I'm charging the call to my card," I told him. "You won't be billed for any of this." Then I realized he wasn't upset about the phone call so much as he was at seeing my feet propped on the edge of the chair I was sitting in.

I dropped them to the floor and sat up straight. The operator came back on the line. "I'm sorry, ma'am. The lines are all in order, but your party does not answer. Would you like to try again later?"

I replaced the receiver, grabbed the fax, and headed for the door.

"Good-bye, Ronnie."

Aldo! I turned to find him standing pitifully next to his some-enchanted-evening dinner setting, and for a fleeting half second I considered staying. Damn. Damn. *Damn.*

"Good-bye, Aldo," I said, and shut the door gently behind me.

32

BLACKIE WAS AT THE BAR in the Quarter Moon when I walked by, so I signaled him from the sidewalk to come upstairs with me. He came out, lugging a fresh Anchor Steam in one hand and trailing smoke from a lighted cigarette he held in the other. His sexy blue eyes caught the amber glow of lamplight and sparkled with excitement.

We took the stairs up through the side door. The crack under Mrs. Parducci's door was dark, thank God.

"Talk to the widow?" Blackie asked as we stepped into my apartment.

"She wasn't much help. She's going to check to see if Mary Solis worked real estate or not. Mitch sent me this." I tossed my backpack onto the table I use for a desk and handed Mitch's fax to Blackie. He read it while I rummaged through the closet for my black sweater and black dungarees.

"What's this?"

"Your guess is as good as mine, Blackie. I tried calling him, but he wasn't in."

"Think he knows something?"

I'd thought about it on the way home. "Mitch is easygoing about everything except work, Blackie. I've heard from him more since he's been on vacation in Tahiti than I have in the last five years. You know why?

'Cause he's bored. He gets bored, so he calls me. That"
—I pointed at the fax in Blackie's fist—"is the product of
boredom. He gets this stupid call from Bink and he
dwells on it. He's probably been sitting on the beach
since Wednesday playing out scenarios on how Bink
could mess up. And since it's Mitch, naturally it's got to
be work related."

"You saying we should write him off?"

"I'll keep trying to reach him, but unless something
major changes, Blackie, we'd probably only be wasting
our time. Did you bring the scanner?"

He slugged the last of his beer and grinned. "Do sea
gulls fly?"

"Great. Give me a sec," I said, and went into the
bathroom to change.

When I came back out, as I slipped on my black
Adidas running shoes, I looked up at Blackie. "How'd he
get away?"

Blackie reached into his breast pocket for a fresh
cigarette and lit it, striking the match slowly and holding
the flame to the tobacco just a beat longer than he
needed to.

"Little fuck torched the kitchen," he finally said.

I stifled a laugh and tried to remember the last time
I'd seen Blackie actually set foot in his trashed-up
kitchen. "I'm surprised you even noticed."

Blackie glanced pointedly across the room at the
stack of dishes in the sink and the general mess that's my
kitchen—the hot plate with the frayed electrical cord,
the blender for mixed drinks, and the dirty frying pan left
over from a twitch of domestic ambition three, maybe
four, weeks ago when I fried myself an egg.

"I noticed, doll. Just like you'd notice."

I tied the knot on my other shoe, grabbed my
backpack full of tools, and stood. "Ready?"

We made it across the Bay Bridge in record time.
Blackie drove his vintage, rust-bucket Buick like it was a

supersonic tank, weaving from one lane to another, swerving every few minutes to avoid sideswiping anybody who dared to come near us, and chain-smoking like a condemned man.

We pulled off the freeway, drove a few short blocks, and headed into Piedmont.

"It's over there," I said, pointing ahead to the house. The police had sealed the front door with a big, yellow police-tape X and a warning sheet nailed to its frame.

"It's a felony to cross a police line, doll," Blackie said.

"Only if you're caught."

It was an easy-access deal. There was a small bin built against the fence in the back alley, and from there it was a cinch to get over the fence. I didn't even need to tamper with the lock on the gate.

"Whose place is this, anyway?"

"A friend of Bink's. The cops said he's in Europe for a year. Bink was house-sitting."

Inside we split up. Blackie took the family room while I looked for Bink's room.

I found it easily enough—it was on the first floor and it was the only room that was a mess. There were clothes scattered all over the carpet, papers piled high on a desk in the corner and all over the dresser too.

I started pawing through the papers, mostly un-opened junk mail, a few blank applications for various private clubs, and some past-due notices from a bunch of credit-card companies and the Saint George Club. At the bottom I found a two-month-old bank statement in an envelope with a bunch of canceled checks.

The statement showed that Bink had closed out August with $13.45 in his account. He'd been fined three times in as many weeks for bouncing checks. During the same period he'd deposited nine thousand dollars in cash on four separate occasions—thirty-six thousand dollars total for the month. That was on top of his regular automatic payroll deposit from Ellis, Pogue.

I rifled through the canceled checks. They covered the range of expenses from the city's most exclusive men's clothing stores to a travel agency. I jotted down the name of the travel agency, searched for airplane tickets or an itinerary, then, when I didn't find any, rummaged through the dresser drawers and closet without unearthing anything else.

A quick reconnaissance by penlight upstairs showed nothing disturbed except a broken vase near the fractured third-floor railing. Everything had a fine layer of dust on it like nobody'd been up there for ages.

Downstairs Blackie was on his knees in front of the huge sectional sofa. With the constant chatter of the dispatch monitor coming through his headphones, he couldn't have heard me walk in, but he knew I was there before I flicked my own light on and off to signal my approach.

Blackie glanced up and studied my face. "Nothing, huh?"

"Not much. But it looks like he had something going for extracurricular cash." I'd give him the details later when we were safely outside the house. "What about you?"

"Tell you in a minute."

He reached under the sofa and brought his hand back out in a fist. "Feel lucky, doll?"

He rose, spread his fingers, and dropped a crumpled piece of paper into my open palm.

"Cops missed it," Blackie muttered. I smoothed the scrap out on the table beside the couch while Blackie shone his penlight on it. It was a ragged-edged clipping from a newspaper.

"It must have fallen out of her purse," I said, remembering the spewed contents on the floor earlier.

The barely audible staccato chatter of the police

scanner filtered through Blackie's headphones out into the room while we read:

MAN MAULED BY LIONS

Clay E. Johnson, 45, president of Johnson Bass, a prominent San Francisco printing firm, died yesterday in what San Francisco Zoo officials are calling "a freak accident." Johnson, the victim of a fatal mauling by three female lions at the zoo, apparently fell or leaped to his gruesome death in the lion cage sometime early this morning. Zookeeper Tippet Harding discovered Johnson's body at approximately seven a.m. as she made her regular rounds. Staff handlers and city medical personnel labored for over an hour before they were able to retrieve Johnson's body.

Zoo veterinarian Howard Ripley stated that the three lions had been sequestered in a normally unoccupied outdoor enclosure so they could be fed a restricted diet. The three lionesses were "obese due to confinement and a lethargic lifestyle." Ripley speculated that had the lionesses not been on a diet, Johnson might have survived the attack. Other zoo officials refused to comment.

A friend and former co-worker of the victim, Allen Carlton, reported that Johnson had been extremely despondent after a recent decline in business.

While Johnson's friends and family seemed convinced the act was one of suicide, San Francisco Police Department has not officially closed the case. Homicide Lieutenant Harold Post said, "Once a cause of death is established, a determination will be made as to how to proceed." Post expects the coroner's report by the end of the week.

Mr. Johnson, a native of San Francisco, is survived by his wife, Fay, his sons, Basil and Edward, and two brothers, Kevin and Erwin.

Blackie scowled, then flicked off his penlight. "Fuckin' Philly Post again," he said. "Shit."

33

"JUST 'CAUSE he won't pick up the phone at his place doesn't mean he's at work, doll."

"Yes it does, Blackie. Philly Post doesn't have a life outside the SFPD."

It was ten-thirty P.M., and we were parked on Bryant Street outside the Hall of Justice.

"What's he gonna do for you, doll? You've talked to him twice already and he hasn't done shit for you."

"He's the law, Blackie. Besides, I keep hoping something I say will click and he'll start working with me on this thing."

"Fuck."

I handed him the Johnson clipping, then reached for the door. "I'll be right back."

Post dropped his hands from his tired face and let them fall with a thud onto his cluttered desk.

"What are you up to, Ventana? That case is a year old. And it's closed." He glanced at his watch. "What are you doing here this time of night, anyway?"

"Let me look at the file."

"Why should I?" His huge, bushy eyebrows narrowed. "This anything to do with that Hanover slag you brought in here?"

"Of course not," I lied. "I took your advice on that."

"Right. I heard OPD held you three hours."

"Small world."

He smiled sourly and glanced at his watch. "You're not seeing the file, Ventana. Not tonight, not ever. It's confidential police information, understand?"

"Okay, maybe I don't need to see Clay Johnson's actual file. What'd the coroner find was the cause of death? Anything in there about foul play?"

Post rolled his eyes. "You won't go away, will you?"

I smiled. "I will if you tell me what I want to know."

With a sigh Post absently picked up a pencil and drummed it on his desk.

"What makes you think I remember the case?"

"How many lion maulings do you get in a year, Post?"

The corners of his mouth twitched. "All right. The cause of death was 'undetermined.' There wasn't enough left of him to test."

"How do you know the body was Clay Johnson's?"

"Dental records." He glanced at his watch again.

"Any suspects?"

"Suspects? It was a suicide, Ventana."

"What makes you think somebody'd want to commit suicide by jumping into a lion pit? This is just a guess, but don't most people want to go out easy? The easier the better?"

Post held my eyes for a split second. Then he reached across his desk for a stack of folders and opened one. Without looking up, he said, "Beat it, Ventana. I got work to do."

"Look, Post, these three guys—"

"Three?"

"I found another questionable death related to Mary Solis—an ex-boyfriend like Art Spenger—in Oakland. There's got to be more to it than coincidence, don't you see? Johnson and Yost—the Oakland boyfriend— both dated her and they both died."

"How's Clay Johnson tie in?"

"Let me see the file and maybe I can tell you."

Post rocked his chair back and crossed his fingers over his flat stomach. "Okay, suppose Johnson's story is the same as the other two. All you're doing is making your bad boy look worse."

"How?"

"Your black-widow theory—"

"Is out—she's dead."

"Sure she's dead. Her next victim—your boy—put two and two together and beat her to the punch."

"Aw, come on, Post. You refused to believe she was dangerous before. Now all of a sudden—"

"Now it fits."

"In his own house? Bink wouldn't—he's smarter than that."

"Not from what I saw."

"He couldn't have killed her."

"Yeah? What makes you so sure?"

"Mary Solis was shoved through a banister three stories up. Bink's acrophobic, remember? He's scared of heights. Take him upstairs and make him look out the window and he turns into paralyzed protoplasm. I've seen him. He can't *function* three stories up, much less commit murder."

Post leaned forward, elbows on his desk. "Remember I told you he was a con man and you said you didn't have anything he'd want? Well, he's conned you, Ventana. You're going to be his defense. 'Poor guy's scared of heights, Your Honor. He's innocent, Your Honor.' "

"Okay," I said. "So convince me. Let me see Johnson's file. If there's a tie-in to Mary Solis, I'll believe you."

Post laughed as he got up and reached for his jacket. "Go home, Ventana. Go home and write this guy off."

* * *

"He wants to bury it," I said to Blackie as I slid into the front seat next to him.

Blackie turned the engine over and stifled a belch as he steered the car onto the street.

"Fuckin' cops," he muttered.

"You're not surprised."

Blackie scowled, and skidded to a stop at the corner. I looked out through the fog-dampened windshield. The red traffic light threw ruby-colored sparkles against the droplets on the glass. They glowed and shimmered like fireworks in the dark.

"How many times I gotta tell ya, Ventana? Cops are no good. It's a club, doll. An' all anybody in the club wants to do is make points. You know how they make points? Closin' cases. And keeping 'em closed. You know that. Nothin' else matters to those guys." He reached for a cigarette and glanced across at me. "I've been telling you all along Post is dirt."

I stared out the window and watched the reflections of light dance across the streets as we sped over them.

"You thought he was different," Blackie said softly. "I know."

We ended up at a Third Street dive called the Dock. I could hear the music from the parking lot—a cool, sweet, soothing jazz.

Blackie jammed the parking brake on and jerked his head in the direction of the music. "Come on, doll. You need some of this tonight. Fuck the cops, eh?"

He flashed his sexiest I-don't-give-a-shit-about-the-world grin at me and opened his door. "Get the lead out, Ventana. I'm buyin' tonight."

34

THE RINGING PHONE sounded like a monster in my ear. I reached for it, knocked it over onto the floor, then fumbled groggily until my fingers bumped against the hard, smooth surface of the receiver. As I raised it to my ear, I could hear a frantic—or was it impatient?—female voice squeaking at me.

"Hello? Hello? Is anybody there? Is this Ronnie Ventana? *Hello?*"

"Wrong number," I growled, then slammed the receiver down and buried my throbbing head under my pillow. I lay there and tried to remember what I'd done last night to make me feel so awful this morning. Everything hurt—my head, my back, even my legs.

Music was involved. Yes. And beer. Lots of—too much—beer. Why?

Before I could remember that part, the phone rang again. I threw the pillow off my head, and this time I opened my eyes before I reached for the receiver.

"Is this Ronnie Ventana?"

"Yes."

"I need to talk to you right away. It's about David Hanover."

I sat up. "Who is this?"

"My name's Carolina Pogue. I'm David's girl-friend."

* * *

I saw her yellow Ferrari before I spotted the red leather jacket she told me she'd be wearing. When she parked across the street from Dianda's, the bakery where I sat waiting, I noticed a small dark-green Sentra pull up down the street. Then she stepped out of her car, and I forgot all about it. Carolina Pogue was the same young, horse-faced woman I'd seen with Felix Ashton two nights ago. She'd been crying then, and from the looks of her now she'd been crying this morning too.

Great. An hysterical girlfriend. Exactly what I needed when I'm facing the hangover of my life. I stood by the door and watched her cross toward the restaurant. She looked the way I felt. Her face was splotchy and her eyes red-rimmed, with big dark circles underneath.

Even if she hadn't been crying, she definitely wasn't Bink's type. She was stocky, for one. Not heavy, but solid and thick-limbed. Bink never dated anybody under five-seven or over a hundred pounds.

Then there was the matter of her face. Taken separately, her features were fine, but combined they made her face seem too long and her mouth too wide. And on top of everything else she had an innocent air, a sweet, fragile aspect about her that made her seem as vulnerable as a kitten.

Christ, I thought, *Bink should be shot.*

"Are you Ronnie?" she asked timidly.

I nodded and offered her my hand. She took it and held on with both of hers. "Where's David?" she pleaded. "Mitchell said you'd know where he is."

Mitch again.

"He said you were helping David. He said—" Her face contorted. She was seconds away from fresh tears.

"Look, Carolina. I need a cup of coffee. How about you?"

At a small table by the window I ordered a double espresso, and she asked for hot chocolate.

"You've got to tell me where David is. I'm so worried about him," Carolina began, fixing me with a supplicating stare. She leaned toward me, and I suddenly noticed a resemblance to the pictures of her father I'd seen in the paper. She had the same penetrating eyes and broad forehead.

"Mitch says you're helping David, that he's in some kind of trouble."

I sipped my espresso and silently cursed Mitchell. She obviously hadn't heard about the murder. I decided not to be the one to tell her.

"He said you would know where he is. Please, Ronnie—can I call you Ronnie?—this is really important. I have to see David. I'll die if I can't see him. I have to tell him Daddy forgives him."

"For what?"

She sighed. "Well . . . the whole thing is really Daddy's fault. And I guess maybe a teensy bit David's for being so sensitive."

I choked on my espresso. After I stopped coughing, I said as mildly as I could, "What are you talking about?"

"We—David and I—were supposed to go to a party at Daddy's Wednesday night, and Tuesday's when he vanished. David played golf with Daddy that morning. I think Daddy said something to David, something that hurt his feelings," she explained. "Daddy swore he didn't, but I know him better than that. He can be an unpleasant bully sometimes."

"Any idea what your father could have said?"

She hesitated. "There've been some break-ins at the office. Well, they're not really break-ins, but Daddy claims somebody's been going through his stuff, you know, files and things, and he thinks David's responsible. Can you believe it?"

"Why would he think of David?"

"Because Daddy hates him, that's why."

"Anything missing?" I asked.

"Of course not. But he says some files were rifled through. It's probably just an untidy secretary."

"What kind of files?"

"I don't know. Files."

I reached into my backpack for Mitch's fax and unfolded it. "Kopar? Teknikker? Basystems? Any of those ring a bell?"

"I don't know. I can't remember."

"Can you find out?"

"Why?" She flounced her hair impatiently. "What does this have to do with David disappearing? Can't you just tell me where he is?"

"Can you get me a list of the tampered files?"

She exhaled impatiently. "Just tell me where he is. Mitch said—"

"I don't know where he is."

"But Mitch said—"

"Mitch's news is three days old. Listen, Carolina, this isn't just some family squabble. David's in serious trouble—not with your father necessarily but with some real heavy hitters. The best thing you can do is get me the names of those files in case there's anything to what your father's saying. Then stay by the phone. If David calls, you call me, understand?"

"But—"

"Here's my card. Go home, Carolina." I rose and placed it on the table next to her mug of hot chocolate. "I want you to call me about those files. And if you hear from David, call me. Don't do anything else. Don't go to him. Don't talk to anybody else. Just stay put and call me. Understand?"

I left her staring at the card. By the time I hit the corner, I'd forgotten all about her. My mind was busy shifting gears from crimes of passion to a whole new territory: white-collar crime.

35

BY EIGHT-THIRTY I was sitting in my ex-probationer Gabriél Juarez's plush bank office in the Marina, watching him stick a pencil into the top of a hamster cage on the mahogany credenza behind his desk. I'd just seen him at the softball-field dedication on Wednesday, but when his wife, Juana, led me into his office, he welcomed me effusively and asked Juana to hold his calls.

One hamster ran circles on a squeaky blue plastic wheel, but the other one saw Gabriél's pencil and lunged at it with teeth bared.

"Look at that! Look at that!" Gabriél cried excitedly. "I love these little guys. They're vicious, you know. They're tiny and cute, but look at the wallop they pack."

The one he'd directed the pencil at reared up, hissed, and finally bit into the rubber eraser with surprisingly long yellow teeth. Gabriél started to lift the pencil, and the rodent held on. When the pencil was about ten inches off the ground, Gabriél gave it a little shake, and the hamster dropped onto the nest of cedar shavings with a tiny grunt.

Gabriél chuckled with pleasure and replaced the lid. "Some kind of spunk," he said in a voice filled with admiration. "Something goes wrong for me, some deal blows up in my face, all I do is stick a pencil in there and watch those little guys hang on. That's all I need to get me to jump back in and keep slugging away."

His deep-brown eyes softened. "I tell that to the kids on the softball team, too, you know. They need somebody to tell them they have to get back up if life knocks them down."

I looked at Gabriél in his thousand-dollar suit and five-hundred-dollar shoes and smiled. Only he could find inspiration in a hamster.

"Did you see Mayor Ashton at the softball kickoff?" he asked. "That's right, you talked to him, didn't you? He's a customer now. Can you feature that? The man has a true heart, you know, giving me business and trusting an almost ex-con with his cash. And I got a bunch of other judges too—his friends. Last year he even opened accounts for his three little grandkids. Ronnie, I can't thank you enough. You did it for me, you know."

I thought of all the people who'd sat across from me at the parole office and who'd ended up back in jail. Gabriél was the only one who'd made himself over into an honest man, then gone even further to make himself an honest hero. I motioned at the community plaques and citizenship awards covering the wall above the hamster cage. "You did it yourself, Gabriél."

He slid into the rich leather chair behind his desk, touched the short ponytail at the nape of his neck, and smiled. "You'll never convince me."

"You can forget any imagined debt you think you have with me if you help me out," I said.

"Anything." He spread his arms expansively.

"I need some information about your old specialty —white-collar crime."

"I'm not sure I can help you, Ronnie. I've done my best to forget about that sort of thing."

"I just need some general info, Gabriél. The basics."

He shrugged, then crossed his arms and leaned back

in his chair. "What I can give you are the basics on insider trading. It's just one way in many of beating the system."

"What else is there?"

Gabriél smiled again. "Fraud. Theft. Insurance scams. Computer crimes. Insider trading's what I know best."

"Okay. Talk."

"I suppose the most basic way would be to buy a boatload of stock before the quarterly report comes out. You know if the report's good, the stock's going to shoot up a couple of points, min. You buy, say, a week or two before, then wait until it shoots up, then unload the stuff. That's the most basic. Depending on the size of the transaction, you might be able to get away with using your own name. Otherwise you could spread it out—use client accounts if you're a broker, make up dummy corps and open up dummy accounts if you're not."

I nodded. "What if you're an auditor?"

"Ah." Gabriél looked pleased. "If you're an auditor, you can collude with the firm and jimmy the numbers to look good even if they're not."

I remembered that Mitch reviewed Bink's files. "Could somebody get away with that even if an honest person was looking over his shoulder?"

"Sure. Just make the numbers look good. That's all that counts—the paper. Listen—" His voice became animated. "Say a company says it's got fifty thousand widgets but really only has twenty thousand. The company writes up vouchers and hands them to the auditor, who sends some scrud down to count the widgets. Now, the warehouse has got widgets stacked to the ceiling, and the ceiling's probably thirty feet high. I ask you, who's going to count every single widget if you've got to take it out of the box to count it? Junior auditor is going to take a sample—he'll look at the first few rows to make sure, then tick off the rest.

"And there it lies. Nobody's going to tramp down to the warehouse to disprove his own auditor—not without a reason." He glanced at me and raised his eyebrows. "See? That's why cheating is so easy—it's all a paper house anyway."

I nodded again.

"Okay. Another auditor option is if you find they cooked their books, you can pretty much write your own ticket. Put the firm accountants, CFO, whoever, through the hoops. But if you get caught, you not only lose your credentials, you go to jail."

He sounded so straight-arrow, it was hard to believe he'd once bilked millions out of the system through insider trading.

"Any of those fit the bill for your cowboy?"

"I don't know, Gabriél. I need to do a little more checking around. Can I come back and ask you some more questions when I know more?"

He rose and walked me to the door. "I'd be offended if you didn't."

36

THE PHONE WAS RINGING as I unlocked my apartment door. The clock on the table by the sofa said nine-thirty A.M., but I felt like I'd already put in a full day. Maybe a run would help me get some energy.

"Ronnie!" The voice on the other end of the line was deep and throaty—Bink's secretary, Marcella. "I just heard about the charges against David. The police were here." She went on breathlessly about how awful it all was, then asked if there was anything she could do to help clear his name.

"As a matter of fact, there is. Do you know if Bink was in any kind of trouble at work?"

"Well, like what?"

"Anybody complaining about his work or things he'd done?"

"No—wait—yes. Marvin Chamber's secretary told me Marvin threatened David for parking in his reserved parking place three days in a row last month. And Nathan Grey called him a brownnose once."

I sighed and said a silent prayer of thanks that I didn't work in an office. "What can you tell me about Basystems, Kopar, or Teknikker?"

"David audited them."

"Were there any problems with the audits or anything else?"

"Nothing I heard about."

"Would you have heard?"

"Of course. David tells me everything. But I'll, like, ask Christian Mullin when he calls in from the Donziger audit—he'll know for sure since he was the senior on the team David managed for all three of those."

As I hung up, I noticed the answering-machine light blinking fiercely from the desk. I smashed the Playback button and listened.

"She's not licensed," Ellie Yost announced triumphantly. "And she never has been."

She then launched into a vivid description of a one-bedroom condo on Nob Hill. "It's a new listing. Hasn't even had a first open yet. I could show it to you this morning at eleven if you'd like. Give me a call."

The second message was from Chuckles, a street contact I'd talked to about Mary Solis on Wednesday. His whiskey-cured voice sounded harsh after Ellie Yost's polished professionalese.

"Your Solis person is a nobody, Ronnie. She's either clean, smart, or from back east, 'cause ain't nothin' out here on her." After a long pause he added, "Do I get the twenty-bucks finder's fee anyway?"

Another dead end. I sat and listened to the tape machine rewind and thought about what I had, white-collar-wise: three dead men, all supposedly killed by a woman who was now dead herself. Tampered files in an accounting office. And Bink. Where did Bink and his own files fit in? Did they connect with Mary Solis and the dead men? If Bink wouldn't tell me, maybe the dead men would.

37

ALDO WAS MORE than happy to accept my apology for last night, especially when I invited him to lunch. It took more convincing to get him to agree to bring the Johnson and Spenger files with him, but in the end he said he would.

With two and a half hours to kill before lunch, Elizabeth Hightower and Allen Carlton were next on my list. I jotted down their addresses, then scampered down the stairs.

A large man in a black suit stopped me on the sidewalk outside the Quarter Moon.

"Ms. Ventana?"

I squinted at him, trying to figure out if he was one of Bink's tankers and decided he wasn't. "Who are you?"

"I'm from Mr. Edwin Pogue's office."

I held on to my backpack and waited.

"Mr. Pogue would like to see you," he said, then pointed to the green Sentra I'd noticed outside Dianda's earlier when I'd talked to Carolina. "If you'd like to step into my car, I'll be happy to drive you."

"I bet you would."

"Pardon me?"

"Nothing," I said, reaching for my own car keys. "I'll drive myself."

* * *

Edwin Pogue wasn't necessarily a big man, but his presence was intimidating—larger than life, smooth and polished. When I walked into his huge office, I found half a dozen secretaries and assistants swarming around his desk, jotting down notes while he barked commands and rifled through folders on his desk. The view behind his desk—the Bay Bridge and Bay, with Oakland beyond —seemed almost insignificant next to him.

"Who's this?" he asked when the secretary led me in.

"Ms. Ventana, sir."

"Good, good." He waved his hand, and the entire staff vanished like a dream.

"So glad you could come on such short notice," he said. "Please, sit down." He motioned to one of two antique upholstered chairs in front of his desk. I slipped my backpack onto the floor beside the chair and sat.

"What can I do for you, Mr. Pogue?"

"You spoke to my daughter this morning."

"That's right. Does Carolina know you're having her followed?"

"It's for her own protection," he said, then smiled engagingly. "May I ask what the two of you discussed?"

"Tampered files, Mr. Pogue. Kopar, Basystems, and Teknikker. Care to tell me about them?"

His expression didn't change. "Why would my daughter discuss something of that nature with you?"

"Why would *you* discuss it with *her*?"

"Carolina hasn't been thinking very straight these days."

"She's thinking straight enough to know you don't approve of her boyfriend."

Pogue cursed under his breath. "Do you know Hanover, Ms. Ventana? Surely you do. You've met him, haven't you?"

I nodded.

"Then you must certainly see my objection. Would you want a relative—any relative—of yours to marry him? Of course not! Using the kindest of terms, let's just say he's not the responsible young man I'd hoped for Carolina."

"How do the tampered files fit in?"

"I thought the specter of impropriety might sway Carolina. As you can see, it didn't."

"Are you trying to tell me you made up the tampered files?"

"Not very original, I must say, but you're looking at a desperate father, Ms. Ventana." He raised a hand and stroked his chin. "Perhaps you could help. As a private investigator perhaps you could look into the matter. Someone like Hanover surely has an indiscretion or dozen in his past."

Out of nowhere a leather-bound check ledger materialized in front of him. "This would be strictly confidential, of course. Someone in my position has to be discreet about these things." He reached for one of the Mont Blanc pens scattered across his desk. "Would two thousand be adequate to start?"

"Save your money, Mr. Pogue. I can't help you."

"Come, come. Surely you won't know until you've . . . looked into things."

"As much as I sympathize with you, Mr. Pogue, you're not going to change your daughter's mind by digging up dirt on Bink Hanover. If she dumps him, she's going to have to come to that decision herself. You're not going to do it for her."

He stared at me like I'd just punched him in the stomach. Slowly he folded the cover on the ledger and cleared his throat.

"Thank you for being candid, Ms. Ventana. I think you might have a point—one I don't particularly like, but a point nonetheless." He cleared his throat again. "I hope you'll hold our discussion here regarding the files in the strictest of confidence. My firm is an accounting firm—"

"I know," I said.

"The firm depends on its reputation of integrity—"

"I know all about it, Mr. Pogue. Discretion."

"Yes, yes. Precisely." The strength and command returned to his voice again. I guess he saw the hesitation in my eye, because he said, "Mr. Hanover and my files have no connection whatsoever. My files are fine. My daughter's situation is not."

He leaned forward in his chair and folded his hands on the desk. "I'm sorry you were troubled by any of this. Rest assured that my firm would never brook any transgression of any sort in the accounting standards. Thank you for coming in, Ms. Ventana. And thanks for your discretion."

My hand was still tingling from Pogue's rigid, bear-like handshake when I neared Marcella's desk. She was poring over a handwritten document so intently that she didn't see me walk up.

"Ronnie!" She smiled warmly, then her face went slack. "Is something wrong? Is David—?"

"He's all right," I said—if anybody who's a fugitive from a murder warrant and possible murderers could be all right. "We need to talk. Can you take a break?"

"Christian Mullin hasn't called in yet," Marcella said. "I haven't asked him about—"

"That's all right. Can you get away?"

"Uh, like now?"

I nodded.

"I guess so."

We stopped at a Pascua's coffee stand on Sacramento, ordered 'lattes and bagels, and started around the block.

"Have you heard anything about Edwin Pogue's messed-up files?" I began.

"Something happened to Mr. Pogue's files? Oh,

wow! You really are an investigator. Nobody's, like, said a word to me."

"How well do you know his secretary?"

"Which one?"

"Any of them. Are you close to any of them?"

"Well . . . there's Inga. We do aerobics together Tuesdays and Thursdays and Weight Watchers on Wednesdays. She does all his filing for him."

"Can you ask her discreetly about the files?"

"I guess. What am I supposed to ask?"

"I need to know if any of his files were tampered with and what exactly happened. Were things missing, altered, or what?"

Marcella walked awhile and chewed her bagel before she spoke. "Okay. It might take, like, a day or two," she said.

"The sooner the better."

I was about to caution her about hiding Bink from the cops if he showed up at her door, when I heard somebody call my name. When I turned around, I saw a handsome, business-suited Mike Neal hurrying to catch up. He looked just as handsome as he had that first day in front of the Saint George Club.

"Hi." His suntanned face was full of pleasure. "Did you talk to Felix all right the other night?"

"Sure. Thanks."

"Sorry I couldn't get you in, but they're pretty strict about the dress code."

Marcella cleared her throat. "I think I'd better get back," she said. "I'll call you, like, when I hear from Chris, okay?"

Mike looked after Marcella with undisguised curiosity. "Is she an operative?"

"She's one better—she's a secretary. The eyes and ears in the office. Do you work around here?"

"Me? Yeah. Over there." He pointed to a glass-and-steel high rise. "Venture capital. I find start-up companies to fund."

"Do you like it?"

"It's a living."

We started down the sidewalk toward his office. "Did you know Art Spenger?" I asked.

"Artie? Sure. We used to play soccer together. Tuesday nights."

"He worked for a law firm."

"Yeah-yeah-yeah—Kindle Laird."

"I have information that he'd been asked to resign."

"Ooooh."

"You didn't know?"

"I'd heard rumors, but you know how it is. Who wants to knock a dead guy?"

"I'm afraid that's what I'm going to ask you to do. I need to know why they asked him to leave."

"I guess it's important?" He was fishing. He was so transparent about it that I had to smile.

"Very. I can't tell you why, though."

"Sure, sure, I understand. Tell you what, I'll ask Johnny Sutliff. He's engaged to Henry Kindle's paralegal. I'll see if he's free for lunch at the club tomorrow. Can it wait until tomorrow?"

"Sure," I said, then watched him amble into the financial-district crowd on his ever so slightly bowed legs.

I made a quick stop at Rob Yost's ex-boss's office on Pine. Eleanor Hightower wouldn't give up anything specific about Rob Yost's problems but suggested strongly that I check any "confidentials" my client had access to.

From there it was around the corner to Montgomery Street to see Allen Carlton, the "friend" mentioned in the Clay Johnson lion-mauling article.

38

ALLEN CARLTON'S SECRETARY had lost her sense of humor years ago, and after two minutes with Carlton, I could see why. He was the kind of guy you don't want to be left alone with in a room. He stood too close, smiled too much, held my hand too long when he shook it, and his breath was bad. I got the distinct impression his main mission in life was trying to brush up against anything female that came into his office.

I took a chair instead of the place on the couch he offered and watched him slide into his seat behind the desk and fix me with the small, beady eyes of a toad.

I gauged him to be about forty-three or -four and fighting every minute of it. The cheap toupee didn't do much for his looks, and his bulging midriff did even less.

He held up my card and pretended to study it. "Private investigator, huh?" He raised his eyebrows. "I'm impressed."

"Wait till you hear me talk," I said, and opened my notebook. "About Mr. Johnson?"

"Right. Clay. Great guy, he was. Terrific. You couldn't ask for a better friend than Clay. Man, I still miss the guy." He stared at his desk blotter, a faint, sad smile on his face. Then he cleared his throat. "So, who are you working for? I can't believe anybody'd be dredging up this crap a year later. It's not Fay?"

"I'm not investigating Mr. Johnson's death per se, Mr. Carlton—"

"Call me Al." More of the slick smile.

"—but the details surrounding his death might help me with the case I'm investigating right now."

"Yeah?" He waited for me to elaborate, and when I didn't, he said, "So what do you want to know?"

"The newspaper hinted that Mr. Johnson had become unstable during the months before his death."

"Unstable? Hell, he went off the deep end. I mean, he just flipped. He got an ulcer, started sleeping around, drinking, and messing up with his work. I don't know what started it all, but it was pretty awful to see a guy fall apart like that."

He was describing exactly what had happened to Rob Yost. "In what order did those things happen?"

"Huh?"

"The ulcer, affairs, drinking, the job—which happened first?"

Carlton thought for a minute. "He messed up with his dick first, if you'll pardon my French. For some reason this babe went after him—man, was she something! I'd trade my wife in for a piece of that anytime. But Clay, boy!" He shook his head in amazement. "He got jaded near the end. He said she was the reason he was in the fix he was in. I can't see how anything that pretty could ever be a problem. I told him so too. I told him to pass her my way, but he just said I'd be sorry and I didn't know the half of it."

"Did he elaborate?"

"Nope."

I asked him if he'd ever seen the woman, and he practically choked on his own drool describing Mary Solis. He finished up with "What a knockout!"

I wondered how much of a knockout he'd think her if he'd seen her dead, contorted body yesterday.

"And here's the killer—get this. I think she kind of

liked me," he said. "The couple of times I met her, we really hit it off. If it weren't for Clay, man, I guess she could have driven *me* crazy, huh?"

I ignored his lewd laugh. "When did Clay Johnson start drinking heavily?"

"That was with her. She was a real party girl. I've never seen anybody that could drink like her. She can drink anybody under the table. Old Clay tried to keep up with her and he couldn't. I don't know how he'd get to work, but a couple of mornings clients came in and found him passed out in the corner. Could be that's why he lost their business. I mean, how many times is a person going to let something like that happen before he looks for somebody sober he can do business with?"

I asked Carlton more questions and finally got around to the day before Johnson's death.

"Yeah, I saw him that day. He told me he broke it off with the babe. I guess he figured if he did, Fay would take him back and maybe he'd get a new job and everything'd be grand again, I don't know."

"Did he seem depressed? Suicidal?"

"I suppose so. He seemed like old Clay, you know? He always seemed like old Clay, even when he was doing the crazy things, he was still old Clay. He never acted *real* depressed. Just cynical, I guess. Yeah. He was a cynical kind of guy and never could see the good in anybody. But I don't know what pushed him over that rail."

We both sat there in silence a minute, thinking our own separate thoughts about why Clay Johnson had died the way he had. After a while Carlton stirred.

"I wonder what happened to that girl."

"She was murdered."

His jaw dropped. "Why would anybody—?" He shook his head in wonder. "I can't believe it. You should have seen her. She was beautiful."

He sounded more like he was talking about a lovely

house that had burned down than about the death of a woman.

Riding the elevator down to street level all I could think was, more "black widow" fodder. Every guy who talked about breaking up or who broke off with Mary Solis ended up dead. It made things look worse for Bink, just like Post had said.

I sighed and stepped out into the lobby. Maybe Aldo's police files could tell me more. I'd hoped to get a run in before lunch, but I couldn't spare the time. It was eleven forty-five. Time to meet Aldo.

39

"**S**O WHERE ARE the files?" I asked him.

We were at Malcolm's Barbecue De-Lite on Grove near City Hall. I'd ordered the super-spicy rack of pork ribs, and Aldo'd asked for a halfback of beef with extra-mild sauce. I sipped an Anchor Steam under Aldo's reproving eyes while we waited for the ribs to arrive.

Since I'd been the one to suggest lunch, I figured I didn't have to wait for the food to come before getting down to business. Besides, I was curious about the file since he'd walked in empty-handed. I was hoping he had copies folded in a back pocket of his starched and pressed blue jumpsuit.

"The files?" Aldo looked up from polishing his silverware with a paper napkin, set his spoon down, and cleared his throat. We were in the center of the restaurant, surrounded by secretaries and clerks and lawyers from City Hall gnawing away at their respective lunches. Nobody was paying the least bit of attention to us, but Aldo leaned forward and beckoned me toward him. "I didn't bring them," he whispered.

"What!"

A couple of lawyer-type faces turned my way. I lowered my voice. "What do you mean you didn't bring them? The whole point of our meeting was so I could look at those files, Aldo. I—"

"Lieutenant Post was the investigating officer, Ronnie. On both of them. Did you know that?"

"What difference does that make?"

"I didn't think I should take them. What if he decides he wants to look at them?"

"Aldo, one case is a year old. They're both closed. Why would he want to see them now?"

"I don't know." He squirmed. "But why do you want to see them? They're not even homicides. They're suicides, Ronnie."

"I know that. I'm not trying an end run around anybody," I lied. "I want to check them out because they're related to something else I'm working. That's all."

"Promise?"

"*Aldo.*"

"Okay, okay. I just—well, I—" With a surreptitious glance at the tables around us, he leaned forward again. "I can tell you anything you want to know. Just ask me. I memorized the files."

"Both of them?"

"They were only a few pages each."

I sighed and looked around at the other diners in the restaurant. What choice did I have? "Okay, tell me about Art Spenger."

"He was a lawyer. He practiced securities law."

"Like stocks?"

Aldo nodded, and straightened his silverware for the tenth time. "He was making gobs of money."

"How much is gobs?"

"The bank records said he had close to five hundred thousand in the bank."

Bink seemed to be swimming in cash too. Only Bink seemed to be having a harder time managing it. An auditor and a stock lawyer. Both would presumably have access to insider information. Both had unaccounted excess cash. "Anything in the file about trouble at work?"

"No. Should there be?"

"I don't know, Aldo. What did you find about Clay Johnson?"

Aldo made a squeamish face. "I didn't read it real close, Ronnie. It was pretty disgusting. You know, he was mauled by lions."

"Okay. Tell me what you remember."

"Well, I—he—there wasn't a whole lot of the remains left by the time the coroner got to him, Ronnie. The lions, they like to eat the abdominal area first and—"

"Why don't we skip that part?"

Aldo looked relieved.

"Did the coroner list a cause of death?" I'd asked Post the same question, but it never hurt to double-check.

"Not really. The lionesses were pretty hungry. There was only about a third of him left, and most of that was bones, so there wasn't much to go from. If you saw the pictures, you'd know what I'm talking about. I think it said something like 'death by hemorrhage brought on by unnatural—' "

Just then the waiter appeared at our table. "Your ribs," he announced with a wide flourish as he set a plateful of meat and bones in front of each of us.

We both stared at our respective plates in horror. I looked at Aldo, and Aldo looked across the table at me. His face turned a sickly shade of green.

"Excuse me," he said, grabbing his stomach with one hand and covering his mouth with the other. He lurched out of his chair and charged unceremoniously across the room.

The waiter and I—and I guess everybody else—watched him vanish into the men's room. In the sudden silence we heard faint retching sounds. I glanced down at the plate in front of me, then at the waiter. "Doggy bags," I said.

Strolling out into the crisp, cool air didn't exactly revive my appetite, but it did clear the queasiness. The sky was a brilliant China blue, endless without a single cloud to mar its surface. Aldo took a deep breath as he stepped out with me, and by the time we hit the middle of Civic Center Plaza, his color was back.

All the benches were taken by homeless people and their dogs and luggage, so we sat on the edge of the drought-dried fountain and pretended not to notice the drug transactions going on around us—or at least I pretended. I don't think Aldo realized what was going on. Otherwise he would have arrested them all.

"What exactly is this about, Ronnie?" Aldo said after we'd sat down. "Does it have anything to do with that fax Mitch sent you?"

"Uh, no. Well, maybe. I don't know, Aldo. It's a long story." I sighed and looked around at the poor beggars in the park. One of them made eye contact with me, so I offered him my doggy bag. He accepted and strolled off to some private place to eat it.

"Would you make a copy of the files for me, Aldo?"

He frowned. "Why? I can tell you anything you want to know."

"Sometimes it just helps to read it yourself. There could be something I'm forgetting to ask you about. Seeing the report could trigger a question."

He thought for a moment and was about to speak when he noticed a guy smoking a joint across the plaza. The guy had lit up when we first sat down, and I'd been wondering how long it would take Aldo to pick up on it.

The joint was down to almost nothing when Aldo spotted him, but the unmistakable way he sucked the smoke into his lungs must have tipped Aldo. Aldo's whole body went rigid. He reached for his gun and his badge at the same time. "Excuse me, Ronnie. I have to arrest a perpetrator."

The stoned-out street person wasn't as far gone as he looked. By the time Aldo reached him, he'd extinguished the butt and swallowed it.

Aldo hauled him in anyway, to the jeers and taunts of the homeless around us. After Aldo left, I gave away his forgotten doggy bag, crossed the street to City Hall, and called Ellie Yost from the pay phone.

"Rob's bank? First Statewide."

"Did he have a lot of cash when he died?"

"Yes. I was surprised, as a matter of fact. He'd opened a private account that I knew nothing about."

"How much was in it?"

She hesitated.

"Please, Mrs. Yost, it's important."

"Three hundred and fifty thousand."

"Could he have earned that on the job?"

"It's possible, but he never could have saved that much. Not with our expenses."

When I called Fay Johnson, she told me the company account had been surprisingly robust for the amount of complaining she'd heard from her husband. How robust? In the mid six figures. And Art Spenger's executor found three hundred thousand dollars squirreled away at Great California Savings.

I hung up, fished out my last quarter, and dialed Blackie.

"Have you had lunch yet?" I asked.

"Lunch?" The way he said it, I knew breakfast hadn't even entered his mind.

"Stay put," I said. "I'm on my way over."

40

I HADN'T COUNTED on the guy coming up behind me in the underground parking lot. I was walking to my car one minute, and the next my feet were kicking the air. I was clawing at the hand covering my mouth and gasping for breath. The arm around my waist felt like a vise.

Before I could get past my surprise, before I could try any self-defense maneuvers or even catch my breath, I was thrown sideways through the open door of a limousine. The door slammed behind me. I landed on my side with a mouthful of carpet, and when I opened my eyes, I saw a spit-polished pair of shoes two inches from my face. I gasped. My heart stopped, then started pounding so loud, I could barely hear.

"Good afternoon," a muffled voice whispered from somewhere above me.

I lifted my head and looked to see who it was. Right off I knew I didn't like him. Maybe it was the hangman's hood over his head, or maybe it was the black leather gloves. Or it could have been the fact that the rest of him was covered by one of those black graduation gowns students wear to get their diplomas.

"Sit down, Ms. Ventana," he whispered in a raspy, guttural voice.

I pulled myself up and slid onto the seat opposite his. It was just the two of us. "W-who are you?"

"A friend. I'm here to give you some advice."

His gloved hands worked on the seat beside him, clenching and unclenching.

"You are your parents' child, Ms. Ventana. You know how these things work. It will be to your benefit to leave well enough alone," he rasped.

"What are you talking about?"

"Don't play stupid with me—I've no tolerance. Stop your prying into matters best left alone!"

"And if I don't?"

His body shifted underneath the graduation gown. I thought he was just shrugging until I saw the sharp edge of a knife appear in his hand. "I'm giving you a warning because of your parents, Ms. Ventana. After today I will have complied with my respect for them." He ran his gloved thumb over the sharp blade. "Understand?"

I suddenly realized the car was moving. How long had we been traveling? I glanced out the window and saw we'd gone just a few feet. We hadn't even left the garage yet.

"Do you UNDERSTAND?"

"Who are you?"

His left hand swung out at me and struck my cheek. I reached to grab it, remembered the knife in his other hand, and thought better of it.

"Back off!" he shouted, then threw open the door and shoved me out.

I hit the pavement and rolled into a parked car. When I looked up, the limo had just turned the corner. A sharp pain stabbed through my shoulder when I tried to get to my feet. I gritted my teeth, forced myself up, and ran after the limo, but by the time I reached the up ramp, it was gone.

I stood there working my sore left shoulder, staring at the parked cars around me, wondering what the hell I'd uncovered.

41

"WHAT THE FUCK happened to you, doll?" Blackie took the cardboard pizza box from my hands and stared at my cheek. I'd checked it in the mirror in my car. It wasn't swollen, just discolored.

"I'm getting close," I said.

"To what?"

"That's the part I don't know."

Blackie looked me up and down. "You all right?"

"I'm fine." I stepped into his living room and, over pizza and coffee, told him what happened.

"Fuckin' bastard," Blackie said when I'd finished.

"Yeah." I crumpled up my napkin and tossed it into the bag the coffee had come in.

Blackie set down his Styrofoam cup of coffee and pointed at the last slice of pizza in the box.

"Sure you don't want that, doll?"

"Positive. Go ahead."

He took a wolf-size bite, shunted it to the side of his mouth, and said, "So what have you got that sends this asshole into orbit?"

I lined up three olives on the oil-soaked cardboard pizza container. "Three dead men. Here. Art Spenger. Rob Yost. Clay Johnson. A lawyer, a banker, and a printer."

Blackie grunted.

"What have they got in common? Unaccountably fat bank balances, trouble on the job, and Mary Solis. And here's Bink." I set a discarded onion slice off to the side. "The auditor."

I looked up at Blackie and he nodded.

"My guess is Mary Solis was their customer. She was buying something from them. The question is, what?"

"Something they had access to on the job."

"Right! Okay, a stock lawyer would have access to dirt on stocks, right? If they're going up or down, right? He's got access to a lot of privileged information. And Bink—as an auditor—goes in and snoops through the bowels of companies to see if they're honest or not. More chance for dirt. More chance to know if stocks are going to go up or down. And the banker, the loan agent I'm not so sure about. But what do people list on loan applications? They give out their whole life stories on those things. More confidential information."

"What about the printer?"

"That's the one that doesn't fit." Clay Johnson's print shop just didn't make sense. But his account was just as fat as the other guys'. What did he know or own that he could sell to Mary Solis or her boss?

I couldn't be sure of exactly what Solis was buying or why, or if she was buying it for herself or the jerk in the hangman's mask. But maybe if I found the answer, I'd find out who killed her.

I shut the pizza box and folded it in half. Then I fished some makeup out of my backpack and covered up the bruise on my cheek. "You want to hold the fort in case Bink surfaces?"

"Sure, doll. What are you gonna do?"

"I think it's time to visit little brother again."

42

HENRY SOLIS RECOGNIZED me as soon as he opened the door. I almost didn't recognize him, though. He was wearing sweatpants and was bare-chested like the last time I'd seen him, but he looked older today and haggard way beyond his seventeen or eighteen years.

"I'm sorry about your sister," I said once I was inside the tacky little trailer.

"Yeah." He propped his buttocks against the arm of the sofa and reached listlessly for his dumbbells.

"I guess the police were already here," I said.

He swore softly under his breath and began flexing his arms, automatically working the hand weights up and down. "Those *pendejos* tried to make it sound like it was her fault. I know María. She's not going to ask nobody to throw her off a third-story floor."

His arms stopped. "You found her?"

"Yes."

He dropped the dumbbells to his side, and his whole body seemed to deflate. "It didn't even look like her," he said softly, staring at the floor. "Her face . . . that picture, the one I gave you, *that's* María. That's how she really looks. Pretty, you know. A little crazy, but pretty."

It seemed important to him, so I muttered something about how beautiful she was. At that he smiled wistfully and stared off into space, lost in some private memory. I let him drift, then broke the silence.

"Who was your sister working for?"

He blinked. *"¿Quien sabe?* The cops, they asked me about your friend, that Bink. Maybe she was working for him. They said he killed her."

"He didn't."

"How can you know?" He started flexing his arms absently again.

I went over the acrophobia theory again and was surprised that some of my conviction had waned since talking to Post. I forced more confidence into my voice. "Bink Hanover may be a real jerk in a lot of ways, but I know he wouldn't kill anybody."

"Why did he run?"

"He's stupid."

Henry Solis snorted. "I don't know if I want you for a friend if you talk about your friends this way."

"He's not a friend, Henry. He's a client. I talked to a guy today—a guy who was afraid to show me his face. His message was I should drop my investigation. Any idea who he could be?"

"No." He flexed his arms some more, rhythmically, up and down, muscles rippling along his bare upper arms. The action seemed somehow comforting and familiar to him. "Will you find María's killer?" he asked.

"If you help me. Who was she working for?"

He pumped the weights up fiercely. "I said I don't know. María never talked about work."

"Do you mind if I take a look through her things? It might help."

"The cops already looked."

"I know." I waited quietly, watching his arms work. Finally he shrugged, set the weights down, and led me down the hall to his sister's room.

It was a modest place for somebody like I imagined Mary Solis to be. A tiny twin bed, beige shag carpet, and

faded crimson velvet curtains. The walls were bare, and
in the corner was a maple dresser with a mirror and
assorted toiletries. Her perfume was stuff I'd seen advertised for two hundred dollars an ounce.

I picked up a lacquer jewelry box and opened it.
The rings and necklaces and earrings inside were all
quality stuff. I was surprised the cops hadn't confiscated
them. I said so to Henry.

"They didn't see it," he said from the doorway. "I
put the box in my room when they came."

I opened the closet. It was half empty, but the
clothes that were there were all beautiful: glitzy evening
stuff with sequins, silk skirts, and soft, cashmere sweat-
ers, all designer labels.

"When was the last time you saw Mary?" I asked.

"Last week."

"Before I talked to you?"

"Yeah. I hadn't heard from her in a while, and I
tried to call her—"

"You have a phone number for her?"

"Yeah." We both ignored the fact that he'd lied to
me the other day. "You want it?"

"I think I'd rather have her address."

He hesitated, then grinned for the first time since
I'd arrived. "You're pretty smart. I guess that's why
you're a detective, no?"

"If I was really smart, Henry, I would have gotten it
from you the first time."

43

I KNOCKED, WAITED, and knocked again. My fingers were actually touching the lock picks inside my pocket when the door suddenly opened. A tall, showy blonde stared out at me. She was barefoot, in a flowered silk robe, with tiny droplets of water glistening on her neck and a towel in one hand, but she managed to look elegant and imposing just the same. Quite an accomplishment for nine o'clock on a Saturday morning.

"Are you the locksmith?" she asked.

"Well . . . I—"

She pointed at the front door. "This is the lock I want changed. Can you do it now?"

I had the tools to do it in my trunk. "Sure," I said, then reached inside and worked the latch. The bolt slid in and out. "Seems to work okay. Somebody move out?"

"My roommate was murdered," the woman said.

I pretended to be shocked, then poked my head farther into the apartment. "Here?"

"No. It happened in the East Bay, but that's close enough for me. I want the lock changed. I don't care if it sounds silly."

"It's not silly at all," I told her. "I think you're doing a very smart thing."

She brightened and actually smiled. "Really?"

"Sure. As a matter of fact, if you want I can look the

place over and tell you if you ought to beef up your other locks too."

"Oh, yes," she said fervently. "That would be wonderful."

"My name's Ronnie, by the way," I said, following her inside.

"Petra Broward."

"Nice place," I said, looking around. The flat was huge, with bleached floors and sparse but expensive-looking modern furnishings. Pink gauze hung from the windows in the living room. It was a far cry from the tiny trailer in Colma.

"These look all right," I told her, sliding the window locks in the living room back into place. They weren't anything grand, but they'd do fine since, looking out, I could see there wasn't really any access from the outside.

We passed through a small dining room, where I checked windows again and moved on to the kitchen. It had black marble counters and matching black European appliances.

"What about the back door? Does this place have a back door?"

"Let me show you." She led me around the refrigerator and into a tiny pantry. "It's right here."

The door was flimsy with a glass window above and a cat door below. The lock was a Schlumb. She might as well send out invitations.

"I'd better change this one too," I said, and hoped the locksmith she'd called didn't show up before I was done.

I tapped the cat door with my toe. "This for your cat?"

She nodded.

"Don't take this the wrong way," I began, "but having this opening here is a security risk. Sometimes burglars can slip through an opening like this. Sometimes they bring a kid along, and the kid slips through, then unlocks the latch from the inside. You might want to keep the cat in for a while and board this up. At least until your friend's killer is caught."

"Oh, I will. Absolutely."

"And the glass—order the unbreakable kind."

She was so enthusiastic that I was tempted to ask her if she'd ever considered installing a burglar alarm. Instead I invited her to show me the bedrooms.

"This yours or your roommate's?" The sunny space was covered in white lace—the brass bed, the windows, the pillows on the rattan chair in the corner—and the air smelled of cinnamon.

"It's mine."

I told her what needed to be done to secure her windows, then asked to see her roommate's bedroom.

"Wow. What happened here?"

The room wasn't as elegant as Petra Broward's—the bed was a simple platform, and the dresser and nightstands didn't even match, but that wasn't what I was talking about. What surprised me was the room had been tossed—systematically, professionally.

Each drawer in the dresser and the twin nightstands had been pulled out and emptied, then flung on the bed. The closet shelves had been cleared, and everything that had been on a hanger was on the floor. Shoe boxes were scattered around, and the medicine cabinet, I could see through the open door to the bathroom, had been emptied too.

"Did the police do this?" I asked.

Petra shook her head. "It was like this when I came home last night. That's why I want the locks changed."

"Anything missing?"

"It's hard to tell. Her address book. She used to keep her personal papers in that drawer there by the bed. All that's gone."

"Did you call the police?"

"I don't want them creeping around my apartment."

"But her killer could have done this. He might have left some clues."

Her face closed up. "I don't care. I don't want them in here. Will you just look at the window and tell me if it's safe or not?"

As I started gingerly through the stuff, the doorbell rang. *Shit*. Now I was going to have to dream up a lie about being here.

"Excuse me," Petra said. "I'll be right back."

I stepped toward the window and, halfway there, glanced down and noticed a bronze metal wastebasket resting sideways on the floor by the dresser. Everything else in the room had been thrashed over, but my guess was the stuff in the can had been overlooked.

I knelt down, righted it, and started rummaging through the makeup-stained tissues and debris. Mixed in with the regular toiletry-type stuff were a couple of crumpled-up checks written by Mary Solis. The first was to Petra Broward. She'd messed up on writing the numbers, had scratched it out, then, I guess, started over with a fresh check. The second one was from a different bank and was written to a department store. It looked perfect, it even had her signature on it, but for some reason she'd wadded it up and tossed it into the garbage.

I stuffed them both into my pocket and kept digging. At the bottom, at the very bottom, was a rumpled sheet of paper. It seemed to be stuck, so I tugged at it, then lifted it away. The paper was a piece of junk mail secured with a plug of chewing gum. Underneath I found a couple of keys taped to the trash can's bottom.

I yanked them free, tape and all, then slid them into my pocket just as footsteps approached from down the hall. A lie. Right. Maybe she'd just sent the other locksmith away. But if she hadn't, what could I tell her I was doing here?

Before I could come up with anything, Petra Broward's imposing, silk-robed figure appeared in the doorway. She looked more upset than I'd expected. This was going to be hard.

"I can expl—" I began, then froze when the idiot Oakland Police sergeant who had questioned me earlier trooped in behind her. A uniformed SFPD officer followed him. Then they all stepped aside, and in walked Lieutenant Philly Post.

44

"WILL YOU EXCUSE ME? I've got to get some tools downstairs," I said, starting for the door and hoping they'd let me pass.

"You're not going anywhere, Ventana." Post blocked the door and scowled at me. The uniformed officer looked sort of apologetic, and the Oakland cop looked just plain shocked to see me.

"What's she doing here?" he demanded.

"What *are* you doing here, Ventana?" Post growled. His furry eyebrows twitched ominously.

"Uh—Ms. Broward needed her locks changed."

Post's eyes swept the trashed-up room. "You lose something?"

"The room was like this when I got here. Ask Ms. Broward."

Petra's narrowed blue-gray eyes darted from Post to me, then back to Post. He'd obviously already established himself as the ranking police officer.

"You know her?" she asked Post.

They all nodded. She turned to me. "Are you a cop?"

I opened my mouth, but Post spoke first. "She's a P.I."

Petra rolled her eyes toward the ceiling. "Great. Cops, P.I.'s. What do you guys want?"

"We just want to look at the victim's personal effects," Post said. "It's routine. What about you, Ventana?"

"I told you—I'm here for the locks."

"But you're a private eye," Petra said.

"I do locks too. And security systems, you know, burglar alarms. If you—"

Post cleared his throat. "Rostow, take her downstairs and wait for me."

"You don't have any right to make me leave. This isn't a crime scene."

Post turned to Petra. "Ms. Ventana here represents the homicide suspect, ma'am. Do you want her in your home?"

Petra stared at me with a mix of horror and confusion, then covered her eyes and shook her head. "I'd like you *all* to leave," she said.

Rostow escorted me out of the room as Post showed Petra his search warrant.

"Looks like you got the inside track," Rostow said, letting go of my elbow as soon as we cleared the apartment. "How'd you know the victim lived here?"

"Luck," I said. "What about you?"

Rostow smiled. "I guess we got lucky too. According to Ewing"—he pointed upstairs, indicating the Oakland police goon—"the phone records show somebody at the homicide scene phoned this place just before the victim got killed."

The next move was supposed to be mine. I was supposed to spill my guts to this nice cop who'd shared his stuff with me as one professional to another.

But I didn't want to tell him about the keys. I didn't want to share anything with the police. They'd only use it to build a case against Bink. And I didn't want the people who'd really murdered Mary Solis—and maybe Rob Yost, Art Spenger, and Clay Johnson—to get away with it. So I just smiled back at Rostow and asked him if Ewing had told him anything else.

He was good-natured and amiable, which made me wonder if Post was using him to play a mild version of good cop–bad cop. We walked up and down in front of the apartment building, each trying to pump the other without any luck.

Finally I gave up and opted for small talk. He was halfway through a story about his kid's debate team, when Post burst out of the building and caught up with us.

"Give Ewing a hand upstairs, will you?" Post said to Rostow.

As soon as Rostow vanished through the door, Post turned to me. "Spill it, Ventana."

"Spill what?"

"You know what I'm talking about. How come you beat us here? What've you got?"

I tried the "I got lucky" bit, but Post wasn't as nice as Rostow.

"I can tell Ewing to hold you for interfering with a police investigation. I can ask him to hold you for withholding evidence. I can even tell him you're an accessory after the fact—"

"Post, you're forgetting I brought Bink Hanover to your office. I asked you to check this out. Remember what you told me? You said—"

"That was before he committed homicide, Ventana. That changed the stakes a little, wouldn't you say?"

"He didn't murder anybody."

Post raised his bushy eyebrows in mock surprise. "Yeah? And I guess you're going to prove it."

"What I'm going to do, Post, is find the person or persons really responsible for Mary Solis's murder. If it turns out to be Bink Hanover and I find him, fine. I'll turn him over. But I don't think that's going to happen."

"Where is Hanover?"

"I don't know."

"Have you heard from him?"

"No."

"I swear to you, Ventana, if I find out you're harboring a fugitive, I'll make your license history. You'll be waiting on tables if you want to work in this city."

I tried my most earnest expression on him. "Are you going to hold this night-shift thing against me forever? I thought we were friends, Post. I honestly thought we had a good working relationship. I mean, look, you're working days again, right? I'm not saying I'm the one responsible for your boss's bad temper, but can't we let bygones be bygones? Can't we work together with Ewing on this?"

It took him about five minutes to say it, but the gist of his answer was no.

45

"**W**HAT MAKES YOU think anybody's going to buy it?" Blackie asked.

It was Monday morning, and we were in my apartment. There was still a faint filling-station odor to the room, but for the most part the place was just like new. My jaw was stiff, but the bruise on my cheek had started to clear. With makeup it didn't even show.

I was at the table I use for a desk, practicing forging Mary Solis's signature. I held the rumpled check I'd pulled out of her waste can next to my latest autograph and compared the two.

"Not bad." I beckoned to Blackie. "Look at this. What do you think?"

He eyed the two signatures sourly. "*R*'s different," he said.

I looked at the two *r*s. "You're right. Mine's more rounded, isn't it?" I tried again. "There. It's perfect now."

He glanced down and grunted. "So what makes you think anybody's going to buy you as Mary Solis?"

"First, I've got the wig. It's her style and color. Then I'm going to show up during the lunch hour. The bank manager and everybody important's going to be out or busy. No flunky's going to question whether I am who I say I am. They don't even think that way until they get to assistant-manager level."

Blackie reached for a cigarette, lit it, and tossed the spent match into my kitchen sink.

"Besides, nobody's going to sweat it over a safe-deposit box. They're worried if somebody rips off the bank, but if somebody walks out with whatever somebody had in his box, it's not that big a deal. Most of the time what's in there's illegal anyway."

"What's my game?"

"You're the distraction. You go in there with this." I handed him a hundred-dollar bill—one of my souvenirs from Bink. "You want to open an account and you've got a zillion questions to ask about interest rates and stuff. Try to get as many people involved as you can so there's less attention paid to me when I walk in."

He blew smoke into the room, then glanced at the two keys lying on the table top next to the checks. "Which one's the ringer?"

"This key"—I picked up the silver one and smiled—"opens a very expensive and special European-style lock called a Rhoemer. It's supposed to be pick-proof. German tempered steel. Laser-designed. Using one for a double-lock safe-deposit box would be overkill."

I set it back down and picked up the smaller, copper-colored key. "If you want to bet, put your money on this one. The real problem is guessing the right bank. And we've got a fifty-fifty chance on that one."

I whisked all my pages of practice signatures into the wastebasket and picked up the black wig. "By the way," I said, "you look great in a suit."

"Fuck."

The Bay City Bank branch listed on the first Mary Solis check was on Van Ness near Turk. I gave Blackie about five minutes to work his way up the line and engage the tellers. There were three and they were all women, so they all broke their necks to get to him.

When I walked in and stepped up to the sign that said Safe Deposit/Payroll, I had to clear my throat four times before somebody came to help me. And even then I could have signed my name "Elvis Presley" and nobody would have noticed. The teller was too busy trying to catch Blackie's eye.

I was in and out of the vault in three minutes. Blackie saw me leave, but it took him another five minutes to extricate himself from the flock of eager women and join me out in the car.

He slid in behind the wheel shuffling bits of paper with names and numbers scribbled all over them. "You see the brunette?" he asked.

"They were all brunettes, Blackie."

"The older one with the smile. Tricia." He shuffled the scraps until he found the business card with "Tricia" written on it, then chucked all the others on the floor under the dash. "She's assistant manager. Has a cabin up in Tahoe."

"Let me guess. She wants you to come up there and ski with her."

Blackie grinned. "I don't think it's skiing she was thinking about, doll." He placed the card into his breast pocket, patted it, then pulled out a cigarette. "Six percent a good rate?"

"It's more than Mary Solis was getting."

I showed Blackie the contents of the open bag in my lap: three long manila envelopes. I'd already gone through two and was about to open the third.

"How much?" Blackie asked.

I reached into the third envelope and ran my thumb across a thick bundle of thousand-dollar bills. "Looks like about six hundred bills altogether."

"Six hundred? What the fuck was she into, doll?"

"Shopping, Blackie. I think we just found Mary Solis's shopping money."

I was ready to take the whole story to Gabriél to get

his take on it, but when I stopped to check my phone messages, there was a brief, desperate message on my phone-answering machine.

"Ronnie, this is David—David Hanover—Bink, okay? You're my one phone call. Come get me out of here. I'm at the Hall of Justice, but they're taking me to the Oakland jail. Bring bail. And a lawyer."

46

THE ONLY PEOPLE hanging around the Oakland jail with any spirit left in them are the attorneys. Everybody else seems bathed in misery: mothers whose sons have been locked up, abject wives and wailing children, sullen brothers and solemn, defeated fathers.

On principle Blackie had refused to come with me. So I waited alone with all the sad souls in a drafty basement corridor while the desk sergeant sorted through paperwork trying to find Bink. I'd been sitting on a hard wooden bench between a sobbing white-haired black woman in a housecoat and a frightened seven-year-old clutching a ragged stuffed toy, and the atmosphere finally got to me. I rose and waited by the exit until the sergeant signaled me over and told me to follow a portly young officer who'd slouched in through a metal door behind the desk.

We passed a metal detector and three locked gates before we hit the visitors' area. A frazzled Bink sat behind glass at the first kiosk in a row of five. When he saw me, he started pecking frantically at the glass with his forefinger and mouthing my name.

As soon as I sat down, he grabbed the phone on his side of the glass and started talking. His words tumbled out at me as I picked up my own handset.

". . . arraignment. You've got to get me a lawyer. And bail. Talk to Barbara. Tell her to use her accident-settlement fund. Tell her I'll pay her back, but she's got to sign some of it over to you now so you can handle bail when they set it. She'll do it if you explain that it's life or death. Just tell her, okay?"

"Bink, you can't expect your sister to—"

"Just tell her, Ronnie." His voice turned shrill, like it had that night he brought the thugs over.

"Why'd you run, Bink?"

He barked out an hysterical laugh. "Isn't it obvious? Look where I am."

"They might have been more lenient if you'd stuck around. It looks bad—well, worse."

"Talk to Barbara. I can't stay in here. They stuck some guy in the cell with me who thinks he's a wolf. I don't want to know what he's got planned for when the lights go off. Come on, Ronnie. Please?"

It crossed my mind that Bink, who'd managed to escape prosecution for a parade of scams, might actually end up paying for a crime he didn't commit.

"This is a capital crime, Bink. If they set bail—"

He blanched. *"If?"*

"They might not, especially since you ran away. But let's say they do, they'll probably set it so high, Barbara won't be able to afford it." He started to protest, but I cut him off. "You actually might be better off in here. They can't get to you. If you remember, this is what I asked Philly Post to do at the very beginning—give you protective custody."

Another prisoner walked by behind Bink—a massive biker-looking type with a shaved head and disgusting tattoos on his scalp. I watched him pass, fascinated by his ugliness, and when I turned back to Bink, big tears were streaming down his cheeks.

"Aw, Bink."

"I c-c-can't stay in th-this place, Ronnie. P-p-p-uhl-ease, Ruh-Ruh-Ronnie."

"I'll do my best, okay? Just stop crying."

He sniffed, and wiped his nose on the sleeve of his jumpsuit, then took a couple of deep, jagged breaths and tried to compose himself.

"Now's the time to come clean, Bink. What was *really* going on between you and Mary Solis?"

"I already told you—"

"You told me she was crazy. I've found out every single guy she was involved with made money, money unaccounted for in any other way—and so have you. What was she buying, Bink? Tell me what the deal is, or you're staying here forever."

"You can't do that. I've got rights!"

I pushed my chair back and started to return the handset to its cradle. Bink lunged forward and grabbed his handset with both hands.

"Wait! Don't you think if there was more to it, I would have told you?"

I sat back down. "No."

"Well, there's nothing to it, okay? I wasn't doing anything illegal. She was a kook, that's all."

"So who killed her?"

"How am I supposed to know? All I can tell you is she was a vengeful bitch." Something flashed across his face. "That's it!" he cried triumphantly. "*She* framed me. Her last act was to commit suicide and make it look like I pushed her."

"She couldn't live without you, right?"

He nodded vigorously. "Yeah, yeah. That's it!"

"Forget it, Bink. Nobody's going to buy that, especially not a judge or a jury."

Half an hour of grilling Bink didn't get us any further. Our time was almost up, and I was way past the being-annoyed stage.

"Think again, Bink."

"Leave me alone, Ronnie. I'm tired. I want to take a shower. Can't we go to a hotel and talk about this crap?"

"Answer the question."

"I told you, I wasn't selling her information. I swear."

"What were you working on at the time?"

"How'm I supposed to remember that? Ask Marcella. She keeps my time logs for me."

"I will. How many times did you see Mary Solis?"

Bink stole a furtive glance at the guard by the wall. "I don't know. A lot."

"How many times?"

"I don't know. Five maybe. Ask Marcella."

"Why would she remember?"

"I'd always come in late the next day because I'd have such a lousy hangover. She marks it down. She knows everything, Ronnie. Why don't you talk to her?"

"Wait a minute. Every time you saw this woman, you'd wake up the next morning with a hangover?"

"We drank a lot. So?"

"Do you ever take files home with you?"

"You mean to work on? Not a chance. I don't work at home, Ron. I don't need to."

I tried to hide my exasperation. "I know this is hard for you to accept, Bink, but it's possible this woman wasn't just interested in you for your body or your charm. I think the evidence points to the fact that she was interested in the information you could give her."

"I keep tellin' you I didn't give her any information."

"Maybe not intentionally. Tell me about your dates."

He sighed. "Are you serious? Get real, Ronnie. Okay. Okay. We'd always start out at Jinx's, you know that bar on Montgomery Street? We'd always start out there. Boy, could that woman drink! We'd hit all the bars in the financial district, then we'd pick up something from that all-night deli off Columbus and drive over to my place. She'd fix drinks, then she'd bring them into the bedroom and we'd drink them."

"Is that how it always was?"

"Yeah."

"Okay. And then what?"

Bink ran a finger along the Formica edge of the kiosk. "Then she'd go fix the deli food."

"And?"

"Then we'd eat and hit it off."

Bink's euphemism for sex. I didn't really want him to get any more specific about his love life.

"Can you think why she'd have six hundred thousand dollars stashed away in a safe-deposit box?"

"That bitch! She was holding out on me!"

"What do you mean?"

"She made me pay for everything, and here she was sitting on a pile of money." I wondered if he felt that way every time he bought Carolina dinner. Or did he view that as an investment?

The officer on Bink's side of the wall came up behind him and signaled me to hang up.

"Looks like I've got to go."

I started to put the phone back onto its hook when Bink motioned me to return it to my ear.

"You'll be at the arraignment?"

"I'll try," I said.

"Talk to Barbara."

"Right."

"And whatever you do, don't tell Carolina."

With that the guard extricated the receiver from Bink's hand and replaced it, then led him out of the room.

I sat there wondering what to do. This was probably the safest place for Bink right now. I didn't feel like getting him out of jail just yet. But if I wanted to investigate the work angle, I needed access to his files. Marcella could get me in, but I'd need Bink's expertise and his knowledge to tell me what was what.

I still hadn't made up my mind what to do by the time I passed through the steel door behind the desk sergeant and into the "room of sorrows," as I'd come to think of it.

"Ronnie!"

I looked up. Carolina Pogue hurried toward me, elegant in a taupe silk suit, but just as gaunt-faced as the other bummed-out people around us. "Is he all right? Did you talk to him? What happened?"

"What are you doing here?"

"I heard it on the radio. They said his name and then they said he killed somebody. Ronnie, what's going on?"

Out of the corner of my eye I spotted a newspaper reporter with a camera. He scanned the room, then brought his eyes back to rest on Carolina and me. I guess we stood out because we weren't wearing housecoats and house slippers.

"Listen, unless you want your picture on the front page of the *Examiner* and the *Oakland Tribune,* we'd better get out of here."

Carolina nodded and stepped in behind me like the true society doll she was. From conception society kids are taught to avoid bad publicity, or at least that's what my mother told me.

When we reached the parking lot and her bright yellow Ferrari, Carolina stopped and fixed me with mascara-stained eyes. "What's going to happen to him?"

I decided it'd be best to focus on technical aspects. "First he'll be arraigned," I began, and went through the whole process with her, explaining that it wasn't likely bail would be set for such a high-profile capital crime.

"But why do they think he killed somebody? I don't understand."

"A woman was found murdered in the house where

he's staying. Instead of sticking around and reporting it, he ran."

"Poor David."

No questions about the woman, no sympathy for the victim. Just "poor David."

"He needs a lawyer," Carolina said. "I'll call German."

"German Daniels?"

She nodded. "He's a friend of Daddy's."

He was also the best and most expensive criminal lawyer on the West Coast. The only case he'd ever lost was his first one thirty years ago. I couldn't imagine him taking on squirrely, looks-guilty-as-hell Bink.

But he showed up forty-five minutes after Carolina Pogue called him. And within the hour Bink was arraigned and released on bail. Carolina paid it.

47

ONE OF THE CONDITIONS of Bink's release was that he stay at German Daniels's house, so I followed them over to a big mansion on Vallejo Street in Pacific Heights. It was just around the corner from the party house where I'd followed Felix Ashton and Carolina Pogue to the other night. Daniels's house was a monstrous sandstone with weathered brass around the windows and a mahogany front door. His foyer was two times the size of my apartment, and the view from the living room spanned both bridges.

Bink had ridden back with Daniels, and I guess they'd talked about the case during the trip, because when they both got out of the car at his place, Daniels looked sort of disturbed. But his sour look could have been from spending thirty minutes locked in a car listening to Bink talk about anything.

Whatever it was, once we were all inside the mansion, Daniels seemed more than willing to part with Bink for a couple of hours when I asked to borrow him to follow up a hunch at Bink's office. It was Carolina who gave us problems.

"I don't want to lose sight of you again, darling," she said, clinging to Bink. "It scares me to death to think something might happen to you again and I couldn't be there to help."

The thought of having a moon-faced, lovestruck society girl tagging along didn't do much for my etiquette. I pulled Bink aside.

"Get rid of her," I told him.

"She paid my bail, Ronnie. She still wants to marry me," he said with a mixture of justified amazement and glee. "I'd be crazy to blow her off now."

So the three of us drove down to Embarcadero Four and signed ourselves in at the security guard's desk in front of the elevators. Everything was going fine until we got to Ellis, Pogue & Lipscomb's front door. Bink kept futzing with his keys until I finally took them from him.

"Which is the right key?" I asked, splaying them across my palm and holding them under his nose.

He looked at them and scratched his head. "I don't get it. It's not there."

I glanced at the lock on the door to see what kind of key we were looking for and did a double take. It was a Rhoemer. I handed Bink's keys back to him and fished Mary Solis's second key out of my pocket. "Let's try this one."

As soon as I tried to insert the key into the lock, though, I knew there was a problem. It fit the slot, but it wouldn't turn. "When was the last time you used this key?"

"Uh, I don't know. A couple of months ago? Let me see that."

I handed him the key and turned to Carolina. "Has your father changed the locks lately?"

"I don't know."

"This is my key, all right," Bink said. "See this nick here, that happened when I dropped it accidentally into Marcella's typewriter. It got mangled, but it should still work." Bink looked puzzled. "How'd you get it?"

"It's a long story. They've obviously changed the locks."

Carolina cleared her throat softly. "Can't you just break in? Mitch said you do things like that."

I weighed the wisdom of breaking into Carolina Pogue's father's office with her watching, then considered the alternatives. I could send her down the hall while I picked the lock, but she'd know I did it anyway. I could ask her to get her father's permission for us to go inside. That would probably add hours of time and the extra hassle of explaining what we were doing.

"Okay," I said. After peering through the double glass doors to make sure nobody was inside, I reached into my pocket for my lock picks. With the lights on I could see everything. Nobody was moving around in there.

"Does anybody ever work late?" I asked. Mitch always did, but I couldn't be sure about any of the others.

Bink shook his head. "Nah."

I checked over my shoulder one last time, then bent over the lock and started working it. It had mushroom drivers and, since it was a pick-proof Rhoemer, it took a couple of seconds longer than usual, but I managed to get us inside in under a minute. My parents would have been proud.

We crossed the open foyer, passed the console in the corner, and headed down the inner hall past the work matrix to Bink's office. As we neared his door, a colorful form glided through the door in front of us. Marcella, one hand clutching an enormous stack of folders and the other a Butterfingers candy bar, froze when she saw me. Then she spotted Bink, dropped the folders and candy on her desk, and squealed as she rushed over to embrace him.

"Oh, David, you're alive! I've been so worried. Are you all right? Did they, like, hurt you or anything?"

Carolina caught my eye, smiled proudly, and whispered. "Isn't it wonderful? *Everybody* loves David."

Bink squirmed out of Marcella's arms, took both

her hands in his, and squeezed them. "Hey, hey, take it easy. I'm okay, Marcella. No sweat."

"You're sure?" She stepped back and looked him over. "God, I was so worried. They didn't hurt you, did they?"

"Never laid a hand on me." The way he said it made it sound like he'd had something to do with it.

Marcella fixed her big doe eyes on Carolina. "It must have been hell for you."

Carolina nodded solemnly. "But we're together now. As long as we can be together, we'll be all right," she said. "That's all that counts."

Marcella's eyes teared up. "You're so brave."

I cleared my throat and stepped forward. "I hate to interrupt, but it's eight-thirty, Marcella. The office is closed. What are you doing here?"

"I got stuck with this thing for Chris Mullin. He's swamped with this Donziger audit, so I'm, like, doing stuff for him. Only I've been so worried, I couldn't concentrate." She smiled at Bink. "God, it's great to see you're okay."

"Anybody else here?" I asked.

Marcella answered like Bink'd been the one who asked the question. "Oh, no. Chris left, like, about thirty minutes ago. I'm just doing the typing, so there was really no point for him to stay."

Which I took as my cue to tell her *our* point for being there. "Those files I asked you about . . ."

"Oh, right. They're right here. On my desk."

"Are they the ones Pogue noticed?"

"No. Those files are in his office. They belong to our big accounts, Janus Tweed and Leavenwood Herbals. I talked to Inga, and she said Mr. Pogue only said somebody'd been in his files. He never said how he knew or what, like, went wrong."

"Are these David's files?"

"Uh-huh. So, like, what do you want me to do with them?"

There were nine bound folders, each about four inches thick. I took one and paged briefly through it, then looked at the next one and the next. All three were Kopar Corp. Basystems and Teknikker each had three folders too. The contents were a mishmash of documents, nothing I was going to make sense of by myself. I took five folders and handed them to Bink, then reached for the rest. "We're going to have to borrow these for a while."

Marcella blanched. "You can't. What if somebody asks to see them? I could get in trouble if they're gone."

"Marcella . . ." I was tired. I didn't want to have to think about any of this.

"Hey, who did this?" Bink exclaimed. He'd been sort of paging through his top folder. "What is this crap? Who changed my opinion?" Marcella came around to Bink's side so she could read what he was reading.

"Oh, that," she said. "Mitch told me to change it."

"Mitch? What gives him the goddamned right? Who the hell does he think he is?"

Marcella backed away, confused. "But, David, he's your supervisor."

"What did he do?" I set my folders on the desk and stepped around to look over Bink's shoulder.

"He changed my opinion. On the annual report we give an opinion of the company's finances. He changed it from okay to a conditional one. Remember I told you how I let a few things go? Well, Mitch changed this deal to show all their problems. What a shitty thing to do."

"It's his job, Bink. And it's supposed to be yours, too," I said.

"Aw, come on, Ronnie. Don't get a conscience on me now." He stared at the folders in his hand. "Now I know why Mitch said check this out. These guys could be pissed at me. I told them things were going to pan out fine. Damn." He dumped his folders and examined mine. "Shit. He did this one too. Let me see that one. Yeah, three for three. That son of a bitch. I can't believe he'd do this to me." He turned to Marcella. "How come I didn't know about this? You knew about it."

"Mitch said he was going to talk to you. I guess he forgot."

"Forgot? Hell! He was too damned chickenshit to do it. Goddamn him."

"That doesn't explain Mary Solis," I said.

"Huh? Oh, her." Some of the steam went out of him. He looked mildly uncomfortable, and I realized he was concerned about what I might say in front of Carolina. *Let him sweat,* I thought.

"Is she the murder victim?" Carolina asked. Marcella nodded.

I turned to Bink. "Is she connected with any of these firms?"

Instead of answering, he caught Marcella's eye. "Why don't you get us some coffee, Marce? You want to give her a hand, babe?"

Carolina popped off after Marcella like a sprightly puppy, eager to have a job to do. The instant they were out of earshot, Bink faced me. "Don't blow this for me, Ronnie. She doesn't know I got laid by Mary Solis, okay? And she doesn't need to know. I don't want to hurt her."

"I didn't ask if you slept with Solis. I asked if she's connected to any of these firms."

"She's not," he snarled. "That's what I've been telling you all along. She's got nothing to do with these." He slapped the stack of folders on the desk.

"Did Mitch know about her?"

Bink thought a moment. "I never said her name. I just told him I got laid by this rocko chick, that's all."

Did Mitch know of a different angle for Bink to get into trouble? One we hadn't even thought of? I stared at the files. If Bink had seen an irregularity on page one, there was no telling what the rest of the contents held. Maybe there was a tie-in to Mary Solis buried in there.

"Okay, Bink. Let's get this over with." I stuck five folders in his arms, took four myself, and headed down the hall. Bink followed.

"Where are we going?"

"We're going to photocopy this stuff. Then you're going to go home to German Daniels's house and go through each file, page by page, and tell me what's there."

It was close to ten-thirty when we left Marcella at her desk to finish her typing. By eleven we'd spread the files out on the floor of German Daniels's study, and Bink had started to whine.

"Can't we do this tomorrow, Ronnie? I'm tired. Look at Carolina. See how tired she is?"

Carolina looked brighter and more alert than I'd ever seen her. "Are you tired?" I asked her.

She started to answer, but Bink butted in. "Sure she is. Aren't you, babe? Come on, Ronnie. Are you going to make us stay up all night?"

That had been my intention, but all I could take was one more hour's worth of steady complaints. After that I left the two of them cooing and cuddling on the divan, ignoring the files, and drove home to my empty apartment.

48

WHEN I CRESTED the last step on the landing, Mrs. Parducci's door flew open. She poked her head out, put a finger to her lips, and motioned me into her apartment. Any other time I would have shined her on, but her wide eyes and the flush of her normally ashen skin told me something was up.

She shut the door carefully behind me.

"He's in your apartment," she whispered.

"Who?"

"Shhh! It's a young man. He was here earlier and asked for you. I don't know how he got inside the building, but he knocked on my door at three o'clock this afternoon and asked if I knew when you'd be back. I didn't tell him. But he's in there right now. I called the police. They haven't come yet."

And they probably wouldn't. Mrs. Parducci called the cops every other day to report "prowlers"—homeless people drifting around on the street outside.

"What's he look like?"

"Real dangerous. And mean. What are we going to do?"

"He's been in there since three o'clock?"

Mrs. Parducci shook her head. "That's the first time he came. See, he went away, then he came back again at nine. That's when he went inside. I've been watching the door ever since and he hasn't come out."

He definitely wasn't burgling the place—my apartment wasn't big enough to warrant more than thirty seconds, a full minute max for a rank amateur. No, he was waiting for me. "How'd he get in?"

Mrs. Parducci shook her head.

"Did he have a weapon?"

"Well . . ." I could tell she hated to say no. "He could have it hidden." The nostrils of her bulbous nose flared. The old lady was practically hyperventilating.

"Have you got a hammer?"

She looked puzzled for a moment, then said no, so I went down to my car and got a tire iron just in case. On the way back I stopped in at the Quarter Moon and asked Marcus the bartender to keep his ears open. "If you hear me yell, call the police and tell them an assault's in progress upstairs."

"Want me to come?" Marcus had a baseball bat under the bar that he'd never gotten to use.

I shook my head. "Thanks. Just call the cops."

I figured the odds were about zero that the guy inside my apartment was one of the thugs. I couldn't picture any one of them waiting three hours for me to come back. But the guy in the limo would. And he'd told me my warnings were over.

With Mrs. Parducci standing guard behind me, her wrinkled face barely visible from behind the crack in her door, I held the tire iron in my right hand and used my left to unlock the door. The next few seconds went by in a slow-motion blur.

The first thing I noticed was the lights were on. Then a tall male figure jumped out of the only armchair in the room and came toward me. His voice was loud and he was saying something—something I couldn't understand. And he was smiling. Smiling? I blinked and relaxed my grip on the tire iron.

"Mitch?"

"Surprised?"

Behind me Mrs. Parducci was shouting, "Do I scream? Do I scream? Ronnie, what should I do?"

Mitch waved a suntanned hand at her over my head. I turned around and said, "Everything's fine, Mrs. Parducci."

She started across the hall toward us. I'd never get rid of her if I let her set foot inside, so I reached over and swung the door shut. Then I turned to Mitch. He was still smiling, looking very tan and healthy and rested.

"You're supposed to be in Tahiti," I blurted.

I might have been nicer if I hadn't just come from spending hours with Bink. But Mitch didn't even flinch at my rudeness. He laughed.

"What are you doing here?" I asked.

"Put your weapon down and I'll tell you."

I glanced down at the tire iron in my hand and shrugged. "Tools of the trade," I said, and instantly felt annoyed with myself for explaining. I set the shank down. "You want a beer? Coffee?"

Mitch glanced at the messy kitchenette. My untidiness had never bothered him when we were married, so I knew he was checking to see how much trouble a cup of coffee would be.

"Instant okay?" I asked. When he nodded, I set a pot of water on the hot plate to boil and reached for an Anchor Steam from the fridge. I crossed the room and flopped onto the sofa bed. "You were supposed to be gone six months. It's only been three."

"I was worried about the Binkster. I haven't been able to reach him since that first call and—" Mitch tried to stifle a yawn but finally gave in to it. "This jet lag's got me. It's only two hours' difference, but there's something about riding in a plane that long . . ."

"You were bored," I said.

"I was worried. Bink's my friend. How am I supposed to relax on the beach when people are trying to kill my friend? How am I supposed to relax when I know that's going on?"

He was bored. I watched him get up to pour the boiling water into his cup. Behind the polished, successful businessman was the ghost of the young boy I'd fallen in love with. Sometimes I longed for that boy, for those days when he was perfect and when he thought I was perfect. Back then I wasn't sure of anything in my life— why my parents had died, where I'd be living next—but I was sure of him. A pang of regret shot through me. I was sure of him still, but now I was sure we'd never be more than friends. Mitch raised his eyes to meet mine and looked suddenly tired.

"So where's the Binkster?" he asked after taking a sip of the rancid instant coffee.

"Why'd you send me that fax?"

"It was the only thing I could think of that Bink could get in trouble for. Did you ask him about those firms?"

"He said it was no big deal. But that was before he saw you'd changed the opinions he'd written."

"Exactly. I thought he might have promised those firms a clean audit, and they might—well, they might not have liked what I did."

"Is there any reason for you to think they'd hire goons to come after Bink? Do those companies have any underworld connections?"

Mitch shook his head. "It was just a hunch, like I said. I don't have any reason other than that's the only transgression of his I know about from the last ten months. It didn't pan?"

"We're still working on it. I left the files with Bink."

Mitch studied my face. "Hey, are you all right?"

"I'm fine, Mitch."

"What's that on your cheek?"

I touched my face. The makeup I'd daubed on the fading bruise must have rubbed off. "It's nothing."

Mitch started to protest, then shrugged, shook his head, and sighed. "Okay. If you say so. Where'd you say Bink is?"

"He's staying with his lawyer while he's out on bail."

"Bail? Jeez. What is it this time?" From his expression it was obvious Mitch figured this was just one more petty scam Bink would wriggle out of.

"Murder."

Mitch gasped. "Good God! What happened?"

"Ever heard of Mary Solis?"

Mitch shook his head.

"She's a woman Bink was dating behind Carolina Pogue's back. Apparently she and he had something going, but I don't know what, and Bink's not talking. Somebody murdered her at Bink's house and made it look like Bink did it. Bink vanished after he found the body, so everybody assumes he's guilty."

"I hope you don't. It sounds like he's going to need all the friends he can find right now."

"From what I've seen, I don't think he'll need anybody besides the one good one looking out for him right now."

"Carolina?"

I nodded, and Mitch smiled. "Isn't she great?"

"Too great for Bink."

"Come on, Ron. She's exactly what he needs. Bink's been looking for somebody like her all his life."

"Somebody worth millions?"

"Don't be so cynical, Ron. This job of yours makes you think the worst of everybody."

"This has nothing to do with my work, Mitch. Bink would be trying to get Carolina Pogue's money even if I were in the dry-cleaning business."

"He told you that?"

"Of course not. He doesn't have to. Bink's been a

scammer since conception. Just because he's never vic-
timized you. . . . Have you seen him around Carolina?
He's phony. He's only after her because she's got a trust
and a wealthy father who happens to own a large chunk
of the company he works for. He's no more in love than
a salamander."

"I think you're underestimating him. He's really
changed, Ronnie."

We could have argued a lot more, but he'd been
saying the same thing for fifteen years, and I knew nothing I could say would change his mind.

Mitch stifled another yawn and asked, "What can I
do?"

At least he was asking me instead of Bink. "Talk to
him. See if you can find out what his scam with Mary
Solis was all about."

"Why does there have to be a scam?"

"Have you ever known Bink when he wasn't up to
something?"

"Ron—"

"Just talk to him."

I set the empty beer bottle on the floor and rested
the back of my head against the back of the sofa. The
Anchor Steam had done what I'd hoped it would do. I
felt relaxed and ready for sleep. Nothing Mitch could say
was going to get to me.

"Are you in any danger, Ron?"

Great, the he-man-protector number. I guess I
should have been ready for it, but I'd been too tired to
see it coming. I took a deep breath. "You're tired, I'm
tired. Let's not talk about this now."

"You're right."

I struggled to keep my jaw from dropping. "What?"

"I said you're absolutely right. Let's both get some
rest. We can talk about this tomorrow, right?"

He rinsed out his coffee cup and headed for the door. As I listened to his footsteps receding down the stairs, I heard the gentle sound of Mrs. Parducci's door closing. It was the last sound I heard.

49

"HE'S WHERE?"

German Daniels's butler dipped his chin slightly to let me know I wasn't being civil enough for his taste. I didn't care. Bink was supposed to be under his lawyer's supervision, and German Daniels was his lawyer. Having Daniels's butler tell me Bink "was out" wasn't good enough.

"Mr. Hanover accompanied Mr. Daniels to the office this morning, miss. I'm sure you'll find him there."

"Did he take the files with him?"

"I wouldn't know, miss."

"They were in the study."

The corner of his mouth twitched with displeasure. "Those would be the papers on the floor?"

"Right. Are they still there?"

"Unfortunately, yes."

"I'd like to have them."

I think he gave them to me just to clear the uncharacteristic mess out of the house.

It took me twenty minutes to drive across the Golden Gate Bridge and up the winding road through the redwoods to Mitch's house. He looked rested and alert when he came to the door, dressed in jeans, loafers, and a Ralph Lauren sweatshirt. His blond hair was still wet from his shower and he smelled of soap.

"Can you take a look at these?" I asked, shoving one stack of files at him and picking up the rest at my feet.

"Sure." He examined the top page. "Ah," he said, and started across the living room. "What am I looking for?"

"I don't know." I followed him inside and set my stack beside his on the glass-and-granite table in the living room. "Anything that strikes you as abnormal."

Sun streamed through the huge glass wall opposite the front door, flooding Mitch's expensive high-tech furniture. The house smelled of burned wood and coffee, and the scent of pine mingled with eucalyptus wafted in from the open door leading to the deck. He'd been having his coffee out there and talking on the phone.

"I haven't got through to Bink yet, but I talked to Edwin."

"Pogue?" I'd forgotten Mitch knew him, was actually a partner in Pogue's firm.

"He's pretty upset about Bink's situation. He wants me to talk to Carolina for him. I told him I would, but that I couldn't advise her to abandon Bink. He understood." Mitch glanced at his watch and smiled wanly. "I'm supposed to meet her at Sam's in Tiburon in half an hour. Can these wait?"

I shrugged. I'd rather he look at them now, but maybe he could get something out of Carolina. "You know Carolina pretty well?"

"I think Edwin made the suggestion more because I'm Bink's best friend. He must think I'll be able to offer some insight."

"Sure. Listen, why don't you ask Carolina if she knows where Bink's been getting his spending money. Find out if she's giving it to him or—"

"No." Mitch held up his hand. "No way. I'm not turning this into a spy mission. This is just going to be a little talk, that's all. To make Carolina and Edwin feel better, because Edwin says she's really loused up over the murder charge, and I don't blame her."

"It'll help Bink," I coaxed.

The sound of a creaking eucalyptus bough filtered in through the open deck door and filled the silence between us. Mitch frowned. "If she says anything pertinent, I'll pass it on, but I'm not going to pursue this actively."

"Sounds fair enough." I let him relax a beat. "Just mention the Corvette and see what she says, okay?"

He didn't say yes. But then, he didn't say no either.

50

G ABRIÉL JUAREZ AND I hit Rudyard Elementary School's front schoolyard right in time for morning recess. A swirling tide of tiny children blew out every exit like so many hyperactive ants swarming out of a nest.

"Your computer whiz works here?" I asked, dodging a tiny black girl chasing an Asian one in pigtails. Across the yard a staid young woman in sensible shoes—obviously a teacher—moved through the kids with all the deliberate speed and dignity of the Queen Mary.

Gabriél nodded as we crossed the threshold. "Teaches math. The principal thinks she's putting in overtime on the computers, but what she's really doing, she's tapped into their modem and going worldwide."

Our footsteps sounded hollow as we marched down the empty, tiled corridor, trespassers in a world where we once belonged.

"Here," Gabriél said, pausing in front of a metal door with a notebook-sized wire-reinforced glass window at the top. He peeked in, then beckoned me to follow him inside.

At a table in the back of the room, past rows and rows of miniature desks, a tiny woman worked at a computer console. Her dress was a simple long-sleeved cotton print, and her shoes were flat-soled canvas kung-fu shoes. She was so absorbed in her work, she didn't hear us come in.

Gabriél grinned and put a finger to his lips, then started across the room on tiptoe. He was halfway there when the woman seemed to sense us and froze.

Gabriél shouted, "Ming Mong! This is the FBI!"

The woman tapped a key, and the computer screen went blank as she turned toward us, a startled look on her face. Then she saw Gabriél.

"Gabriél! You rascal. You're lucky I know the FBI would say, 'Freeze!' not 'This is the FBI,'" she said in perfect, unaccented English.

"Don't think we're even, Ming." Gabriél turned to me. "This woman sent her cousin over to the bank last week to 'audit' our books. He told me he was a bank examiner. He spent five minutes on my computer, then told me I was seventeen million dollars short. I was ready to blow my brains out when Ming strolls in and says, 'Gotcha!'"

Ming offered me her hand. "My name is Ming Mong. I'm honored to meet you," she said.

"Ronnie Ventana."

"Ronnie was my probation officer. Remember I told you about her? Her folks were the Ventana cat burglars."

Ming arched her eyebrows. "Gabriél thinks very much of you. And I, I admired your parents very much. They were very clever outlaws."

"We need your computing skills," Gabriél said. "Can you locate some stock profiles for us?"

Gabriél had explained on the way over that the best place to start looking for signs of insider trading was to get a profile of the suspected target firms—their stock prices for a period of time, bios of the principal managers, and the last couple of annual reports. From that we could have a base line to study for any blips of unusual activity or actions.

"And this is all on computer?" I'd asked.

"Sure. Any brokerage firm keeps tabs on this stuff. And the stock exchanges too."

Ming Mong seemed to know exactly what we wanted. "NASDAQ or New York Stock Exchange?"

Gabriél looked at me.

"I don't know," I said.

Ming smiled. "That's all right. I only asked because it's easier to elicit the data from one than from the other."

Gabriél handed her the names of the stocks he'd written down at his office.

She read them, then asked, "How far back do you want me to go? A year?"

Bink had started working at Ellis Pogue ten months earlier. "A year should do it," I said.

Ming nodded, then sat down at the computer terminal once again. "May I quickly finish what I began?"

"By all means." Gabriél was effusive.

As her fingers worked the keys, entering numbers, she spoke softly. "Much of the information you seek is available from a variety of financial data bases, but the brokerage houses have more comprehensive and reliable information. They really dig deep when they research a firm."

Ming continued typing, entering codes and getting responses from the computer.

"There," she finally said, tapping a key that made the screen go blank. "Do you own a computer, Ronnie? May I call you Ronnie?"

"Sure. No."

"Then I must explain to you how this works. I type the telephone number here." She tapped out seven digits. "Then I tell the machine to dial it." She touched the "return" key, and a small square box on the back part of the table started beeping out the same tones you hear when you dial the phone. The line rang a couple of times, then the connection was made.

"The modem, over there, enables me to make the connection. Oh, darn." She sighed. "I'm afraid their computer's down right now. I was hoping this brokerage firm would do it for us, but I'm afraid this will take some time. May I call you when I succeed? How urgently do you need the information?"

"I'm lucky to be getting it at all, Ming," I said. "Anytime is fine."

She nodded gratefully, then walked us to the door. When I handed her my business card, she apologized again and promised she'd keep trying. Then she assured me she'd phone as soon as she had the data.

As we walked out to Gabriél's car on the street, I said, "The four guys I'm dealing with all had different jobs. Could they be selling the same type of information to somebody?"

Gabriél circled his red Jeep Wagoneer and got in. When I sat down beside him, he said, "That depends. What kind of work are we talking about?"

"One's an auditor and one's a stock lawyer. Those two are pretty obvious."

He nodded and waited for me to continue, holding his keys in his hand while he listened. The shouts of the children playing in the schoolyard filtered into the silence of the car.

"Another one's a bank loan officer."

"If it's corporate lending, it'll work. Whenever a company buys another one, it needs financing. The bank would know ahead of time who's buying what."

"How does a printer fit in?"

"Ah." Gabriél smiled. "That's a nice touch. When a company goes public, they issue a lot of printed matter that goes out to prospective buyers. When a company buys another company, hundreds of documents need to

be printed up. The printer, Ronnie, is going to be privy
to a ton of inside information."

Gabriél stuck the key into the ignition and started
the engine. We drove off, leaving Ming Mong's school-
children playing in a world far more innocent than the
one they'd inherit.

51

T HE PHONE-ANSWERING MACHINE was blinking frantically when I walked in the door. Mrs. Parducci had detained me for about fifteen minutes out on the street. She'd been on her way to the market but decided the vegetables in the bins on Columbus would wait while she grilled me severely about Mitch.

"Your ex, is he? I didn't know you'd been married, dear. How long were you married? When did you get divorced? I never saw my ex again once we signed those papers. He could be dead, for all I and the kids know. He was a piece of garbage, to tell you the truth. A real deadbeat. Did I ever tell you about the time he broke my nose?"

She hadn't, but I said, "Sounds terrible, Mrs. Parducci. Will you excuse me? I have some calls to make."

Then I darted through the door before she could open her mouth again.

There were three messages on the answering machine. The first one was from Ellie Yost. I called her back, but according to the receptionist, she was out showing "a property."

"I can give you the number of her car phone, or you can leave a message with me." I left a message.

Then I pressed Playback again and recognized the crisp, carefully clandestine voice of Aldo Stivick. I could almost hear his palms sweat. "I've located the sports equipment you want to borrow, Ronnie. Call to set a time. I'm free for lunch tomorrow."

I didn't really want to phone Aldo, so I played the final message back instead. Mitch. I dialed his number from memory.

"What have you got?"

"Ronnie?"

"Right. Did you get a chance to check out the folders?" Breakfast with Carolina would have taken an hour minimum, two hours max. I checked my watch. Two-thirty. That meant he'd only had a couple of hours to look at the files.

"A quick glance," he said. "I'll go over them more carefully later."

"And?"

"Everything looks okay. No irregularities. If they're going to show up, it'd be in the work papers."

"Work papers?"

"The stuff in these folders. It's documentation for the whole engagement, a paper trail: copies of what's been examined, memos explaining what's been done, spreadsheets. It all looks good and it's all ticked and tied."

"Great. Where does that leave us?"

"I think you need to start looking at other possibilities, Ron. Focusing on Bink and his work isn't going to tell you who killed the Solis woman."

I felt my defenses rise. "Yeah?"

"Isn't it obvious?"

I started to remind him that checking out the three firms was his idea, then decided it'd be "nonproductive," as our failed marriage counselor used to say. "Find out anything from Carolina?"

White noise sang in the silence between us.

"Mitch?"

"I want you to know I felt very uncomfortable doing this, Ronnie. When you ask me to betray a confidence, I feel like I'm taking advantage of the person. Carolina's pretty vulnerable right now."

He went on for about five minutes about how "difficult" things were for Carolina right now, how she was having trouble "processing" all the mess Bink had brought to her doorstep, et cetera. I listened because I knew Mitch. He'd found out what I wanted in spite of himself.

Finally, when I was on the verge of interrupting, he said, "She hasn't given him any money, Ronnie."

"Would she tell you if she had?"

"She wouldn't lie, Ronnie." His tone was sharp. "She's not that kind of person."

"It would have been better if she *were* bankrolling him—for him, I mean, not for her. This way we're looking at two major problems: If it's not coming from Carolina and he claims it didn't come from Solis, then where'd he get the cash for the sixty-thousand-dollar Corvette? And the Saint George Club dues are a thousand a month. Even if he cuts back on his Armani suits, ski vacations in Gstaad, and God knows what else he throws his money away on, it still won't buy him the membership. Where's he expect to come across the twelve thousand a year that's going to take?"

"All I can tell you is that Carolina is not paying for his lifestyle."

Something about the way he said Carolina's name this time made me pause, but before I could put my finger on what bothered me, Mitch said, "I'm meeting Bink tonight at German Daniels's house for cocktails. Carolina has some sort of obligation with a fund-raising party. She wanted to take Bink, but German didn't think it'd be a good idea for him to be seen socially, so I'm taking her instead."

"You're going to a fund-raiser?"

"It's the least I can do for them."

"A *society* fund-raiser?"

"You're jealous," he announced in a mildly incredulous tone.

"Jealous? Why would I be jealous?"

Only after I hung up did I realize I'd forgotten to ask him to grill Bink about the source of his cash. Maybe Bink would be more forthright with Mitch.

I sat there a long while thinking about what had just happened. Mitchell and I have been divorced eight years —three more than we'd been married—and we've both dated a variety of people over that time.

I'd demanded fidelity from my husband but not from my ex-husband. Something about the divorce papers allowed me to let go. Not once had I felt possessive or jealous. But Carolina Pogue bothered me. If only I could figure out why.

The ringing phone jangled me out of my musing.

"Ellie Yost here," the voice on the line announced. She sounded breathless with excitement.

"What's up?"

"You're not going to believe what I saw."

"What?"

"I think I'd rather show you. Can I pick you up in ten minutes?"

52

ELLIE YOST PARKED her sleek green Jaguar on the paved roadway parallel to Marina Boulevard. To the right, not more than fifteen feet from us, sailboats bobbed and clanged in the water. Across the street to the left, million-dollar homes sat, reconstructed and reinforced after the earthquake of '89 had shaken them silly.

"What are we looking for?" I asked.

Ellie pointed at a Tudor-style house with a For Sale sign in its front yard. For a minute I wondered if she was going to try to sell it to me.

"I brought a client of mine here this morning," she began. "They're asking a million two, which is just a teensy bit beyond her budget, but I think her husband will go for it if she really kicks up a fit. I don't think the sellers are going to come down any more. You really get a feel for people after a couple of years selling property, and these people have hit rock bottom on their price."

I cleared my throat. "Yes?" I couldn't keep the impatience out of my voice. She immediately smiled and apologized.

"Oh, I'm sorry, darling. See the house next door?"

It was a huge, three-story yellow stucco with grand picture windows looking out on the Marina from each of its three floors. Four glossy cars were parked in the drive

—two silver BMWs, a black Lincoln, and a white Saab. They all had tinted windows.

"I showed my client this house this morning. We were outside talking afterward, in the drive, and a woman came out of that house next door. There was something familiar about her, otherwise I wouldn't have given her a second glance. She was with a stocky man in a suit."

It took every ounce of my willpower not to say, "So what?"

"They drove up in that black car and went inside."

"Who was she?" I asked.

"Well, that's the part that's bizarre. That picture you showed me the other night—the woman Rob, uh, be-came involved with?"

"Mary Solis?"

She nodded. "It was Mary Solis."

53

"WHAT DO YOU MEAN she's alive?" Philly Post scowled at me from across his report-littered desk. "Then who's the stiff the Solis people buried yesterday?"

"I don't know. All I can tell you is that I staked out the house for two days and I saw her."

The harbormaster had let me set up a chair by the window in his office with a clear shot of the yellow stucco house. He'd even brought me sandwiches and coffee and had his night-watch person do the same for Blackie when he relieved me.

Most of the time all I saw was the garage door go up and a BMW with tinted windows would drive out or in. I followed the car twice and lost it both times. Two days straight and Blackie and I hadn't seen a single person. Until now.

"She finally popped out this morning," I said. "I saw her. Mary Solis is alive."

Post ran a thick-fingered hand through his gray-brown mop of hair and swore softly under his breath. "Why are you doing this to me, Ventana? No cop likes to tell another cop he blew it. Especially not across jurisdictions. Jesus."

I didn't say anything. What could I say—they should have reconstructed the dead woman's face? Mary Solis had never been arrested, so they had no fingerprints to compare for identification. Henry Solis must have been too distraught to really look at his dead sister. It was an understandable mistake. Nobody's fault.

Post glared at me. "All right, all right. I'll bring her in for questioning. But don't tell anybody about this until I talk to her. Keep your mouth shut, understand?"

"On one condition."

Post arched one of his bushy eyebrows and waited.

"Call me when you bring her in. I want to be there when you question her."

"Give me a break, Ventana."

"I'd hate for this to leak to the papers."

"Is that a threat?"

I smiled. "Is that an invitation?"

I stopped by Aldo's office on my way out. He looked surprised to see me, I guess because I hadn't phoned him back since his call two days ago.

"Still have that paperwork you called me about?" I asked.

"Sports equipment, Ronnie. Remember, you asked me about *sports equipment.*"

"Right, whatever. Have you got it?"

"Why, uh, yes." I figured his hesitation was due to the fact that he realized if he said yes, he couldn't stall me into a lunch. He glanced at his watch to make sure it was way past mealtime and sighed, then handed me a brown manila envelope.

"They're copies. Burn them when you're finished, Ronnie. I don't want anybody to know you've got them."

"Right."

"I'm serious. I could lose my job." He looked around and lowered his voice. "What exactly are you trying to prove?"

"I'm trying to get Bink Hanover off the Mary Solis murder rap, for starters."

"Wow! You're working for German Daniels?" Aldo's bland face brightened with approval. "Ronnie, that's marvelous. He must be the best criminal defense attorney in the country."

A sudden frown replaced his beaming smile, and he glanced suddenly at the manila envelope in my hand. "You won't tell where you got that, will you? You won't let Mr. Daniels see it, will you? He likes to talk to the media, Ronnie. I really meant it when I asked you to read it and then burn it. Really."

"Consider it done."

"I mean it. I—"

"Don't worry, Aldo. I'll take care of it."

I pointed at the computer screen behind him and said, "Think you can scare up anything on a guy called Rob Yost? He went off Highway One near Devil's Slide last year."

"Ronnie."

"Hey, it might not even be in there. I don't think anybody considered it a homicide. Do you get CHP reports?"

It turned out he had access to the data base, but he needed to use a different computer down the hall to get to it.

"I might have it by tomorrow," he said. "Are you free for lunch?"

I went home, put on my running shorts, and went for a nice hour's run along the Bay out to Fort Point and back. When I jogged home onto Grant Avenue, I spotted a man in front of the Quarter Moon. As I got closer, I recognized Mike Neal. I waved and shouted, "Mike!"

He turned and hailed me. "Can I buy you a cup of coffee?"

I pulled on the sweatshirt I'd had tied around my waist, ran my fingers through my sweaty hair, and said yes. With our two espressos on the tiny table between us, we both watched an old Italian woman cross the street to take a bench in the sun in Washington Square.

"I had lunch with Sutliff," Mike said. "He had some pretty rotten stuff to say about Artie."

My heart quickened.

"Artie was hooked pretty bad on nitrous oxide. I guess you knew about that."

I nodded.

"He was even tanking at the office near the end. He'd bring in a little tank inside his briefcase and leave his legal briefs at home." Mike shook his head. "Pretty sad."

"So why'd they ask him to leave?"

"The scuttlebutt says he was giving out confidential information."

"To who?"

Mike shrugged. "I don't know."

"How did they know he was giving it out?"

"His secretary turned him in. She had a thing for him, but he jerked her around for the woman he gave the stuff to. Get this, he even asked the secretary to photocopy the papers he passed on."

"Didn't anybody tell the police?"

"Are you kidding? A company like Kindle Laird isn't going to have a scandal. They'd rather just ask the guy to leave and sweep the whole thing under the rug. They told the police he was doing a bad job, that he was incompetent. Period."

"So the cops don't know about the inside information?"

"And they probably never will. If word gets out that a company's secrets aren't safe at Kindle Laird, they'll lose clients in droves." Mike glanced at his watch. "Gotta go. Let me know if there's anything else I can help you with."

* * *

I went home, showered, dressed, and checked my phone messages. Philly Post hadn't called.

Half an hour was all it took me to review Aldo Stivick's folder on Johnson and Spenger. I made a half-hearted attempt to reach Johnson's wife by phone, but didn't have any luck, so I pulled out the big envelope of stock data Ming Mong had dropped off with Mrs. Parducci. The flap had been steamed open and amateurishly reglued, but I didn't care. There was nothing Mrs. Parducci could figure out from the stuff anyway.

I spread the documents all over the table I use for a desk, grabbed a beer, and started reading.

Teknikker was founded five years ago by a Silicon Valley financial wizard named Randy Tabing, who'd come up with some kind of specialized approach to chip manipulation. The company went public three years later, and Tabing cashed out all his shares and options the next year and retired. The report said he was twenty-nine years old.

The stock price profile that Ming Mong printed up for Teknikker came in two different styles. One was a list and the second one was a graph. I picked up the graph and studied it.

The line went up and down, up and down, sometimes more, sometimes less. The general trend was upward except for the last six months. The stock had started out at seven two years ago, peaked at forty-two, and yesterday had closed at twenty-five.

Ming had given me two years' worth of quotes, even though I'd told her one would be enough. In the lower corner of the page was a note, handwritten in tiny letters: "Since the company has only been traded publicly for two years, thought you'd like to see it all. M."

I stared at the graph again. Up and down, randomly. I picked up a sheet of paper and covered everything on the page except the last ten months. The line went up for four months, with tiny peaks and valleys, then started a downward slide that seemed to have stabilized a month ago.

I set the Teknikker graph aside and looked at the stuff on the other two companies. Kopar Corporation was a glassware manufacturer based in Novato, and Basystems made some kind of underwater-pressure measuring device.

According to the reports, the companies were older than Teknikker, but they'd had the same kind of history: going public, having the price of the stock eventually take off, then drop over the last few months.

I reached for the phone, dialed Henry Solis, and asked him about his sister's jobs again. Then I called Mitchell's number and got his answering machine. I hung up and started to dial German Daniels's house, then hung up. If Mitch was there, I was sure he hadn't brought the work-paper folders with him. They were probably still at his house.

I stuffed Ming Mong's papers back into the manila envelope, shut off the light, and drove to Marin.

54

CAROLINA POGUE'S yellow Ferrari took up most of the extra space in Mitch's drive, so I ended up parking out on the roadway, next to a huge shrub that scratched probably a year's worth of grime off the Toyota's right side.

"Ronnie!" Carolina Pogue swung the door open and smiled. It was the first time I'd seen her smile, and she looked genuinely pretty in spite of her large teeth and long face.

"Who is it?" Mitch called from the kitchen.

"It's Ronnie," Carolina answered, and beckoned me into my ex-husband's house. I smelled garlic and oregano. He was cooking for her?

I walked in, feeling suddenly awkward—not because of her or the fact that they were having dinner, or that I'd interrupted them. Knowing Mitch had switched on his answering machine so they wouldn't be disturbed didn't even bother me. It was just that they seemed so . . . well, domestic.

Then I spotted Bink on the couch. He was drinking red wine, and from the looks of his flushed face he had already had a few. The hors d'oeuvres on the table in front of him hadn't been touched, but one bottle of wine was already empty and a second was three-quarters gone. He grinned sloppily. "Ronnie, old pal. Whatcha doin' here? Checkin' up on me?"

Mitch popped out of the kitchen in a chef's hat and an apron with "It's Nice but It's Not California" written across its bib. "Ronnie. What a surprise!"

Did he look guilty, or was it my imagination?

"I called and got your answering machine." For some reason my voice came out sounding stilted. "I assumed you were out."

"We were," Carolina said. "Mitch and I ran out for more wine. Would you like some?"

"I came over to look at the work papers again."

Bink rolled his eyes. "Give it a rest, Ronnie. Have some wine. Have some pasta."

"Why don't you?" Carolina chimed in. "Have some pasta, I mean. Doesn't Mitch's sauce smell great? It's almost ready, isn't it, Mitch?"

"Half an hour," Mitchell said, reaching for a glass and filling it. "Just enough time for a leisurely sip of Barbera." He extended the filled glass to me.

I shook my head. "Thanks. I think I'll just take a look at the files, if you don't mind."

Mitch exchanged glances with Bink. "I thought we already decided the files checked out," he said in a neutral tone.

"I found something else."

The forced party atmosphere fizzled like one giant sigh. I realized too late that they'd been trying hard to forget the very thing that I'd brought in the door with me: Bink's murder charge. Bink turned from a party drunk into a sullen drunk. And Carolina suddenly shrank and looked tired. The cheerleader smile gave way to dark smudges that seemed to appear suddenly under her eyes.

Characteristically Mitch refused to let his spirits sag. He sipped the wine he'd offered me, then turned to Carolina like nothing had happened. "Do me a favor?"

Carolina's smile was mechanical.

"Grate the Parmesan."

She nodded, and vanished into the kitchen.

"And watch the sauce. It's got to be stirred every couple of minutes," Mitch called out as we headed down the hall to his den.

Mitch closed his office door and turned to me. "What's going on?"

"With what?"

"With you, Ronnie. You're all stiff and formal. What's the deal?"

I looked around the room for the work-paper folders.

"Ronnie . . ."

"I'm fine, Mitch. I expected an empty house, that's all, not a party. I thought I'd just come in, take a peek at the files, and go."

"It's Carolina, isn't it?"

"What's Carolina?"

"Look, she's a good kid. And she's very much in love with Bink, okay? I happen to like both of them a lot, and they're going through a really tough time right now. Tonight is just a couple of hours for them to forget the mess Bink's in." He smiled. "Stay. Have a home-cooked and kick back. This stuff will be here tomorrow."

"Can I use your phone?" I reached for the telephone on his desk without waiting for an answer.

"Did you hear me, Ron?"

"Sure, I heard you." I dialed my phone machine and pressed a couple of numbers. If there were any messages, the last two digits would signal the machine to play them back.

I waited, listening. Nothing.

"Damn." I replaced the receiver and scanned the room for the folders again. "Where are they?"

"Ron—"

"Look, Mitchell, things are happening on this case

that you don't know about. Stuff that's got to be addressed now, okay? So you guys have your party, and I'll
just look at the files. It's no big deal. Just pretend I'm not
here."

He frowned. I could tell he was earnestly torn between helping Bink and Carolina by escaping for a few
hours and helping them by helping me.

Finally he seemed to make up his mind. "If you're
helping Bink, so am I. They're right here."

Mitch opened a deep drawer and pulled out the
folders. "What are we looking for?"

There was a soft tap on the door. "Come in," Mitch
said, and Bink skulked into the room.

"What's the deal?" he asked.

"Ronnie's checking something out."

"Yeah?" He leaned against the door frame, hands
in his pockets. From the solemn expression on his face I
guessed he was coming down off his alcoholic high.

"What's the date on that final Teknikker audit?" I
asked.

Mitch ran a finger down the inside front page—a
chronology of the engagement. "September thirtieth."

I pulled out Ming Mong's graph for Teknikker,
picked up a red pencil from Mitch's desk, and put a dot
above September 30. The price of the stock had plum-
meted steadily for weeks after. I checked Basystems and
Kopar Corp. Same deal.

"What are you getting at?" Mitch asked.

"I called Mary Solis's brother today. He said she
sometimes worked for a stockbroker."

"You think she was using Bink's stuff for insider
trading?"

We both turned to Bink.

"Don't look at me." He squirmed and sunk his
hands deeper into his pockets. "Hey, I told you, if she
got my stuff, I didn't give it to her. She never even came
within a hundred yards of any of those files."

"She had the key to the office," I said.

Bink swore softly under his breath. "What am I, Einstein? How am I supposed to know what she was doing?"

Mitch and I waited.

"Are you saying I sold her those reports?" he asked. His incredulousness was pretty convincing. Mitch wavered.

"You had the means, motive, and opportunity," I said.

"Yeah? What's my motive?"

"Money," I said. "Money to burn."

Bink swore again and glanced over his shoulder down the hall toward Carolina and the kitchen. He stepped inside the room and closed the door. "That's got nothing to do with Mary Solis, okay? I didn't have anything going with her, and you know it. Why do you keep diggin', Ron? I mean, isn't it bad enough I'm arrested for a murder I didn't do? You've got to try to peg insider trading on me, too, so I won't even be able to work anymore? You want to take away my livelihood? What'd I ever do to you?"

His voice had risen to a plaintive whine by the time he finished. Bink was good at this: the "poor me" scenario.

I glanced at Mitch. His earnest blue eyes were full of sympathy for his friend.

"What if," I began, addressing Mitch, "what if Bink was selling this stuff to Mary Solis?"

Bink sputtered a protest, but I ignored him. So did Mitch.

"What if he gave her the stuff he'd written up, never expecting you to change it. Mary Solis bases her decision to buy stock on what Bink's told her, then the stock goes down instead of up, and all hell breaks loose. She lets it go by once—it could have been a mistake—but by the third time she's furious and she brings her thugs out to teach Bink a lesson."

"Great story," Bink said sarcastically.

"*Is* it a story?"

Bink forced air past his lips, then rolled his eyes. He glanced at Mitch. "I'm not buyin' it, Mitch. What about you?"

"Well . . . it makes a lot more sense than just saying she's crazy," he admitted. "But who killed her? And why?"

I could have told them both that Mary Solis wasn't really dead, but I knew Carolina'd be on the hot line to German Daniels within seconds. And from there it'd be just minutes before it got back to Philly Post. Even though he hadn't called yet, I still expected him to let me in on the questioning.

I packed up Ming Mong's stock portraits and as many of the work paper folders I could carry.

"That's the part I'm working on," I said, and walked out the door.

I crossed the Golden Gate Bridge fully intending to storm into Post's office and demand to see Mary Solis, but once I hit Doyle Drive, I just kept going. Marina Boulevard was straight ahead.

I checked my messages from a pay phone near Gas House Cove, then parked the Toyota close to where Ellie Yost had parked her green Jaguar three days ago.

The lights in the elegant yellow stucco were on, and nobody'd pulled the curtains shut, so the whole interior of the first-floor living room was lit up like a movie screen. Only there wasn't any action inside; the room was empty.

I reached into the glove box for binoculars and was about to raise them to my eyes when I sensed a shadow outside the car, behind me. I jerked my head around and saw a torso—a man's torso in a heavy dark coat—outlined in the rear side window. He was moving toward my passenger door, coming fast. I reached over and engaged the lock on the door just as his hand vanished below the window. He tried the door handle, then rapped his knuckles against the glass. As I reached for the ignition, his face came into view: Philly Post. He glared through the window at me, bushy eyebrows fog-laden, their moisture sparkling in the light from an amber streetlamp ahead.

"Open the door," he barked.

"I don't like your tone."

"What?"

I reached over and rolled down the window a crack. "I said, I don't like your tone."

Post's face flushed. "Open this goddamn door before I break it, Ventana. I want to talk to you."

"Have you picked up Mary Solis?"

"No."

I snapped the lock. Post swung the door open, fell into the seat, and closed out the cold.

"What are you doing here, Ventana?"

"What are *you* doing here? You're supposed to be questioning Mary Solis."

"Who appointed you boss? You know whose house that is?"

I sighed. "If Mary Solis is inside, who cares?"

"Edwin Pogue."

"What?"

"Edwin Pogue. You know, the honorary International Chamber of Commerce representative? The mayor's brother-in-law? Founder of—"

"I know who he is. He lives there?"

"Owns the place. Rents it to his niece, the mayor's daughter."

"The twin?"

"Huh?"

"Felix Ashton has a twin sister."

"Felicia Ashton."

Felix and Felicia.

"So when are you going to question Mary Solis?" I asked impatiently.

Post scowled. Close up, in the dim light from the streetlamp down the way, he looked pretty unhappy, like a lion with a toothache.

"You must have it out for me, Ventana. What is it with you? You trying to set me up?"

"I'm just trying to solve this thing, Post. Don't you think Mary Solis ought to have some of the answers?"

"How do you know she's in there?"

"I told you—I saw her," I said through gritted teeth. "I staked out the place for two days, and she finally popped out. I told you all this. She walked with some other woman down to the Safeway." I jerked my thumb over my shoulder. "Probably Felicia Ashton. Then they walked back to the house and went inside. What's the problem? Don't you want to solve this—this—mess?"

He stared at the boats bobbing in the dark beside us. After a while he brought his eyes back to the yellow stucco down the street. "All right, Ventana. I'm doing this ex officio. Anything happens, I'll—"

"Thank me," I said.

His answer was half snort and half sneer.

He left my car and walked back to a nondescript brown sedan about ten yards behind me. I'd driven right by him without even noticing. Either that or he'd come up after I'd already parked. I really should have noticed him.

Post drove past me, all the way to the end of the roadway, then doubled back once he'd pulled out onto Marina Boulevard. I turned the ignition on and sort of coasted up a few yards with my lights out, then stopped directly opposite the house. Since the traffic was still pretty thick along Marina Boulevard, I doubted I'd hear anything, but at least with my binoculars I'd be able to see if the person who answered the door was Mary Solis.

Post left the car at the curb, ambled up the walk, and rang the bell. He waited what seemed like forever and had just started to turn away when a dark-haired woman answered the door—the same woman I'd seen with Mary Solis earlier. She looked sluggish, like she'd been asleep, but she seemed to listen attentively after Post showed her his badge.

When he finished, she shook her head. Once. Then twice. She talked for a little bit, then listened some more to Post, and finally shook her head again. A slow smile. It looked like she was asking Post inside.

"Go for it!" I urged. But he backed away and put up his hands defensively like she'd pointed a gun at him. The woman shrugged, then closed the door.

Post's scowling face looked yellow under the glow of the streetlamp as he walked back to his car. Great. I turned over the ignition again and backed up to the spot where I'd been before. Post pulled up beside me, pointed forward, and signaled me to follow him.

I shook my head. He scowled savagely, cut his engine, and slammed his door when he left his car. He slammed my door, too, when he got in.

"I'm dead meat," he announced. "She took down my badge number. The minute the captain hears this, I'm back on nights."

"Was that Felicia Ashton?"

He nodded.

"So why didn't you go inside?"

"She was drunk, Ventana. Drunk and horny. My only chance is going to be if she mixes herself a couple more cocktails before her lights go out. She might just forget she ever saw me."

"What about Mary Solis?"

Post glared. "Nobody's staying there, Ventana, so get off your trip."

"But—"

"Somebody was, she said. An in-law cousin on her mother's side. Not Mary Solis. But she's gone now. Went to stay with her brother."

"Felicia's brother or the cousin's brother?"

"Felicia's."

Felix Ashton.

55

BEFORE HE LEFT, Philly Post made me swear I wouldn't bother Felix Ashton. Then, just to make sure I got the point, he tailed me home.

Like a good girl I drove straight home, parked the Toyota in a legal parking space, and went upstairs. He didn't like it when I waved down at him from the window, but that was the point. I didn't like being told who I could and couldn't talk to.

Fifteen minutes later when I looked out the window, Post's car was gone. I grabbed my coat, opened the door, and ran smack into Mrs. Parducci. She'd been standing at my door, fist raised, ready to knock.

"Oh, hi," I said unenthusiastically, and tried to squeeze past her. She held her ground.

"I just heard you come in and—"

"I'm sort of in a hurry, Mrs. Parducci. I've got to go someplace."

"That's all right, honey. This isn't a social visit. I just wanted to drop this off like that nice young man asked me to."

"What young man?"

Something rustled in her hand. It was an envelope. "Let me see that."

Mrs. Parducci had steamed this one open, too, but

her handiwork was less obvious than on the first one. She was getting better.

I ripped the seal and read the hand-printed note inside: *Be at the Holocaust Monument outside the Palace of the Legion of Honor tonight. 11:00 p.m.*

I looked at Mrs. Parducci. "What did he look like?"

"The young man? Oh, he was nice-looking. Clean-cut and real polite. Not like my lousy kids. They wouldn't even bother to check with the neighbors to make sure I get something. Oh no, they're too busy for that—"

I prompted her for details and got sandy-colored hair, brown or blue eyes, mid-twenties to mid-thirties, and not too tall. In other words, Mr. Anybody. And he'd knocked on Mrs. Parducci's door fifteen minutes after I'd left for Mitch's. "What was he wearing?"

"Brown slacks and a sweater. Looked like a college boy—a smart one."

"Smart? Why smart?"

"He was wearing glasses."

That ruled out the thugs. But Mr. Hangman's Mask was still a possibility.

I stuffed the note into my backpack, headed Mrs. Parducci back into her apartment, and started to shut my own door when the phone rang.

"What's up, doll?" Blackie's familiar, cigarette-cured voice crackled across the line.

"Can you meet me out front at Johnny's Spot at ten-thirty?"

"Out in the Avenues? Easy, doll. Somethin' cookin'?"

"I've got a nibble."

He grunted his approval. "Need tools?"

"Just some backup, that's all."

"You got it."

I was seven blocks out of North Beach, traveling west on Broadway, before I spotted the dark sedan tail-

ng me. Instead of staying on Broadway and going on to
Felix Ashton's condo, I turned left onto Van Ness and
headed south. The headlights turned left with me. I took
a right on Turk and doubled back, but the lights stuck
with me. I drove through a parking garage, and he was
waiting for me half a block down from the exit when I
came out.

Whoever he was, he was good. I used every evasive
tactic I knew and still couldn't shake him. So I headed
for the Bay Bridge. And that's where I lost him. He
stayed behind when I took the on-ramp. I stepped on the
gas and cursed Philly Post. The tail had been a cop, a
San Francisco cop with no jurisdiction outside the city.

I doubled back at Treasure Island and drove straight
to Felix Ashton's apartment. It was ten o'clock. The windows visible from the street were dark, and his car wasn't
around, but I rang his bell anyway. There was no answer,
so I hung around a few minutes more, then drove over to
Johnny's Spot Lounge and waited for Blackie.

He was right on time. I kicked aside a couple of
empty cigarette cartons, some fast-food containers, and
half a dozen forgotten beer bottles and slid into the front
seat of Blackie's vintage Buick. He was grinning, blowing
smoke from a newly lit cigarette. His blue eyes glistened
through the haze.

"Still trying to clear the asshole?" he asked.

"I don't know." I told him about the note.

"Sounds like a setup."

"Or it could be somebody who just wants to talk."

"Maybe." Blackie's expression told me he didn't
think it likely. "What's the plan?"

"I want you close but out of sight."

Blackie nodded.

"We'll take my car, and you can wait under cover
outside. I won't need you unless something goes wrong,
okay?"

Blackie flicked his cigarette butt out the window and coughed. "Gotcha."

"Ready?"

"Do buzzards fly?"

We might as well have saved ourselves the trouble. I sat in my car for an hour, my veins singing with adrenaline, jumping at every sound. Each time a car came by—and it happened three times—my heart stopped. And every time the headlights swept by and continued around the curve and down the road, I cursed.

By midnight I gave up and winked my lights at Blackie. He popped out of the underbrush nearby and tapped the window on the passenger side of the car seconds later. I let him in.

"Fuckin' no-show," he said, rubbing his hands together, then cupping them and blowing into them to warm them up. I started the engine and switched on the car heater. I was cold, but not half as cold as Blackie must have been.

He said what I'd been thinking the last half hour. "Looks like somebody wanted you out of the way. Where's the asshole tonight?"

"With Mitch."

Blackie grunted, reached inside his breast pocket for a cigarette, and lit it. He squinted at me through the smoke. "He could be the mark."

That was a possibility I had considered.

Blackie and I tossed around other possibilities and had just decided we needed some Anchor Steam to clear our heads when I spotted a figure skulking behind the monument.

"There he is!" I cried, then threw open the door and hurried through the dark toward him. Behind me I heard Blackie's door open.

As I circled the barbed wire of the enclosure, the guy spotted me and froze. Instead of hailing me, he dropped whatever it was he was carrying—it looked like a big bundle—and took off running through the trees.

"Hey!" I shouted. "Hey! Wait up!"

I broke into a run and had just reached my stride when I tripped over the thing he'd dropped. I shoved it aside and sprang to my feet, cutting through the woods at an angle to head him off. The branches whipped my cheeks, so I raised my arms to protect my face and kept running.

He was a small, dark hulk in front of me, darting through the underbrush.

The proximity of the snapping twigs ahead of me told me I was gaining on him.

In a few quick strides I doubled my speed and was nearly on him. I could actually hear him panting—sucking in air and blowing it out in the dark. If I reached forward, I could almost touch him. Close enough. I took one last deep breath and sprang at his back, throwing my arms around him to bring him down.

We both tumbled to the ground with a grunt, me on top and him facedown. I pushed all my weight against the back of his shoulders, scrambling to straddle his back and pin his arms to the ground. I expected a fight and was surprised that he just went limp and gave up.

I sat there on the middle of his back, gasping for breath while my body rose and fell with his heaving chest.

He was a small guy but bigger than me. If he'd been in shape, he probably could have outrun me.

We both stayed where we were, me sitting on his back and him flat and facedown in the dirt until Blackie caught up with us. The sweet smell of tobacco smoke preceded him.

"Good work, doll," he said, planting a foot on the guy's neck and offering me a hand up.

I took it and rose, then noticed Blackie held a valise in his other hand.

"What's that?"

"He dropped it."

We both looked at the guy on the ground, then at the valise. The guy was still puffing, still trying to catch his breath.

"What's in the bag?" I asked.

"Clothes," he gasped. "Clothes and papers. I looked, but I didn't touch anything. I swear."

Blackie and I exchanged looks. "What kind of papers?" I asked.

"I don't know. Please, can I get up?"

"Just a sec."

Blackie kept his foot on the back of the guy's neck while I reached into the guy's back pocket and pulled out his wallet. His driver's license said he was Herbert Noonan and he was all of nineteen. His address was in Berkeley. He had two bills in his wallet. Two crisp fifties.

I tossed the billfold onto the ground beside him and patted him down for weapons. Finally I nodded at Blackie. He reluctantly took his foot off Herbert Noonan's neck and stepped back.

Noonan struggled to his feet and stood there in the middle of the woods, rubbing the back of his neck and cowering. It was pretty obvious he was terrified.

"Who are you, Herbert?" I asked. "And what's the deal with the valise?"

"I don't know anything about what's inside the bag, man. I—"

Blackie stepped in close. "You hear what she asked? She asked 'Who are you?' "

Poor Herbert Noonan's eyes went round and white. "I'm a student, man. I'm nobody. Please don't hurt me. I didn't do anything. She asked me to bring this over, and that's all I know. She said it wasn't illegal."

"Who is *she*?"

"This lady. She was in a wheelchair."

"A wheelchair? What'd she look like?"

He grimaced. Now he looked positive we were going to shoot him. "She was in a wheelchair, that's all I remember." He seemed to sag. "Are you going to kill me?"

I opened the valise and rummaged through it. Clothes and papers. He hadn't lied. "You were supposed to be here at eleven," I said.

"I got tied up in traffic," he babbled. "That's why I was late. Then I got lost and ended up in the Presidio. The MPs pulled me over and gave me a ticket. My car broke down over on Thirty-second Avenue. I had to walk here. Shit. I'm sorry I ever met that lady."

He turned down the ride I offered him, probably because he thought we'd murder him in the backseat, and set off walking toward Geary, looking over his shoulder every few minutes until he was out of sight.

"You know the wheelchair broad?" Blackie asked.

"Bink's sister," I said.

Blackie laughed. "She into James Bond?"

"I think she was trying to hide the fact that she lied to me, Blackie. Feel like rousting her?"

"A wheelie? Forget it, Ventana. Have a heart."

I picked up the valise and lugged it to the car. The minute the parking-lot lights hit it, I recognized Bink's valise, the one he took with him when we left his house in Piedmont. The same one he took with him when he vanished from my car at the supermarket on Park.

I yanked it open and rummaged through the clothing he'd stuffed inside, tossing each article on the parking-lot pavement at my feet. Under three shirts, two pairs of jeans, and some underwear was a stack of papers. I pulled them out and scanned the top page.

"We've hit pay dirt, Blackie. These are some kind of stock-transaction records."

"The smoking gun?"

"It could be the bullet itself."

* * *

"You know what he was doing, Blackie?"

We were in my apartment sorting through copies o
Bink's stock transactions. We'd put the flimsy carbon tis
sue forms in chronological order, then bunched them
together by stock name.

Blackie reached for a cigarette and fixed warm blu
eyes on me. "What?"

"He was shorting these stocks."

"Yeah? What's that mean?"

"It's when you sell a stock before you own it, the
hope its price goes down before you have to deliver it
You pocket the difference when you pay the origina
seller later."

"That illegal?"

"Only if you're trading on inside information. Al
these stocks went down, and that's exactly what Bink
wanted them to do. That's how you make money short
ing stocks. And naturally Bink had a sure thing, since h
knew exactly when the bad quarterly reports were going
to make the stock take a plunge."

"Your buddy Gabriél was busted for something like
that, wasn't he?"

I nodded and reached for Ming Mong's printouts
"Look. See, Bink sold short right here when Teknikke
was at forty-eight. Then he covered his sale here, when i
was down to twenty-eight. He did a thousand shares, s
he made twenty thousand dollars. And here"—I picked
up another set of carbons from the Basystems stack—
"he made fifteen thousand here."

Blackie took a long toke off his cigarette, then
smashed its burning end into the bottom of the ashtray
"Yeah," he rasped, blowing smoke out along with hi
words. "But if everybody's making money, why the fuc
does Solis kill the bastards?"

"They'd outlived their usefulness. Yost got fired
Spenger and Johnson wanted out. And they all probably

knew enough to hang her, so she decided to eliminate hem."

Blackie squinted at me through smoke. "So who'd she whack at the house, doll?"

I stacked all the transaction records in one pile, put hem in an envelope, and slipped the envelope into my backpack.

"Well, Blackie, I guess we'll just have to find her and ask her."

56

FELICIA ASHTON LOOKED like she just woke up from a binge. It was eight o'clock in the morning, and maybe she had, but her clothes looked fresh and ironed and her short, straight brown hair was combed. It was her face that looked bad—puffy and red, like an alcoholic's.

She was awake enough to look puzzled when she opened her front door and found me standing on her front steps—as puzzled as I'd been after sending Philly Post to her and coming up empty.

"Yes?" Her voice was crisp and impatient through well-educated syllables.

"Felicia Ashton?"

She nodded. I held up a business card. "My name's Ronnie Ventana. I'm a private investigator, and I'd like to ask you a few questions if you don't mind."

Her bloodshot eyes narrowed. "About what?"

I glanced over her shoulder into the opulent interior of the living room. "Can we talk inside?"

"I'm not sure I want to talk. What do you want to know?"

"It's about your houseguest."

Her expression didn't change. "I don't have one."

"The one that left."

"Sorry. I don't know what you're talking about."

She started to close the door, but I retreated with her, stepping forward so the door struck the toe of my shoe.

Felicia looked down, then brought her eyes back to meet mine. If she was alarmed or nervous, she didn't show it.

"Her name's Mary Solis," I said, keeping my foot where it was. "Is that the name she gave you?"

Felicia blinked. "I don't know who you're talking about or what you're doing here. You must have the wrong address."

I reached into my pocket for the picture Henry Solis had given me. "Is this the woman who stayed here?"

She didn't take her eyes off mine. "No."

"I think you'd better look at the picture, Ms. Ashton." I raised the photo between our faces.

Felicia Ashton eyed the picture and did a double take. "That's Felix!" she exclaimed. "Where did you get that?"

"From Mary Solis's family. They're concerned about her. They think she's dead."

"Dead?" Felicia Ashton took the photograph from my hand and studied it intently. "Felix just started wearing his hair longer like that last January. What did you say her name is?"

"Mary—María—Solis. Your brother's in love with her. She could be in danger, and so could he."

"How?"

"Several people connected to her have turned up dead. Look, I saw her come out of here Wednesday."

Ashton shook her head abruptly and shoved the snapshot at me. "I'm sorry. I can't help you. I've never seen this woman before in my life."

"Somebody was staying here."

"I'm not going to discuss my relatives with a complete stranger," she said, and reached for the door again. "Especially when you're trying to mix Felix up with a murder."

"I didn't say it was murder."

"Get out! Get out of here before I call the police."

I withdrew my foot and let her slam the door in my face.

I parked the Toyota behind Blackie's monster Buick on Sacramento and joined him in the front seat. Felix Ashton's condo was half a block down the street.

"Did she bolt?" I asked.

"Not yet. You get anything off the sister?"

"Nothing. She's a cold customer, but she knows something. She sort of lost it at the end. Has Felix shown?"

"Somebody opened the drapes half an hour ago, and that's it."

"What about—"

Blackie stiffened. I followed his gaze to the brown-shingle building down the street.

Felix Ashton popped out the front door carrying a set of golf clubs and shoes.

"Don't these fuckers ever work?" Blackie asked.

"He's the mayor's son, Blackie. He doesn't have to work."

Ashton loaded the clubs into the trunk.

Blackie reached for the ignition. "Do we tail him, doll?"

"I will," I said. "You keep watch here for Solis. Felix could just be a diversion so she can sneak out later."

I followed Ashton to the Mount Vesuvio golf course, watched him park his red Beemer in the members' lot, then saw him go inside. That's where the I'm-off-to-play-golf charade fell apart: He left his clubs in the car.

I parked in the visitors' parking lot and sat there thinking, wondering how long it'd be before one of the valets noticed and rousted me. I didn't really want to go inside—sometimes it's best to keep your distance.

While I waited, a huge new Lincoln Continental pulled into the members' lot. The size of the car was awesome, and that's what first caught my attention. It probably handled like a Boeing 747.

The Lincoln circled the lot a couple of times, like a great white shark looking for prey, then finally settled into a space near the club's front entrance.

The car's passenger door opened, and out stepped Chuck Vardigan—Gabriél Juarez's nemesis from the SEC. He checked his watch, frowned, then hurried inside. I guess I wasn't surprised to see him—he'd been out here the other day, and he was the type to join clubs and climb the social ladder.

What did surprise me, though, was the monster-sized bodyguard who climbed from the driver's side and hurried inside at Vardigan's elbow. He was the same guy who'd worked the phone lines outside my place a week and a half ago. Vardigan's bodyguard was one of Bink's tankers.

57

I F CHUCK VARDIGAN and one of Mary Solis's thugs were meeting Felix, I couldn't just sit there and let whatever was happening happen without at least trying to spy on them.

I pulled a wool tweed blazer out of my trunk, dusted it off, and hoped it didn't stink too much of exhaust fumes. With my hair tied back and sunglasses and a gym bag for props, I hoped they wouldn't recognize me.

I bought my way past the valets, tightened my grip on my gym bag, and braced myself as I hurried through the doors, pretending to check my watch. My "I'm late" routine sometimes works and sometimes doesn't.

Instead of a gauntlet of checkpoints, though, I found an empty lobby and a vacant reception desk. I couldn't believe my luck. I started across the room, making a beeline for the door marked Dining. It seemed like a logical place to start.

Midway there a big male voice boomed out behind me. "Miss," the voice said. "Are you a guest, miss?"

The maître d' at the dining-room entrance turned alarmed eyes on me, so I reversed directions and circled back to the desk.

"Ronnie? It *is* you, isn't it?" I'd expected a surly face, but here was a sumo-wrestler-sized guy behind the reception desk, grinning at me with teeth so white against skin the color of deep, rich plowed earth.

"Squire?"

"How ya doin', Ronnie?" He reached across the desk, took my hand, and squeezed it. "What a surprise," he said warmly. "How long's it been?"

I knew to the minute: nineteen years, three months. Before that we'd hung out a lot, kicking around his dad's old warehouse, playing hide-and-seek while our parents talked business. Squire's dad was a fence—one of the best, one my parents used a lot.

I didn't know back then that probably fifty percent of the stuff in his building was hot. I'd just thought of the place as a fantastic castle, with carpets rolled up and antiques spread around just for us to hide behind.

But after the fiery crash of my parents' car and Squire's discovery of his dad's lifeless body choked by exhaust fumes in the garage, it was just too hard for him to be around me. And I guess it was hard for me to be around him, too, because after I went to his dad's funeral and he came to my parents' funeral, I never spoke to him again.

Seeing him now, though, was great. I gripped his hand and squeezed back.

"It's been too long, Squire."

"What you doin' here? Better not be a member. Your daddy'd kill you he see you joining a place like this."

He wore a dark, navy blazer with the club's emblem embroidered discreetly over the breast pocket. "What about yours if he saw you working at a place like this?"

Squire's belly shook when he laughed.

"You right about that, Ronnie. Damn straight. But a guy's gotta pay the bills, ya know. I got kids to support now. I got a little girl so smart, it'd be a crime not to send her to college. Gonna be a doctor. Can you believe it?"

A door opened behind him, and a Vanna White look-alike appeared.

"Thanks, Squire," she said. "I'll help this lady if you—"

"She's a friend a mine, Kitty. I'm takin' care of her just fine."

Vanna/Kitty glanced at me disinterestedly. "That's nice." She picked up a bunch of mail and started to flip through it.

Squire took me through a side door to a closed room behind the reception desk. Compared with the opulent lobby, the club's security room looked like a dungeon. No windows, gray paint on the walls, a monitor sitting on a rickety desk, and three stiff-backed metal chairs. The monitor was tied in to a surveillance camera trained on the front door and lobby.

"Coffee?" Squire asked, and when I shook my head, he said, "You here on business, ain't you? I heard you was an investigator. You're lookin' for somebody, ain't you?"

I pulled out the picture of Mary Solis and Felix Ashton. "Have you seen this guy? He came in a couple of minutes ago."

Squire took the photograph and held it up to the light. "Sure, I seen young Mistah Ashton come in. He's here all the time. He's in the dining room right now. Him and Mr. Vardigan, the guy that always tries to steal my pen when I work the desk."

Squire reached over and switched channels on the console. The screen filled with tables and bobbing heads. I squinted at the picture and managed to pick out Felix Ashton's dark head and Chuck Vardigan's broad shoulders.

"See 'em?" Squire asked.

"Um-hm." I turned away from the screen and saw Squire was staring at the picture in his hand, his sweet face furrowed with confusion. "You lookin' for Mistah

Ashton," he asked after a moment, then pointed at Mary, "or Miss Lopez?"

"Lopez? Do you mean her?"

He nodded.

"You've seen her before?"

"She's Mr. Felix's girlfrien'. She's down the hall, Ronnie, staying in Mr. Felix's private room for a couple a days. You wanna see her? Talk to her? I can't take you—I gotta stay here an' watch this shit—but I'll tell you how to get there. Here." He reached for a plastic badge. "Anybody ask, show 'em this pass."

"I think I'm going to need more than a building pass, Squire."

A chuckle purred out from somewhere deep in his chest. "She don't wanna talk to you, huh? Okay. Try this." He handed me a passkey. "It's faster than pickin' the lock."

Felix Ashton's private room was on the ground floor of the east wing and looked out on the woods. I noticed the view after I used Squire's passkey to let myself in and found the sliding glass door gaping wide open. I spied a flash of red amid the green foliage outside.

"Wait! Mary, wait!"

I bolted into the woods after Mary Solis. If she hadn't been wearing high heels and a tight skirt, I would have felt more challenged. She ran like a gazelle, but I ran faster. Twigs snapped under my feet as I quickly gained on her. I was right behind her, gathering up my muscles to spring forward and tackle her, when she stopped and pivoted, not aggressively, not defensively, but with unmistakable confidence. I almost skidded right into her.

In spite of having just run for her life, in spite of being breathless and disheveled, she looked more stunning than she had in Henry's photograph. Her tight red dress set off an incredible mass of thick black hair, flawless olive skin, and a figure that would have made Barbie jealous.

Black eyes set deep in an oval face gleamed at me with defiance and, just barely, a trace of fear.

"Who are you?" she demanded, eyeing me and gracefully gulping air.

"My name's Ronnie Ventana. I want to help you," I said.

"What"—deep breath—"makes you"—deep breath —"think I need help?"

"Most people don't run when there's a knock on the door."

"You didn't knock," she said, then glanced over my shoulder at the building behind us. I didn't turn because I knew that trick. She'd bolt the minute I looked away. But I prayed nobody was coming up from behind.

Whatever she saw made her relax. And seeing her relax made me nervous. I took a step forward and to the side, then glanced furtively toward the club. The distance was filled with trees and nothing else. She'd been bluffing.

"I know about David Hanover and you," I said. "I know you were working with him on insider trading."

Her black eyes burned back at me. "You're crazy."

"He didn't know that's what you were doing at first, right? Then he figured it out and threatened to blow the whistle unless you let him in on the deals. Isn't that how it happened?"

The tiniest of smiles curved the corners of her lips. "You're guessing."

"I'm right, aren't I? He forced himself in on the deals."

"That's exactly what he did. But you haven't got any proof and you won't get it from me."

"I've got Bink's transaction records and his bank statements."

"That fool."

"And I've got the six hundred thousand dollars you left in your safe-deposit box."

She blanched. I could see that she wanted to ask how I'd found the money. Instead she asked, "What do you want?"

"Who did you murder in Piedmont?"

"What?"

"The dead woman—the one you pushed through the banister—who is she?"

"I didn't kill her. She's nobody—a prostitute from Davis Avenue. Somebody made a joke about how much she looked like me and, well, they thought it'd be clever to frame Hanover. But I didn't kill her. I haven't killed anybody. And you can't prove anything anyway. You have nothing. Please return my money and go away. Leave me alone. Don't you understand your meddling's going to get both of us killed?"

"Four people have died already. You can't walk away from that."

"Yes, I can. And I will."

"Henry will be glad to hear you're alive," I said, trying a new tack.

"Don't talk to Henry."

I'd struck a nerve.

"Don't tell him I'm alive. Please. I beg of you. He's got nothing to do with any of this. I—I want to resolve this before I see Henry again."

"Then come with me. Talk to the police."

"That's exactly what will get me killed."

"They'll put you under protective custody if you co-operate."

She glanced over my shoulder again. "I can't explain now, but I'm working this out my own way. Please. If I promise to meet you, will you leave then?"

"I'm not leaving here without—"

I didn't see her fist come at me. I barely even felt its impact. All I remember is stumbling and falling backward, then seeing the sky go dark. After that everything around me turned to soft black velvet.

58

BEFORE I OPENED my eyes, before I really felt the pain in my head, I knew I was in a hospital. The antiseptic smell was unmistakable. And the swishing sounds. Nurses always swish when they walk. Doors in hospitals swish when they open and swish when they close. People whisper, and everything's subdued.

So I wasn't surprised to see a white room. What surprised me was seeing Felix Ashton sitting next to my bed, looking haggard and ragged.

I moved my head and was instantly sorry. Somebody groaned. When Felix looked up, I realized the noise had come from me.

"Ronnie, it's me, Felix Ashton. Are you all right?"

I looked around. "I can't afford a private room."

"The club's paying for it. They're real concerned about liability. I told them you slipped and fell in my room."

"Why?"

"Squire told me to. He came with you in the ambulance but had to get back to work. He asked me to tell you he's sorry he couldn't stay."

I reached up and touched the back of my head. The skin wasn't even broken. The doctors hadn't used a bandage or stitches or anything, but there was a lump on my scalp the size of a lemon.

"It was a rock," Felix said. "You hit your head against a rock."

I looked at him and for a fleeting second wondered if he'd helped the rock find my head. Hadn't Mary Solis seen somebody coming up behind me? I couldn't remember. I closed my eyes. "Why were you hiding Mary Solis in your room?"

"She was scared. She came to me Wednesday night and she was terrified."

"Of what?"

"She's in some kind of trouble. I don't know what's going on, but I love her. I couldn't not help her. You don't know what it was like seeing her after I thought she'd died. It was as though we'd been given a second chance. I thought I'd lost her forever, and now she's gone again. What did you say to make her run away?"

I was starting to feel jaded about all these people in love. Bink had professed love for Carolina, and now Felix was declaring his undying love for Mary Solis. I didn't care. I didn't care if they were as fated and destiny-driven as Romeo and Juliet. All I wanted to know was why he'd hidden her in the room. So I asked him again. "I want details, Felix. Specifics. What exactly is she afraid of?"

"You know my brother-in-law, Chuck Vardigan?"

"The SEC guy? *He's* your brother-in-law?"

"Right—Felicia's husband."

"*He's* the one she's running from?"

Felix shook his head hastily. "Chuck knows how to reach the guy, that's all. He's a point of contact."

"Who is he contacting?"

"That's the part she wouldn't tell me. She asked me to ask Chuck to tell the guy, whoever he is, that she wouldn't breathe a word to anyone about anything if he'd just give his word not to hurt her. Pretty crazy, huh? Do you know what this is about?"

"Where's Mary now?"

"I don't know. When I got to the room, she was gone. She took her stuff and vanished."

"Give me a hand, will you?" I pushed aside the bedcovers and dragged my legs over the edge of the bed. My toes barely touched the floor.

"What are you doing?" Felix reached over and laid his hand against my shoulder, forcing me gently back into bed.

I jerked my shoulder away, then winced as the pain shot up the back of my head. "Dammit, Felix, stop. I'm getting out of here—now. Are you going to help me or not?"

59

THE BUMP ON MY HEAD was painful, but it wasn't bad enough to be hospitalized over. The old geezers at the Mount Vesuvio Club were probably turning over in their upholstered leather chairs wondering whether I was going to sue them or not. *Let them worry*, I thought, as Blackie tooled his vintage Buick toward the Marina.

I'd showered and changed and even wolfed down a plate of pasta Blackie brought up to my apartment while I was in the shower. I was actually starting to feel alive again.

"Let me see if I got this straight," Blackie said, turning left onto Union. "This guy used to work for the government—"

"The SEC."

"Yeah—Seck. And he was go-between for a couple of inside traders?"

"Right."

"Did he tell the cops?"

"I don't think so, but why don't we find out? He just might be our man."

A servant showed us to one of the rooms Felicia Ashton refused to let me see yesterday, and asked us to wait. A few minutes later Chuck Vardigan burst into the room like a meteor. The servant trailed after him with a silver tea service and china cups.

Chuck shook our hands, exclaimed over Blackie's boxing career, then sat down and poured tea. He doctored his own cup with enough cream to make a soufflé while Blackie fingered the delicate china cup in front of him and watched Vardigan like he was the Boston Strangler.

"How did I meet Mary Solis?" Vardigan began. "Well, it's rather complicated, you know. She's really a friend of Felicia's. That's how we met. Felicia introduced us. Felix met her that way too—through his sister."

I glanced toward the hall that led to the rest of the house. "Is Felicia home? Could we talk to her?"

"That's impossible. I'm sorry."

"This is important."

"You don't understand. My wife's not at home."

"When do you expect her?"

"I—I can't. She—" Vardigan hesitated. He looked at Blackie, then back at me. "Is this confidential?"

"What's the problem, Chuck?"

Chuck joined his hands together and stared down at them. "She's ill," he began. "Felicia's very ill. I'm afraid you can't talk to her. No one can. She's in—in a program, you see. She checked herself into a program this morning, and the next few days are crucial. That's what the doctor said. I can't let you speak to her. I can't even see her myself."

"Do you know what hospital she's in?"

He shook his head. "The doctor refused to tell me. He said it was standard practice."

I handed him my card and said, "If he phones again, will you tell him it's urgent that he call me?"

"Absolutely." He took my card, patted his pockets, then looked at me. "Have you got a pen I can borrow? I'd like to jot this down, if you don't mind."

I handed him a ballpoint out of my backpack and

said, "Felix mentioned that you were a go-between for Mary Solis and somebody else."

He looked up, surprised, then said, "That's right." He wrote "Urgent to call" on the back of my business card, then absently slipped my pen and the card into his breast pocket. "Mary phoned me at the office one day and said she had something personal to talk to me about. When we met later, she asked me to deliver an envelope for her. Of course, she played down its importance the first time. But she did ask me not to look inside. That request wasn't too difficult to honor. I generally don't read other people's mail. I dropped it off and—"

"Where?"

"At the park above the crooked street."

"Lombard?"

"Vermont. Just up off the freeway. There's a stand of bushes there. Anyway I assumed this—this delivery was a one-time event, but a week later she asked me to do the same thing again. I delivered a second sealed envelope to the same place. This time, though, there was a package in the spot where I was supposed to deposit the envelope. It had Mary's name on it. She didn't mention it beforehand, but seemed to expect it when I brought it back."

Blackie and I exchanged glances. I could tell from his expression he was thinking the same thing I was. "Why couldn't Mary deliver the envelope herself?"

Chuck looked startled by the question. "I don't know," he said after a moment. "I suppose she could have. I never thought to ask."

"Did you ever ask her what you were delivering?"

"Once. She said it was nothing. And if I minded doing it, she'd ask someone else."

"And you left it at that?"

He lowered his eyes. "I didn't want to press her. You see, I was flattered that she'd asked me. She's such a beautiful woman. I imagined scores of younger men vying to do her bidding."

I thought of the breathtaking beauty who'd turned to strike me at Mount Vesuvio, then looked across the table at colorless, short, and chunky Chuck Vardigan, the boring bureaucrat with the drunk wife.

"I enjoyed having something to share with her, an excuse for meeting with her."

I waited for him to continue, but he didn't. "Did you sleep with her, Chuck?"

He seemed relieved to admit it. "Yes," he said.

Mary's brother had been right. When men met Mary, they forgot themselves.

"I think Felicia knew," he added. "I think that's why she's been so ill lately. She must have known."

"If she knew, why would she let Mary stay here?"

"I've been out of town—I didn't know she was here. But you'd be surprised at the things people do when they drink."

"Mary told me you knew who she was dealing with."

"I didn't. I never have."

"Did you ever hang around the park to see who picked up the envelopes? Weren't you curious?"

"No. You see, as soon as I had the return envelope, I'd take it to Mary. That's all I could think about, seeing her again."

"Did Mary ever mention anything about the person —directly, indirectly?"

"No. She never even opened the envelopes until after I left. I remember coming back once. I'd gotten as far as my car and realized I'd left my tie with her. She let me in and went back to the—uh—to the bedroom to get it. While she was gone, I noticed the open envelope on the coffee table. I reached over and peeked inside, but it was empty."

We listened to him try to explain how remarkable a woman Mary Solis was, but I was already convinced she was unusual. How many twenty-two-year-olds get mixed up with murder?

"About your driver," I said.

"Duke is actually Felicia's driver. She had her license taken away some time ago."

"I'd like to talk to him."

"I'm sorry. I let him go. Without Felicia there's not much point in having him around. The doctor said it could be months before she comes back home."

Chuck looked down at the Oriental carpet and sighed. "It looks as if I've made a perfect disaster out of my life. Felicia's gone. Mary's gone. My self-respect is gone." He looked up and his eyes were pleading. "You won't report me, will you? The only thing I've got left is my reputation. I don't know what I'd do if I lost that."

His self-pity blanketed the room. I stood and Blackie followed.

"If you hear from Mary, or if your wife improves, give me a call," I said.

He started to rise, but I waved him back into his chair. "That's okay. We'll see ourselves out."

60

FELICIA ASHTON'S doctor never called. I'd phoned every drug rehab facility and all the hospitals and had pretty much given up finding her or Mary Solis when the phone rang Friday morning.

"That you, Ventana?"

"Post? Did you talk to my witness?" I'd convinced Post to ask Squire about having seen Mary Solis at the club two days after her funeral. It wouldn't hurt to have the police looking for her too.

"Forget the witness," Post said. "I got news."

"You found her?"

"Yeah." In person Post was practically inscrutable. Over the phone he was impossible to read. His tone didn't give a single hint about what was going on—either with him or with his case.

"And?"

"Come down to the Hall, Ventana. We need to talk."

I knew she was dead before I even walked into Post's office. It was the only reason he would have phoned. It was the only reason he would have thought to include me. He was investigating a murder now.

"What happened?" I asked after he confirmed my hunch. I was sitting on the hard wooden chair in front of his folder-strewn desk while he sat across from me and

fiddled absently with a blue pencil. The office reeked o
his trademark dirty-gym-clothes smell.

"Her throat was slit. We found the body dumped i
an alley in the Mission. You know, where the hooker
hang out. Coroner says she died last night."

*I could have saved her. She was alive these last tw
days. If I'd worked harder or faster, she'd be alive now.*

Post's hard, black eyes were on me when I looke
up. For a second I thought I saw remorse in his eyes too
Then they went cold and impersonal.

"As far as we know, you were the last person to tal
to her."

I knew he didn't mean to imply that I was a suspec
but I had an uneasy moment thinking maybe I was. H
kept me guessing all the way out to the Mount Vesuvi
Club. We walked out to the spot where Mary Solis and
had had words.

"Show me where you were standing."

"Do I need a lawyer, Post?"

He shook his head, raised an eyebrow to reassur
me, and asked me again to show him where we both ha
stood.

"I was about here." I moved into place, facing th
woods with my back turned about three-quarters awa
from the building. "And Mary was here. She was lookin
this way."

Post circled the spot with his eyes, then pause
when his gaze hit the rock I'd landed against.

"This it?"

I shrugged. "Looks about right. What's this abou
Post? You think there was somebody else out here?"

"Maybe."

I'd been grappling with the same possibility since
woke up in the hospital. If there had been a third person
Mary Solis had viewed him as a friend. Her expressio
hadn't shown fright or panic. I tried to remember more

ut everything related to those moments just before she
it me were in a dark, hazy fog.

"Tell me again what went down between you two."

I repeated my edited version of the conversation,
eaving out the money part because I knew he'd blow a
asket over my going into her safe-deposit box or, for
aat matter, my not telling him about the money. I gave
im the truth, just not *all* the truth.

If he suspected I was holding out on him, Post didn't
t on. He just took it all in and kept asking me question
fter question. Finally he seemed satisfied. He dismissed
endall, who'd been scribbling furiously as I talked.

"We picked up your friend," he said as we walked
owly across the back lawn to the car.

"Bink?"

Post nodded. "He's got an alibi."

"Oh?"

"Carolina Pogue. How's that squirrel rate a nice girl
ke her? She's too good for a flake like him." He
lanced at me sideways. "Think she'd lie for him?"

"Is she his only alibi?"

Post nodded. We'd reached the car, but he didn't
aake a move to get in. "That's all he needs. Her as an
libi and German Daniels. Oakland's already dropped
ll charges. I don't know if they should have."

Post glanced at me again to gauge my reaction. I
ied giving some of his inscrutability back to him, but it
idn't work.

"You don't agree?"

"I've told you before, Post. Bink's a scam artist, not
killer."

He slapped his forehead. "Right. I forgot," he said
arcastically, then opened the squad-car door and mo-
oned me inside.

Settling into the backseat beside me, Post signaled
endall to drive, then turned to me. "So if your guy is
ean, who do you think did Mary Solis?"

Bink had the best motive. Mary Solis could have threatened to sabotage his relationship with Carolina by exposing either Bink's infidelity or his insider-trading dealings.

I looked up and found Post studying me intently.

"Tell me this," I said, "were you really going to call me when you found Mary Solis?"

Post blinked and screwed his normally scowling lips into a tight, unpracticed smile. "Sure, Ventana. I did, didn't I?"

"If she'd been alive—would you still have called?"

"Sure."

I turned and gazed out the window to hide my discovery: The inscrutable Philly Post smiled to hide his lies.

"So who's good for this homicide?" he asked.

I could have told him about Vardigan's courier duties. Instead I just shook my head and said, "Your guess, Post, is as good as mine."

61

"I DON'T KNOW where to go next," I said, staring at the mountain of papers strewn on the table in the conference room across from Mitchell's office.

It was Sunday evening, and Mitch and I were the only ones there. I'd asked him to let me see the original folders for Teknikker, Basystems, and Kopar again in case we'd missed something the first time around.

Bink had admitted to insider trading and had said he never told Mary Solis he wanted to stop. He'd known about the others and thought they were fools for trying to walk away from a good thing. He admitted all this to me and to Mitch, but swore he'd clam up if we brought in the police. None of it explained his trouble or Mary Solis's death, though.

Mitch stirred in the chair next to mine, stretching his arms above his head, then rubbing the back of his neck. "Want some more coffee?"

I reached for the stack of computer data Ming Mong had generated and shook my head. "It's got to be in here. We're just not seeing it."

Mitch slumped back into his chair. "There are such things as unsolved cases, you know. Why don't you just turn over what you've got and let the police take care of it. Bink's cleared of murder. That's all we were concerned about, wasn't it?"

"No." I skimmed the stock reports, laid them down, then reviewed the price charts. Nothing.

"Tell me again what these financial reports can be used for," I said.

"IPOs," he answered wearily. "Do you want me to explain that again?"

"Uh-uh." I knew IPOs. The letters stood for initial public offering—the process where a stock goes public and begins selling shares traded on the stock market. "What else?"

"The SEC requires the information in the reports firms have to file."

"Okay."

"The financial statements from the audits go into the company's annual report—the report card of how they've done for the year."

I nodded. "What else?"

"Bank loans. Banks look at the financial statements when they decide to extend a line of credit to a company. They require an audit to make sure the company's healthy before they agree to risk a loan."

"What else?"

Mitch sighed. "Come on, Ronnie. You're pushing too hard. We've been over all of this a hundred times. Let's take a break. Maybe something will come to you if you just step away from it."

I fingered the files on the table in front of me. Kopar. Basystems. Teknikker. Bink hadn't worked on any other firms. "None of these guys have applied for a loan. Not even a line of credit. They're all publicly traded already, so that rules out the IPO business. And you can't find anything fishy about the stuff, right?"

"Everything looks *fine.*" His tone had turned testy.

I drummed my fingers on the top file and forced my brain to focus.

No weird stuff in the audit. No applications for loans or lines of credit by Teknikker, Basystems, or

Kopar. Nothing. There was a pattern of insider trading, but Bink hadn't tried to quit like the three dead guys had.

Ming Mong had even broken into the trading accounts of the principals of each firm to see if they'd purchased substantial amounts of stock before the annual reports were issued. Losing their shirts would have been a great reason for them to murder Bink if he'd assured them of a cover-up. But I'd come up blank there too.

I threw up my hands, shoved my chair back, and stood. "Okay, Mitch. You win. Let's walk down the Embarcadero and back. Maybe something will hit us after we've had some air."

Mitch followed me out the conference-room door and nearly ran into me when I tripped over a stack of files on the floor. I reached out to steady myself, and my eyes fell on the huge matrix calendar covering the wall. I'd passed it that first day when I'd followed Marcella down this very hall. Along the matrix's top border were dates, and along its left border were the names of clients and their respective auditors.

"What is this?" I asked.

"Work schedules. We plot everything everybody's supposed to do over the course of the quarter. It's to make sure we don't miss any filing dates or anything."

I studied the tiny penciled-in squares, then saw Bink's name beside the notation "Kopar Sys." The date was August 13. I followed the squares to the week before last and found Tuesday. I put my finger on it.

"What does this mean?" I asked Mitch.

He read out loud. "Donziger. Hanover. It means—"

Something clicked inside my head. "This is it, Mitch!" I cried, tapping the matrix with my finger. "This is it!"

I danced around Mitch, then kissed him. "We've been looking at the wrong firms. It's not what Bink's done—it's what he *was going* to do. This *has* to be it."

"What are you talking about?"

"Don't you see? For some reason these guys—Donziger—didn't want an audit from Bink. So they deflected him."

Mitch looked skeptical. "With thugs and Uzis? Come on, Ronnie, I don't buy that for a minute. This is a corporation."

"Think about it. This has got to be the key. We've combed our way backward and forward through the other three. They're the only firms Bink's worked on since he's been here. The only ones besides Donziger. Right?"

Mitch nodded.

"So it *has* to be Donziger."

"But—"

"Shhh. Don't let your *should*s and *shouldn't*s get in the way, Mitch. Let's just follow this one up."

We searched Bink's entire office for the work papers on Donziger and couldn't find them. The archives turned up blank, too.

"Wait a minute! Didn't Marcella say somebody else was doing Donziger?"

"Right, Chris Mullin—the senior on the engagement."

We scurried over to his office and rummaged through his desk.

"Bingo!" I said. "It's right here. Look." I waved a sheet I'd found tucked casually inside a folder amid the pile of notebooks on his desk. "It says Donziger's applying for a loan worth two million dollars."

Mitch was dumbfounded. I guess he hadn't really expected me to find anything. I shunted the petty annoyance I felt aside and tried to focus on the victory.

"We're getting close, Mitch. This is great."

Then I eagerly read farther down the page, and my heart sank. The bank writing the loan was Barnweather Bank of London—Gabriél Juarez's bank.

62

I DIDN'T WANT to think Gabriél had gone bad again. I wanted to believe in Gabriél as much for my own sake as for his.

"What does he gain by giving a loan to a company that doesn't deserve it?"

"Simple," Mitch answered. "Donziger gets the loan, the company's president or whoever siphons off the funds, then declares bankruptcy. The bank CEO and the company CEO split the profits—each gets a million that's been stashed away in some Swiss account. The first step to the two million is a clean audit."

I sank into Chris Mullin's chair. "Then I think our theory's got problems."

"Why?"

"Bink's the most bribable guy I know. If they wanted a clean audit, they could have just waved ten dollars under his nose and he'd be lapping at their heels."

"Give the guy some credit."

"Come on, Mitch. You know it's true. Why wouldn't they include him in the deal?"

"Maybe they knew he was planning to marry Carolina and wouldn't need the money. They must have realized that and decided to get rid of him."

I wasn't convinced, but I wasn't about to tell Mitch.

We'd be here till dawn trying to persuade each other. "Do you think Chris Mullin's in on it?"

Mitch shook his head. "He wouldn't have to be. Chris is fairly fresh to the field. Bink hired him for senior because he's got an impressive degree. Not much experience, though. It wouldn't be that hard to get something over Chris if he were in charge of an audit."

"I think we'd better check out Mullin's—what do you call them?"

"Work papers?"

"Yes, we'll check out the work papers first. Maybe Donziger didn't get a clean audit."

Mitch reached for the phone beside the stack of folders on Mullin's desk.

"Who are you calling?"

"I promised Carolina I'd take her out to dinner this evening to talk about Bink. Looks like I'm not going to make it."

I buried the tiny but surprising flit of satisfaction that coursed through me. "How long do you think this is going to take you?"

Mitch grinned. "You mean us?"

"I don't do accounting."

"Sure you do, Ron. I'll show you."

Three hours later we'd pretty much exhausted every angle they could have used. Nothing in the work papers showed anything that could be considered deleterious to Donziger's reputation or mode of doing business.

"Looks like they're going to get a clean audit," Mitch said.

"Unless we come up with something."

"Maybe we're wrong. Maybe it's got nothing to do with Bink's work."

I'd noticed Mitchell's skepticism mounting with each ticked and tied sheet we reviewed. Three hours was enough time for him to start thinking that I'd made it all up.

"Maybe," I agreed. "But there's only one way to find out."

"What's that?"

"I'll tell you later," I said, trying to avoid a lecture on how I was going to end up in jail someday just like my parents.

It was eleven o'clock by the time we finished putting Chris Mullin's files back in order. Mitch phoned Carolina again and asked if she was still up for a meeting. I left him on the phone, talking in a low, intimate tone that made me feel left out.

63

I DIDN'T FEEL like going upstairs when I got home, so I slipped into the Quarter Moon and found Blackie hanging out, trying to avoid some woman who'd trailed him through three bars and a restaurant before he managed to give her the slip.

"Want to go for a ride?" I asked.

Blackie grinned. "This got anything to do with larceny, doll?"

"Not yet," I said, and led him out to the car.

We found Donziger Associates easily enough just off the freeway in the southeast corner of the city. The building was huge, about twenty thousand square feet, painted a chalky white color so that even in the dark it stood out like a pearl amid acres and acres of drab, gray warehouses and industrial-type buildings.

Like most of its neighbors, Donziger had tall, high-powered lamps stationed at each corner of its lot. But whoever ran the place seemed a little more paranoid than the others. Nobody else on the block had the tall wire-mesh fence topped with cut-wire, the huge Beware of Dog signs posted, or the Warning—Private Property decals at every entrance. On the positive side, there was no sign of a security guard.

I parked the car near the fence in the alley in back. "Wait here a sec, Blackie."

I walked up to the fence, grabbed it with both hands, and jiggled it. Within seconds a monstrous black hulk bounded into view, snarling and growling so loud, I heard it before I actually saw it. He flew into the light, and I saw him—one hundred pounds of solidly lethal Rottweiler—flying at me. I let go of the fence and jumped back just in time.

The dog hit the wire and bounced off of it like a demented rubber toy. When he landed on the pavement, he didn't even hesitate. He roared for effect and flew at the fence again. The spot where he'd hit the first time bulged out. There were similar bulges all along the fence.

I let him have a couple more runs at me while I studied the electrical wires leading off the street into the building and the wires running along the exterior of the building. I sketched a quick schematic on a notebook out of my pocket, then headed back to the car.

Blackie was smoking and looking skeptical when I slipped into the driver's seat beside him.

"I don't know about you, doll, but Spike there's about talked me out of this one."

"Don't be such a chicken, Blackie. I've got it covered."

"Yeah?" He rolled down his window and flipped his cigarette butt out. The red ash arched through the darkness and landed in a burst of sparks about twenty feet from the car.

"You free tomorrow night?"

Blackie rolled the window up slowly and said, "Fuck."

64

I SPENT MOST of Monday getting ready. A drive down to Donziger to case the building in the daylight and to double-check the absence of security guards, a phone call to my cousin Myra, whose friend ran the Purple Poodle Farm up in Kensington, and a stop at the tool-rental shop for a few incidentals. My final trip was out to Kensington and back. Then I drove over to Blackie's.

"What the fuck is that?" Blackie said as soon as he got in the car. The white toy poodle Myra's friend at the Purple Poodle Farm had lent me growled furiously at Blackie from the backseat.

"What's it look like, Blackie? It's a dog."

"Fuck, Ventana. Are you nuts?"

I laughed out loud.

"Hardly, Blackie. Conifer's Princess Daisy of Twilight here is our ticket into Donziger."

Blackie grunted. I could tell he wasn't convinced.

"Think love, Blackie, not war."

"Fuckin' animals," he muttered.

He didn't say anything else until we pulled up in the alley behind Donziger. We both got out of the car, and I handed him the leash with the dog attached.

"Whatever you do," I said. "Don't let that monster lose interest in her, okay?"

We both stared down at the curly-haired little poodle trembling at Blackie's feet. The light from the streetlamp overhead gave Princess's coat a yellow cast and turned her eyes and nose purple.

Blackie snorted. "What makes you think she's his type, doll?"

"She's in heat, Blackie. That means she's everybody's type. It makes her a canine Madonna." I pulled a bunch of tools out of the trunk, then checked my watch. "What time have you got?"

"Ten thirty-eight."

"Okay. Give me four minutes, then jiggle the fence and get Conan over here."

I'd already decided the best route into the building was to go in via the back entrance, through the warehouse, instead of the front office. Once inside, I could take my time getting into the office section of the building, where I was sure their files were kept.

"Give me five minutes to get inside, then put Princess in the car." I didn't know much about canine love habits, so I couldn't be sure how long Conan's unfulfilled ardor would last. Five minutes seemed like a safe bet.

"When I'm ready to come out, I'll flash a light from that window there. I'll need as long as you can give me, 'cause I don't know what I'll be carrying."

I crept around to the side of the building, out of sight of Blackie and the dog, to a spot where some shrubs were growing up against the fence. I ducked behind them, slipped my gloves on, pulled out the bolt cutters, and waited. The fence jiggled, and I heard the dog's roar, then total silence. A second later a coy little *yip* reached my ears.

"Yesss, Princess!" I whispered, and snipped the wire fence. The bolt cutters were good and sharp. They went through the metal like a hot knife through snow.

I cut a V, with each arm about two feet long, then pushed the cut section inward and slipped through. It

was harder to bend the fence back the way it was to
cover the gaping hole I'd made, but I needed to keep
Conan inside and any suspicious night patrols in the
dark. As soon as I had the fence so that it looked untouched, I headed for a small door in the back.

I worked the Evertrust lock, slipped inside, and, figuring on a sixty- or ninety-second grace period before
the alarm went off, searched my surroundings in the dim
light for the most logical place to hide a burglar-alarm
control unit.

There was a desk stationed beside the door. Behind
it was a stationary partition with cabinets and some
shelves. One quick, wide glance around me just to make
sure. There were rows and rows of boxes stacked on
pallets straight ahead of me and three forklifts parked in
the corner. Another set of different-sized boxes were on
my left. The cabinet had to be it. *Otherwise I'm dead,* I
thought.

I circled the desk, jerked open the first cabinet door,
and flashed my penlight around inside. Nothing. Without
bothering to close it, I reached for the next cabinet door.
My hand slipped off the knob. It was stuck. I grabbed it,
held on tight, and pulled. It finally swung open, and the
rays from my penlight caught something red. An LED
readout. The control box. It said I had fifteen seconds.
Fourteen. Thirteen.

The seconds ticked off in my head, keeping time
with the silent red countdown on the face of the box. I
positioned my electric drill on the screws in each corner
and removed the faceplate from the panel. Nine seconds.
With my penlight in my mouth I took a set of wire
diverters out of my left pocket and clamped each end
simultaneously onto the two leads that would trigger the
alarm. Five seconds. Then I reached into my right pocket
for the nippers and clipped the lead wires. The red numbers stopped at three.

I let my arms drop and took a deep breath. It was

the first time I'd ever broken into a place without thinking, at least for a fragment of a second, of my parents. They were nowhere with me this time. I felt suddenly lonely and abandoned. Just as my spirits started to sink, I took another deep breath and suddenly felt the energy of my father's warm brown eyes on me and the sunshine of my mother's radiant smile. *I still need you guys,* I whispered, then replaced the cover panel and closed both cabinet doors. Onward.

I marched down the center aisle, where the boxes were stacked about twenty feet high in some spots and four or five deep. I'd gotten as far as the opposite end where the boxes were piled only two and three high, when I heard a soft whirring noise from somewhere on the other side of the warehouse. I froze and listened. It sounded like a small motor. Probably a soft-drink or coffee machine.

I swept my penlight around in the dark. Nothing. Then I happened to glance up and saw the two red beacons atop posts on either side at the end of the row of boxes.

"Shit!" A robot sentry! The whirring got louder. All it would take was one little microwave to sense my presence and send a signal to the security office, wherever it was. My best chance would be if they were off-site. Most likely they were, but I couldn't be sure.

The soft, purring motor was getting closer. Where to hide? Microwaves penetrate everything but metal. I scanned the dim space around me. Metal . . . metal . . .

The boxes were filled with metal components! Yes! I pocketed my penlight and scrambled for a toehold in the mountain of boxes. Scaling the wall of cardboard was tough, but I finally made it to the top.

The boxes were piled five deep. If I went too far across the top toward the middle of the stack, the microwaves might sense me from the other side, but if I stayed here, resting on the top box of the first row, the little whirring monster would recognize me for sure.

I rested a second longer on the first box, listening for the maddeningly gentle sound of the robot's tiny motor. It was coming very close. I needed to move. Tentatively I scooted my weight to the next box over. The minute I put my weight on it, its top caved in. I fell into that box, through the one beneath it, and partway through the next one.

From where I lay, gasping, wedged in the dark, deep between four walls of cardboard, I could hear the little machine turn the corner and whir down the aisle. Shit.

At least I knew what Donziger was hiding now. Empty boxes meant they were inflating their inventory. A greater inventory meant they were worth more, worth enough on paper to qualify for a two-million-dollar loan. But unless I could climb out of here, I'd probably never live to tell anybody.

I shifted my weight cautiously and slid through another two boxes, landing on the back of my shoulders, feet up. Unless I moved, I'd never get out, but I was afraid I'd slide through another set of empty boxes and eventually end up twenty feet down.

Trying not to move anything but my arm, I reached toward the side, feeling for the wall of cardboard. My fingers hit something dull and flat. I worked them upward until I reached an edge. Then I curled my hand around it and pulled up to right myself. I spread my feet out so they rested on the outside corners of the box, figuring I'd be less likely to slip that way.

With each foot in a corner and one hand holding on to the edge of a box in the stack closest to the aisle, I pulled my penlight out of my pocket with my free hand and surveyed the damage. Each box was about two feet tall. I counted five boxes over my head. I'd fallen through more of them than I thought I had.

I held on to the penlight with my teeth—for some

eason the hole I'd found myself in wasn't as scary with
he light on—and searched my pockets for a screwdriver.
knew exactly where to look.

Praying that my movement wouldn't send me down
hrough another set of empty boxes, I lifted my screwdriver and plunged it into the side of the box in front of
ne. It sunk through without any resistance from the in-
ide. I did the same thing on all four sides and hit some-
hing hard only on the stack closest to the aisle.

Chris Mullin's report had said each box contained
omputer parts worth forty-five hundred dollars. And
he warehouse was full of boxes. Thousands.

I would have done the math, but I heard, on top of
he constant soft drone of my trash-can-sized nemesis,
he clink of metal against metal. Keys working a lock.
ust as I snapped off the penlight, the overhead fluores-
ents flickered on. Then I heard voices.

"You checked the roof?" a voice said.

"Uh-huh."

"All right. Get the office area. Lucifer and me'll do
he warehouse."

Lucifer? What parent in his right mind would name
child Lucifer? And what grown child would insist on
sing that name? I held my breath and prayed that Luci-
er and his friend wouldn't think to look up.

I heard footsteps, then a door closing. Guard num-
er two was gone. I prayed I'd left everything intact in
he offices. Over the whirring of the robot and shuffling
f the guards, I distinctly heard the panting of the mon-
ter Rottweiler. *Lucifer.* Lucifer was the *dog.*

I wasn't sure if that made me feel better or not.

I stood frozen amid the empty boxes, my limbs get-
ing stiff and my mind going numb. Guards, robots, and
ogs. What now, Mom? How about it, Dad? How would
he infamous Ventana cat burglars get past this one?

"Will you shut that thing off?" a voice shouted.
The damn thing keeps tripping."

"It's Lucifer," another voice answered.

"I don't care what's doin' it. Just shut it off before we get canned."

A door slammed. Seconds after that the whirring stopped. I relaxed, but only slightly. Even with the robot turned off, I still had two humans and a dog to contend with. I stood, listening to them circling the huge space checking corners and crevices, for what seemed like days. Finally I heard a voice say, "Come on, boy."

Next I heard a door shut, and the warehouse was silent.

They'd left the robot off and the warehouse lights on. Should I scale the rest of the cardboard boxes and try to make a break for it while the guards and the dog were in the offices? I'd just about convinced myself to run when I heard voices again. As they got closer, I could also make out the unpleasant panting of the dog.

"I say the thing's busted."

"Yeah?"

"I say leave it off, or we'll be back in thirty minutes when the damn thing shorts out again."

"Manual says we oughta reset it."

"Go by the manual and your whole watch gets screwed up. You wanna go home when your watch is over or not? Nobody's going to blow a gasket we leave the goddamn thing off. Perimeter alarm's still up."

"Right."

Only it wasn't. The diverter I'd installed on my way in completed the system's electrical circuit. The alarm bypassed every window and door in the place. You could drop a nuclear bomb on the building and the guys monitoring the alarm back at the security company wouldn't even know it.

The warehouse went dark, and I heard a door shut. I listened hard for the panting dog and heard nothing. Time to go.

Blackie was behind the wheel when I slid in next to

him. Princess was yapping out the window from the backseat. The whole inside of the Toyota smelled of dog. Outside, Lucifer stood forlornly behind the fence, transfixed by the sight of the tiny poodle bouncing against the glass. For half a second I felt sorry for him.

"So?" Blackie said, throwing the car into gear and speeding toward North Beach.

"They've got about a zillion empty cartons in there, Blackie. And they're calling it all merchandise."

He grunted and reached for a cigarette. "Pumpin' up the books."

"Exactly."

"Where's the little fuck fit in?"

"Bink? That's the part he's going to have to tell us."

"Sure, doll."

The way he said it, I got the feeling he thought I'd have better luck getting the pope to say he believes in Santa.

65

"**W**OULDN'T I HAVE told you already if I knew anything about it?" Bink demanded indignantly. "Talk to Mullin. He took over the engagement for me. Maybe he's in with them. Talk to Patty Boniface. She's the one set everything up. She's their controller, for Chrissakes. How are they going to pull something like this over without having her in on it?"

"I'm not saying you knew, Bink. I'm just asking you to help out by telling me what you know about their operation."

His expression stayed wary. "How do I know you're not trying to get me thrown back in jail?"

"I got you *out* of jail, Bink, remember? Why would I try to get you arrested again?"

"You're the one who knows all the bad guys."

"What are you talking about?"

"The banker, right? What's his name? Juarez. Well, you know him, don't you? And Vardigan. You've been friends with Chuck Vardigan for a long time too."

I barely knew Vardigan, but that was beside the point. "Vardigan's not a bad guy. He's barely even involved. And anyway, he works for the SEC. He's like a cop, only for stocks."

"You're not going to con me, Ronnie."

"What are you talking about?" I was so frustrated, I had to force myself not to shout.

"Vardigan's not with SEC, Ronnie. He's their CEO. He's Donziger's CEO."

66

I COULD TELL Post smelled a promotion. He'd stopped snarling at me and was actually listening, paying attention, and asking questions—intelligent, pointed ones.

"This guy, Juarez—you're sure he'll talk to you?"

I'd already convinced Post he should work the case and make the arrest instead of turning it over to the Fraud Unit. There were at least two homicides involved.

"Gabriél used to be one of my probationers," I said. "He thinks he owes me for keeping him out of jail."

Post snorted. "He'll really owe you once you do this to him."

I cringed inwardly. I'd hoped Gabriél's honest life-style had been real. It was hard to believe he'd been lying to me all this time, lying to the whole Latino community, to the kids he'd brought along out of the *barrio*. I wondered how I could have been so wrong about somebody. Then I looked across the desk at Post. "Will you do it?"

"The wire's yours," he said.

"I want you out there monitoring it, okay? Nobody else."

"I gotta have a backup."

"Kendall."

Post shook his head. "Kendall's a pencil pusher. What if this guy gets violent?"

I thought about the long-fanged hamsters in Gabriél's office and how they'd lunged at the pencil he'd
stuck in their cage. I considered Gabriél's admiration of
their miniviciousness and wondered if he'd react the
same way when his own back was against the wall.

"Then I want Blackie."

"Coogan?" Post nearly spat the name. "No deal. I'd
take Kendall over that lush any day. You're not telling
me who I can and can't work with, Ventana. I'm using
whoever I want for backup."

"Suit yourself," I said, gathering my backpack as I
rose from my chair.

"Hey! Where are you going?"

"I want Blackie."

"Sit down, Ventana."

I stopped, but I didn't sit. Post launched into a big
bureaucratic explanation that was nine-tenths subterfuge
and one-tenth bluster.

I listened, and when he finished, I said no.

"Come on, Ventana. Be reasonable."

I headed for the door.

"Wait!" he shouted.

With my hand still pointedly on the doorknob I said,
"Blackie Coogan, Post. It's Blackie or no wire and no
bust."

"Jesus." His head barely moved, but he actually
nodded before he slumped against the back of his chair
and scowled.

67

DOWN IN THE POLICE garage Blackie and Post circled each other warily like two alley cats. Until we'd actually reached the car, neither one of them had realized they'd have to ride together. Neither one wanted to get in first.

I sat in the backseat of the unmarked police car, wires and microphone taped to my torso. I was starting to wonder how smart I'd been to insist they work together.

I reached over and rolled down the window. "Hey!"

Post's surprised expression told me all I needed to know: He'd already forgotten I was even there. Great.

"Will you two stop acting stupid and get in the car?"

Blackie muttered obscenities under his breath, but he slipped into the passenger seat up front.

"Separate fuckin' cars woulda been better, doll."

"We've already been over that, Blackie."

He grumbled as Post got in and started the engine. Neither one spoke to the other the whole trip down to Gabriél's bank.

When we pulled up half a block up the street from the bank, Post turned on the receiver and caught my eye in his rearview. "Say something."

I did and heard it echo over the radio. "Perfect," Post said. Blackie nodded. I opened the back door.

"Good luck," Post said.

Blackie gave me a thumbs-up signal and winked.

Gabriél's office door popped open the instant Juana announced my arrival over the intercom.

"Come in, Ronnie," Gabriél exclaimed. He stood behind his desk, arms spread in a hearty gesture of welcome.

"This is great. Did you come to take me to lunch? No? Then I insist on taking *you.*"

I shut the door, crossed the room, and stood before him, both hands resting lightly at my sides. I didn't know what to expect.

"We've got to talk, Gabriél."

"Of course, Ronnie," he said, still not quite keyed into how serious I was. Then he cocked his head to one side, and his eyes narrowed. "Something is wrong."

"Something is very wrong, Gabriél. We need to talk."

"By all means. Sit down. Sit down, please."

I did and waited until he followed suit. "I think you've been holding out on me," I began.

"How so?" The vestiges of his earlier smile lingered uncertainly on his face. "I don't understand."

"The Donziger loan," I prompted.

His expression didn't change. "Yes?"

"You arranged to lend Chuck Vardigan two million dollars."

"Donziger, not Chuck," he corrected mildly.

"I want a piece of it, Gabriél."

"A piece of what?" He still looked very puzzled.

"I'm not asking you to do something for nothing. Cut me in on Donziger and I can bring in another firm. It's twice as big as Donziger. We can do the same thing with them, for twice as much. But I want a piece of Donziger first."

"I don't know what you're talking about."

"Come on, Gabriél. I'm not a parole officer anymore. I'm not going to report you—not as long as you let me in."

"Ronnie, I honestly don't know what you're saying." He sounded exasperated.

"The loan, Gabriél. You know exactly what I'm talking about. Your bank lends Chuck Vardigan's firm two million dollars. Chuck's firm goes belly-up, and you write it off as a bad loan."

"Why would Chuck's firm have any problems? His preliminary financials look fine. If you know something about Donziger you're not telling me, I think you'd better fill me in."

Things weren't working out the way I thought they would. "Stop playing so hard to get," I said. "You've got to deal with me, Gabriél. Either way you've got to deal with me. Why not choose the one that holds all the pluses—money, freedom. Come on."

Gabriél reached down and pressed a button to activate the intercom on his desk.

"Juana, bring me everything we've got on Donziger."

The squeak of the hamster wheel broke the silence while we waited. Juana hauled in the files, started to speak, then closed her mouth and left us alone. As soon as she left, Gabriél opened the thickest file, spun it around on his desk, and shoved it toward me.

"Show me," he demanded furiously. "Show me what you're talking about."

I glanced down at the first page in front of me. It was filled with numbers and figures. At the top were the words *Preliminary Financial Report,* and at the bottom was a lengthy disclaimer about the contents.

"The paperwork's fine, Gabriél. You know that. It's not going to show up on paper."

He stared into my eyes until I had to look away. His

voice barely a whisper, he said, "I learned my lesson nine years ago. You helped me learn it, Ronnie. You believed in me when I wasn't even sure if I should believe in myself. I'd never do anything stupid like I did before. I thought you knew that."

Shit. What was I supposed to do now? I'd blown the whole plan, and Gabriél hadn't admitted to anything. If Blackie and Post hadn't strangled each other already, they were probably sitting in the car shaking their heads.

I got out of there as fast as I could, feeling stupid and misdirected.

"What the hell are you doing, Ventana?" Post screamed as soon as I opened the car door. He'd swiveled, one arm crooked over the backrest of his own seat, to face the rear passenger side where I slid in. "I can't believe you bought that stooge's story. Why are you wasting my time?"

"I'm not sure if he's in on it," I said.

"Not sure? Jesus Christ, Ventana, you want a signed confession? Ever heard of circumstantial evidence? If it looks like shit, smells like shit, and feels like shit, it's gotta *be* shit, dammit!"

Blackie leaned toward him imperceptibly and said, "What do *you* know, asshole?"

Post whipped his head around and jabbed a finger at Blackie. "YOU stay outta this!"

"She was in there, asshole. *You* see the guy's face? *You* got history with this guy?"

Post's color deepened. "Shut up, you old—"

"POST!" I shouted. "Stop it, both of you. I don't know if he's lying or not, okay? I just couldn't tell. If I'm wrong, if Gabriél's not in on any of this, I've just destroyed my credibility with a very good friend."

Post rolled his eyes. "What about all those dead bodies lined up outside Donziger's door? You wanna walk away from them? You wanna forget all about them?"

All I could think of was the haunting hurt and confusion in Gabriél's expression when I left. Was he betraying me? Or was I betraying him?

68

I WAS SLOUCHED in a chair in the back corner of the Quarter Moon working on my fourth Anchor Steam when somebody walked up, stood next to the table, and cleared his throat. I hadn't seen Philly Post walk in because I'd been staring hard at the bottle on the table for at least a half hour.

"It's eleven o'clock in the morning," he said, taking the chair opposite mine.

"So?"

He frowned.

"Go away," I said, and reached for the beer. His hand covered mine and held the bottle on the table.

"I wanna nail this guy. Don't you?"

"I'm not a cop, Post." I tried to pull my hand away, but he wouldn't let go.

"I can't do it without you," he said.

He released my hand, and I pulled it away empty, leaving the beer on the table between us. "What did you say?"

"I said, Ventana, that I can't do it without you."

I leaned back in my chair and stared at him, wondering whether I was so drunk that I'd misunderstood. He repeated himself a third time, leaning fiercely toward me to make sure I got the point.

I got it, all right. I got it so hard that it made me

laugh. I'd been waiting what seemed like forever to hear Post say those very words, since I'd met him, since I first suggested we work together. And now he was saying them. He was sitting there asking me to work with him, admitting he couldn't put a hero and a friend of mine away without me. What a joke.

I stopped laughing and said, "Forget it, Post. Leave me alone."

"He's a con, Ventana. He's scum."

"Have you met his wife?"

"Some of them have wives, some don't. It doesn't make them any more honest."

"How about his kids? He doesn't have just his own. He's got about two hundred. Did you know that, Post? They call themselves Gabriél's kids. Even their own parents call them Gabriél's kids. And they say it proudly."

"You were all for it yesterday."

"That was yesterday." Before I'd seen Gabriél's confusion. Before I'd seen the raw sense of betrayal in his eyes.

For a few brief moments yesterday Gabriél had been the same messed-up but sensitive man who had walked into my office years ago, eager for a second chance. And even though he'd taken his chance and run with it, done more than I or the judge or his public defender or anybody had thought possible, it was like I'd taken all that away from him yesterday. As if by doubting his honesty, I'd stripped him back down to that confused guy of so many years ago.

I reached for the Anchor Steam, and this time Post didn't stop me. After a long, deep slug, I set the empty bottle down and looked across the table at him. My eyes wouldn't focus the way I wanted them to.

"Go away," I said. "Leave me alone." I waved at Marcus to bring me another one.

Post scraped his chair back and rose after Marcus

brought over a fresh bottle and cleared the empty one. "You know what you are, Ventana? You're pathetic."

I stared at the untouched bottle, then looked up at him. Anger cleared my vision. His face was full of disdain. "You think you're perfect, don't you, Post? You think because you've got no feelings for anybody, you're perfect. Try helping somebody out sometime. Try watching them fall. Then come back and tell me how pathetic I am."

"The guy conned you, that's all."

"Then he conned the whole world, Post."

"Most crooks do. You going to get sober and work this with me or not?"

I looked at the bottle on the table, then looked back up at him. "Or not," I said, reaching for the beer.

Post snatched it away. "Dammit, Ventana! I need you on this."

"I don't work for the PD, Post. I'm free-lance, remember?"

He went to the bar, taking my Anchor Steam with him, and came back with a cup of coffee. "Here, drink this."

"I'm not working this case for you. I'm not going to work it for anybody, understand? If Gabriél's guilty, I'm not going to be the one to put him away."

He sat down and pushed the cup and saucer a little closer toward me. "Drink it."

I drank the bitter coffee and felt my brain cells start to clear before I'd even finished the cup. "Okay," I said, when the coffee was gone. "I'm sober now. The answer's still no."

After Post left, I considered having another beer, but realized he had sort of ruined my little session of mourning by injecting a second layer of guilt.

I settled the bill with Marcus, then stepped outside and squinted into the clear, blue sunshine. The crispness and light didn't seem right. The day should have been

one of those doughy-gray fogged-in San Francisco day
when you have no hope of ever seeing the sun.

I was fumbling with the downstairs front door when
I heard my name and turned to find Juana Juarez on the
sidewalk behind me. She looked solemn. She didn'
smile; she only dipped her head in greeting when ou
eyes met.

"May I have a word with you, Ronnie?"

"Uh—sure. What are you doing here, Juana?"

"Please." She glanced around as if to say, "Let's no
talk on the street."

"Come on upstairs," I said. Juana wasn't the kind o
woman you'd take into a bar. I motioned her to go ahea
of me and wondered if she smelled the alcohol on m
breath as she passed by. My discomfort at that possibilit
was more sobering than Post's coffee.

Upstairs I offered her the only armchair, and I sat a
the table I use for a desk. "Would you like coffee
Juana? It'll just take a minute."

She agreed, I think more because she wanted me t
have some than because she wanted any herself.
tinkered around with the hot plate, got the water boiling
then spooned some instant into a couple of mugs.

Back at the table I set the mugs down and faced her
"What can I do for you?"

"It's Gabriél," she said softly. "I must know wha
you said to him yesterday."

I flinched. "Why?"

"He's not himself. He walked out of the bank afte
you left and he refuses to go back. He didn't coach th
Potros last night. The children were very disappointed
This morning he refused to leave his bed. I don't under
stand. When I ask what's wrong, he only shakes his head
Ronnie, what happened yesterday? What did you say t
him to make him this way? Did you tell him somethin
bad about me?"

"Of course not. Why would you think that?"

"He won't speak to me, Ronnie. I come into the room and it's as if I weren't there."

"I'm sorry, Juana."

"You must tell me," she insisted. "This situation cannot persist. It cannot go on. Gabriél must run the bank. He must help the children. What have you done to him, Ronnie? Tell me. What did you say to make him like this?" There were tears in her eyes. She finally gave in to them and wept.

I let her cry herself out, then I rose, and she stood reluctantly, her good manners not allowing her to press me further.

"I'll do what I can to straighten this out," I said. "I just need a little time."

But if "straightening things out" ended up meaning putting her husband in jail, I wondered how polite she'd be to me then.

69

"**S**OUNDS LIKE A GUILTY conscience to me," Mitchell said.

We were in his office combing through the Donziger files for the third time, flagging the items where we suspected they'd cheated. Everybody else in the office had gone home hours ago. In fact they'd gone home hours before I'd phoned Mitch and insisted he meet me at the office. It was now five in the morning.

"Either that or I've really rocked him somehow."

"If he's acting this way and he's *not* guilty, then he's nuts. What kind of power do you think you have over this guy?" Mitch narrowed his usually generous blue eyes in suspicion. "Is there more between you two than you're telling me? He's not the guy . . . ?"

Mitch didn't need to finish. I knew what he meant. "No, Mitch, he's not the man I had an affair with when we were married."

Eight years and he still hadn't forgotten. But I guess I hadn't forgotten his transgression either. Mitch watched me a moment longer before turning back to the file. That's what had broken us up, the suspicion, the constant effort to read between the lines that had started the instant I told him about my affair.

"Okay," I said. "Let's forget about Gabriél. Let's

focus on Chuck Vardigan. I want to talk to Pogue about him."

"Carolina?"

"Her father."

"Oh." Did his silence mean he'd finally realized she was always on his mind? "Why?"

"He might know where to find Felicia."

"I'll ask Carolina. She's her cousin, after all. Think Felicia knows something?"

"She might. Otherwise why stash her away at some dry-out clinic? I'd just like to talk to her and find out. And I'd like to talk to Pogue anyway. He might know something without realizing it."

Mitch gestured at the papers spread across the table in front of us. "We've got enough here to put *somebody* away. Aren't you going for overkill?"

"This will get us fraud. There's got to be a way to incriminate Vardigan for the murders."

"What about Juarez?"

I reached for another folder and ignored his question. He didn't press me for an answer. Instead he started lifting papers and documents, searching for something. He noticed I was staring.

"My pen," he said. "Did you see what I did with it?"

"That's it!" I shouted. I slammed my hand on the table and jumped out of my chair. "That is it!"

Mitch looked up at me, bewildered. "What?"

"You've done it again!" I bent over him, took his face in both hands, and kissed him squarely on the nose. "You're a genius, Mitch," I said, and headed out the door.

70

"**A**LL RIGHT, Squire, this cost me a bundle, so we've got to make it work."

We were in the security room behind the Mount Vesuvio Club's front desk. I couldn't tell Squire that the "bundle" had come from somebody else's stash, specifically, from Mary Solis's safe-deposit box. It would have looked bad. And besides, I felt pretty crummy about raiding her money. But I figured if I could use a tiny bit—relatively speaking—of her cash to nail her murderer, she wouldn't mind.

After I'd left Mitch, I'd spent the rest of the dawn tracking down Blackie to find out where he'd hidden the money for safekeeping. I finally found him at an after-hours jazz joint in Chinatown, and by the time I got him sober, he told me he'd actually rented his own safe-deposit box at the same bank where Mary Solis had. It was close to nine by then, and the bank opened at nine.

After that I looked up Skippy—an ex-parolee of mine who hadn't done as well as Gabriél. Skippy lived in a back alley in the SoMa district and was still into electronics—illegal surveillance electronics. He liked making bombs, too, and tried to sell me one after I bought the mike, but since bombs are what got him into trouble, I declined.

Now Squire and I were in the security room at the

Mount Vesuvio Club, and Squire was admiring Skippy's handiwork.

"Looks like a regular pen," he said, holding it up and twirling it under the light. "Uh-huh, a regular ole pen. That's something, ain't it?"

I thought so. And for what it cost, it should be.

"So all's I do is slip it to him when he signs in?"

"Right."

Squire chuckled. "Where you going to be?"

I nodded toward the front door. "Out in the parking lot. Can you clear me with the valets?"

"Easy," he said. "You got a van?"

I shook my head.

"Use mine. You can stretch out in it." He jingled his keys in front of me. "Go ahead. He won't be here until noon. Never is."

I parked Squire's van across from the front door, then stretched out in back with the receiver turned on low. I wadded up a sweater I'd dug out of my backseat to use for a pillow, but gagged when I put my head on it—it reeked of Princess, the sexy poodle dog. Tossing the sweater on the floor in disgust, I set the alarm on my wristwatch for eleven-fifty and managed to doze.

Before the alarm sounded, I switched it off and settled into the front seat. Vardigan's Lincoln rolled into the club about five minutes later. As he disappeared into the club with his bodyguard—the very guy he'd told me he'd fired—I reached over and turned up the volume on the receiver.

Squire's voice came in loud and clear.

"How are you today, Mr. Vardigan?"

"Fine, Squire. Just fine. Say, have you got a pen? I seem to have misplaced mine. Thanks." When he spoke again, his voice came in louder. "And yourself, Squire? How are you today?"

"Couldn't be better."

I listened as Vardigan made his progress through

the club. The maître d', the waiter, the idle chat wit
other club members, and nine holes of golf. I was s
bored, I was ready to turn the whole thing over to th
SFPD by the time Vardigan finally showed outside th
club again.

He was standing at the front door chatting with
bald-headed man named Ross while he waited for h
bodyguard to bring the car around, when suddenly, a re
Jeep Wagoneer screeched to a halt in front of them. Ga
briél Juarez jumped out and waved the parking atten
dant away.

I sat up and listened as he disappeared behind th
Jeep.

"You're fucking with me, Chuck," he shouted.

"Hey—hey—what's the—take it easy, Gabriél. Wh
don't—"

"If you ruin my bank, I'll take you to court, miste
I'll sue you for every single penny you've stolen."

"Ross, will you excuse us?"

The bald-headed guy disappeared into the building
The parking valets all backed off too.

"Now, calm down, Gabriél. Calm down." His voic
was strained. "Now tell me, Gabriél. I'm listening. I wa
to hear what you have to say. What's the problem?"

"The problem is you're fucking with me. You'r
fucking with my bank. You're going to blow everythin
I've worked so hard for. You're trying to kill my ban
and I won't let you."

"Nonsense, Gabriél. Kill your bank? Why? Wha
makes you think I'd do something crazy like that? Who'
been filling your head with crap like that? We're in bus
ness together, we need each other. Isn't that right?"

"I don't need your kind of business, Chuck. I'm n
going to let you ruin my bank."

"Nobody's asking you to. I've never heard suc
crazy nonsense. Who've you been talking to, Gabriél?"

"I've been looking at the papers, the audit."

"And what did you find? Tell me, did you find anything that told you I'm screwing things up?"

There was silence. "I want to see your inventory."

"Sure, Gabriél. You want to see it, I'll show it to you." Vardigan was getting smoother by the minute. "Now, tell me this, Gabriél, who's been spreading these tales out of school? You know me. I'm a former officer of the government, for Pete's sake. Why would I do anything like what you're saying? Whoever's telling you this crap—this kind of talk is bad for the business. Makes me look bad. It's slander, that's what it is. I want to know who's spreading these lies."

Chuck Vardigan was so persuasive, I held my breath and waited for Gabriél to say my name. But he didn't. Instead he demanded to see the inventory again.

"I've got to see it, Chuck. Now."

"Sure, Gabriél. Of course."

The bodyguard pulled up in the Lincoln. Vardigan opened the door and motioned for Gabriél to get inside. "Let's go."

"I'll drive myself," Gabriél said.

The three vehicles formed a sort of caravan. I was positive Gabriél would die the instant he set foot inside the warehouse, but there was no way to warn him without alerting Vardigan. There was no way to alert the cops or Blackie, either. For this one I was on my own.

71

EXCEPT for Lucifer, the dog, the warehouse yard was deserted. And the building was locked up tight. Gabriél and Vardigan circled to the front of the building, parked, and got out. I slowed the van and pulled into the alley in back of the complex, then parked near the V-shaped hole I'd cut into the wire the other night.

As I listened to their hollow-sounding footsteps and Vardigan's soothing patter through my headphones, I sized up my options. The work I'd done on the burglar alarm the other night was to my benefit if I wanted to sneak inside. Odds were nobody'd noticed the bypass I'd installed and left in the system. The way I'd set it up, everything seemed to be on and in working order, but in fact anybody could break into any window or door in the back without triggering the alarm. If I could make it past the dog, I had an easy entry.

Then there were the receiver and the recorder. They weren't small enough to be portable, so if I went inside, I'd have to leave them behind in the van. I wouldn't know what they were talking about. I'd be on my own, going in blind.

What would I do once I got inside? I didn't have a gun. I needed to do something, though. I couldn't just let them murder Gabriél.

I'll figure that out when I get there, I said to myself, then tucked my lock picks into my pocket, loaded a fresh cassette into the recorder, grabbed the Princess-scented sweater off the floor, and headed for the fence.

"Lucifer," I called out softly. "Oh, Luuciferrr."

He came bounding toward the fence and choked off the beginnings of a roar as soon as the romantic scent of my sweater hit his slathering black nose. I made a mental note to toss the sweater out when I was done—no way could I ever get the Princess smell out. I tied the sweater up high on the fence so Lucifer could get some exercise while trying to get a noseful of his girlfriend's perfume. If the sweater wasn't enough to keep him busy while I ran across the lot, at least he'd be tired.

I circled the fence until I reached the cut V, pulled the wire back, and stepped inside. There were a million ways I could get caught—the dog, somebody seeing me from the window inside, or just plain walking into the warehouse and running into them.

"Don't think about that," I whispered to myself, and took off across the back lot to the door.

It was locked, but the dog was still busy bouncing up and down next to the fence, so I had time to work the keyhole. The door squeaked when I opened it. I slipped inside and closed it behind me.

Inside I held my breath and listened. When I'd left the van, they were in the front office. Vardigan had just offered Gabriél a drink, and Gabriél had refused. "The inventory, Chuck. I want you to show me the inventory."

I guess Vardigan was still stalling, because I didn't hear a sound inside the warehouse. Then suddenly a soft whirring sound hit my ears. The robot! Damn! I'd forgotten all about it.

I looked around for metal to hide behind, zeroed in on the lockers housing the burglar-alarm central unit behind the desk, and hopped behind them.

The whirring got louder, then receded. Then I

heard a door open, and the sound of footsteps echo
loudly through the massive building.

"Didn't you turn that thing off?" Vardigan asked

A gruff voice said, "It's on standby."

"Forget standby. Shut the whole thing down. I ca
stand the noise."

A door opened and closed, and Vardigan started
his jovial-sounding patter with Gabriél again. He ke
pressing to know who was spreading the "lies" abo
Donziger, and Gabriél kept avoiding the question a
insisting on seeing the inventory. Then suddenly t
whirring stopped. The door opened and closed aga
Footsteps followed.

"It's off, boss."

"Come with me, Gabriél." More footsteps. "A
right, pick a box, Gabriél. Any box you want . . . Th
one. Okay. Duke, get down that box."

Footsteps again, then the high whine and clicks
the forklift engine kicking into gear. Vardigan raised
voice over the humming of the machine. "That on
Duke. No, higher. Yeah. That's the one, right, Gabrié
Bring the whole stack down, Duke."

"All five?"

"Right. Go for it."

I crept out from behind the lockers and starte
toward their voices. So far they hadn't done anythi
illegal. But I couldn't wait until they'd killed Gabriél ju
to make a case. If it was save Gabriél or make a case,
had to save Gabriél.

Before I reached the edge of the row where th
stood, I heard the door open, then footsteps. Gabri
cried out.

"Juana! Juana, my God." His voice turned mea
"I'll kill you if you hurt her. I swear to you."

Vardigan laughed. "Don't worry. I won't—as long
you listen."

In the silence I could make out heavy breathing—probably Gabriél—and the sound of rustling papers.

"Are you all right, Juana? Have they hurt you?"

I didn't hear an answer, but I hoped she was nodding. Chuck Vardigan spoke again.

"See this? If you sign this, I'll let her go."

"What is it?"

"Her ticket out of here."

A long silence. Then Gabriél said, "You can't get away with this. You'll never get away with it. This loan has to be—"

"What? Approved? That's why you're signing it, buddy boy. Can't get much higher than the CEO, huh? Go ahead. Sign it. Do it for your wife." He chuckled like he thought he'd said something clever.

"It won't work, Chuck."

"Sure it will. By the time anybody notices we got approval before the audit was in, we'll have the cash in our own little numbered account and we'll be long gone."

"But why?"

Chuck laughed again. "You wouldn't understand, Gabriél. You give away all the money you make like it's candy. You pull down a ton of cash, but you don't even spend it on yourself or your family. Instead you give it away to a bunch of indigent kids looking for a handout. Try working twenty years as a GS-Eleven. Try pulling down chump change for twenty years. Try getting used to the idea of four- or five-hundred-dollar annual raises while you watch guys embezzle hundreds of thousands of dollars and get away with it."

"But your wife is wealthy. She can provide—"

"That's *HER* money!" he shouted. "Ever have to ask your wife for money? Try it sometime. See how much of a man it makes you feel. How would you like to be living in a house your wife's family paid for, driving a car

she bought and paid for. Think about it, Gabriél, an
maybe you'll get a clue what this is all about."

"I'm not signing this."

"Sure you are, Duke."

"Umph!"

"That one's for you. The next one goes to you
wife."

"Let her go," Gabriél moaned.

"Sign."

"Let her go first."

"Sign the goddamn thing, or you can watch her di
inch by inch. What's it going to be?"

"Juana . . . You promise you'll release her if
sign?"

"That's what I said."

"I will take you at your word."

Juana hadn't made a sound. I wondered if she wa
too hurt or drugged to speak. Slowly I tiptoed to th
edge of the row the voices were coming from. Then
stuck my head out to see.

There was a small crowd gathered on the other sid
of the loaded-up forklift. Vardigan, three of the thugs I'
seen at my place, Gabriél, and Juana. Most of them ha
their backs to me, but Juana and her keeper were facin
me. Juana wasn't even tied up or gagged or anything.
guess they figured they didn't need to restrain a woman

Gabriél bowed his head.

"Are you going to sign?" Vardigan demanded.

Gabriél's answer was barely audible. "Yes," he whis
pered.

I watched him take the pen from Chuck and scrib
ble something on a couple of sheets of paper.

"Atta boy, Gabriél. Attaboy!"

As Chuck took the papers from him, Gabrié
slugged him in the jaw. The two thugs jumped Gabrié
and pummeled him with his fists. Juana ran to Chuck
who was splayed upright against a wall of boxes.

"Are you all right, Chuck?" She reached out and
ran her hand lovingly along his cheek. Chuck ignored
her, watching instead the goons beating Gabriél, who by
now was writhing on the cement floor.

"That's enough," Chuck finally said. The goons
backed off. Gabriél pulled his battered head up and
stared. Juana had her arm around Chuck.

"Juana, why are you—Juana, what . . . ? I don't
understand."

Chuck glanced down at Juana, who was clinging to
his side, then turned to Gabriél and laughed. Gabriél
struggled to get to his feet, but after making it halfway
up, dropped to the floor with a grunt.

Juana said, "If you're going to kill him, do it now.
Don't make him suffer."

"What do you care?" Chuck asked. "You with me or
not?"

"Of course, Chuck. But after all, he is my husband."

"You don't see me pleading over Felicia, do you? I
tuck her in that drunk farm, didn't I? Shit, don't give me
that 'don't let him suffer' routine. You're either with me
or you're not."

Juana shuddered. "Chuck, I love you. You know
that."

"And you love the two million dollars I've got more,
don't you?"

"That's not true. I love you for yourself. You know
that. We met before you had any idea about the bank."

"I was short-selling then. You couldn't exactly say I
was poor then. A few hundred thousand a hit. Trading
on my own cases so nobody would know. Monitoring
myself. Ha-ha-ha. What a gag!" He sobered instantly. "I
suffered then. Why shouldn't this guy suffer now?"

"But—"

"Shut up. You want him to end up like Rob Yost,
going accidentally over the coast highway? Or like Johnson, eaten alive by lions?" He chuckled. "Those were

clever accidents, wouldn't you say? They were Mary
ideas, and I put them into action. So, Juana, it's up t
you. What do you think we ought to do with your soo
to-be-deceased husband? Make it clever, darling."

Juana stared at Chuck as if she'd seen a real mon
ster for the first time. "I don't want him to suffer."

Chuck's hand flew out and slapped her chee
knocking her back a couple of steps. Clutching her red
dened cheek with both hands, she started to weep.

"How are we going to do him, Juana? You'd bette
make it good, or I'll be sorry you talked me into killin
Mary. Her ideas were always so clever. Come on, Juan
how are we going to do this?"

Just then the dog barked in the back lot. Chuc
cocked his head to one side, then grinned maliciously
"How about it, Gabriél? You like dogs? No? That's un
fortunate, because I don't think Lucifer will try to get o
your good side. No, no, no. That's too obvious. Come
Juana, think. What are some of your soon-to-be late hus
band's hobbies. Surely we can tie one of them into this.'

Juana was staring at Gabriél, who was in turn star
ing at her. "Juana," he whispered. "Help me, Juana."

Chuck closed the distance to Gabriél and kicke
him fiercely in the stomach. "SHUT UP," he screamed
"Don't you talk to her."

A tear dripped slowly down Juana's cheek. Sh
turned away.

"Juana! Come on, use your imagination. What's h
like to do?"

"Hike," she said in a bare whisper.

"What?"

"He likes to hike in the hills of Marin."

Chuck laughed. "That's perfect. Get the van
Duke."

I crept slowly back to the lockers that housed th
burglar alarm. Trying not to make any noise that woul
bring them down on me, I pulled the locker door open

then worked the screws loose from the control unit's front. My shunt was still in place. All I had to do was disconnect it, and the alarm would send a message to the off-site security guards. I reached up and pulled one alligator clip off. That should do it.

I closed the locker without bothering to replace the front of the alarm box. *Hurry.* When I crept back to the end of the row where they'd been, they were gone. Shit. They were going to get away.

"Chuck," I shouted without even thinking. "Chuck!"

I heard a scrambling up ahead near the office doors. I crouched down, trying to make myself invisible.

"Who is it? Who's there?"

"Let him go, Chuck. The killing's got to stop. You can't kill everybody."

"Ronnie? Is that you, Ronnie?"

"I have everything you've just said on tape. There's no way you can get out of it this time."

He didn't answer.

"Chuck. You've got to stop."

I crouched back behind the row of boxes and listened. They were whispering fiercely. I stuck my head out from behind the row of boxes and heard a loud pop. *Shit.* They had guns. I dropped and rolled along the floor to the next row of boxes, then crouched and listened.

"The police are on their way," I shouted. "You don't have a chance. Give up."

Another shot rang out in response. A woman screamed. "You shot him! You shot Gabriél. My God. Let's go, Chuck. Let's just leave right now. Before the police come. Hurry."

"She's bluffing," Chuck said, then raised his voice. "Aren't you, Ronnie? Nobody's coming to save you. And for every minute you don't come forward, I'm going to plug another hole in your friend here."

"Don't do it, Chuck. Give yourself up."

Another shot. Another scream.

I ran for the back door and opened it, then whistled for the dog. He was lying on the ground at a spot just beneath the Princess-scented sweater, exhausted, I guess, from bouncing up and down for the last half hour. But seeing me, all his frustrated hormones made him crazy all over again. He charged the open door.

I slipped behind it and crawled up on top of the lockers.

Then I heard Chuck. His timing was perfect. His voice rang out just as Lucifer hit the threshold. "Fifteen seconds for bullet number three, Ronnie. It's up to you."

The dog didn't even pause at the door; he just kept right on going straight toward Chuck's voice.

"Holy Jesus! It's Lucifer. Run! *Run!*" I heard the clank of metal hitting the concrete floor, then clambering footsteps that stopped suddenly.

I prayed that the snarling that followed wasn't Lucifer making a meal out of Gabriél.

A head peered in through the back door. "They're over there," I shouted to the security guard. "The dog's got them."

He shot off down the aisle toward Lucifer's snarling and snapping. A second guard popped his head inside. His pimply face was contorted with fear, but his pistol was drawn and he was pointing it at me.

"All right, miss. Come down from there. Take it real slow and keep your hands out where I can see them."

When my feet hit solid ground, I wanted to kiss him, but I was afraid he'd shoot me if I tried.

72

"**Y**OU'RE LUCKY you're not dead," Post said, snapping off the tape player and fixing me with a scowl.

"Is it enough to convict?"

"It's not admissible. But we've got Juana Juarez. Once he hears what she's spilled, he'll sing and try to cut a deal. You can bet money on that."

I slouched deeper into the hard wooden chair across from Post's desk and wondered why I always felt so crummy when I finished a case. Post's eyes bored into me, solid and piercing.

"Why so glum, Ventana? You got your bust."

"I was thinking of the murder victims," I said. "It just seems so pointless. Five people murdered for money."

"Stupid, isn't it? But, hey, they were greedy too. It's not like they were innocent victims minding their own business. They got looped in with this guy because he promised them some fast bucks."

"What about the prostitute?"

"The only reason she bought it was because Solis wanted out. She figured if she faked her own death and framed Hanover, Vardigan would let her off and she could marry Felix Ashton." Post shrugged. "The hooker just happened to be in the wrong place at the wrong time."

I rose. "I've got to go, Post. I want to catch Gabriél before visiting hours are over."

"You dating this guy?"

"He's a friend, Post. He's just found out his wife was shafting him fifteen different ways and was willing to kill him. He's got two bullet holes in his body, and right now he feels pretty crummy."

"So *you're* going to cheer him up?"

"I'm going to keep him company, Post."

Once I got to the hospital, though, Gabriél didn't look like he needed more company. He was surrounded by kids and parents and baskets of flowers and fruit. His room was packed, and he seemed in the best of spirits. I stayed in the background until the nurse came in to clear everybody out.

"Nurse," Gabriél said. "Please, may I have a word with this young lady here?"

The nurse nodded and shepherded the rest of the crowd out the door.

"Only a minute," she cautioned, then closed the door behind her.

Gabriél's face was transformed as soon as the room emptied. He looked suddenly tired and sad and old. He beckoned me toward him and took my hand.

"Thank you, Ronnie. I owe you my life."

I squeezed his hand. "I owe *you* an apology."

He frowned. "Nonsense. You were justified. I did it once. You had no way of knowing I might not do it again."

"I did, Gabriél. And I'm sorry."

"I was wondering, Ronnie, if you . . . Can you tell me, how is Juana?"

"She's in custody, Gabriél. She's confessed to the whole scheme and wants to testify against Chuck."

He nodded. "Does she have a lawyer?"

"I don't know."

"I want to pay for her lawyer, Ronnie. Will you make the arrangements? Find her a good one. Don't tell her, though. Don't tell her I . . . don't say it's from me."

He smiled weakly, then closed his eyes. "Forgive me, Ronnie. I think I'm falling asleep."

His grip on my hand relaxed just as the nurse poked her head inside the door.

"Time to go," she whispered, then opened the door wider to let me pass.

73

THE BUZZER SOUNDED, so I stuck my head out my apartment door and looked downstairs to see who it was. The figure was lithe and male and well dressed. I peered closer and heard myself groan. Bink.

"Go away!" I shouted.

He cupped his hands against the glass and peered up the stairs. When he saw me, he pounded on the door. "Open up, Ronnie. Open up! I've got to talk to you."

I sighed, reached inside, and buzzed him in.

"Man, oh, man, Ronnie. I'm glad you're home," he said, hurrying up the stairs. "We've gotta do something before he gets away with this. He's pulling the rug right out from under me."

The floor behind Mrs. Parducci's door squeaked. Whatever Bink's problem was, I didn't need her grilling me about it later.

I sighed again. "Come on in, Bink."

He followed me inside and started pacing the tiny open area of the apartment. "He's screwing us over, Ronnie. You've gotta—"

"Slow down, Bink." I glanced nervously toward the window. "Should I be looking out there? Did anybody follow you?"

"Huh?" He looked puzzled, then it suddenly dawned on him. "No, no. It's nothing like before."

"Okay, then what are you talking about?"

"That son of a bitch husband of yours—"

"Ex, Bink. He's my ex. What did Mitchell do?"

"He hasn't told you, has he? That's 'cause he's too chicken to face you. That tells you what kind of man he is."

"If you're angry with Mitch, that's between the two of you. It's got nothing to do with me."

"Sure it does. That prick—that lousy son of a bitch stole my fiancée."

"Carolina?"

"Who else was I getting engaged to?"

"Carolina and Mitch?"

"Yeah. Can you believe it? She took me out to breakfast this morning—a Dear John breakfast—and told me she's going to Tahiti next week with Mitchell—on their honeymoon."

I reached for the chair behind me and sort of fell into it. "Their honeymoon? They're married?"

"Not yet. That's why I'm here. We gotta do something, Ronnie. You gotta talk him out of it."

Mitch married? To somebody else? To Carolina Pogue? I looked up at Bink, who'd stopped in front of me, his lips tight, his expression grim. *Mitch was getting married.* Somehow a weight lifted somewhere inside me. And somewhere else a great sadness welled up. I wasn't sure what I felt. Mitch and Carolina.

"You gotta talk to him, Ronnie."

"What do you want me to say, Bink: 'I don't want to be married to you, Mitch, but I don't want you married to anybody else'?"

Bink waved his arms impatiently. "Tell him—tell him he can't steal my girlfriend."

"He didn't steal her, Bink. She's not a property to be stolen—she's a human being. They're both adults. And believe it or not, so are we."

Bink's jaw dropped. "You're going to let them do this to us?"

"Come off it, Bink. You were planning to bilk her out of her inheritance. You're in love with her money, not her."

"And Mitch is?"

I paused. "I guess so."

"But he—"

My doorbell sounded again. I reached over and buzzed the downstairs door open. A second later there was a knock on my door and Mitch walked in. He took one look at Bink, then turned to me.

"I guess you heard," he said solemnly, trying to keep the excitement out of his voice until he could gauge my reaction.

I nodded, surprised at the tightness in my throat. He looked so happy. Had he looked this happy when we'd decided to marry?

"I wanted to be the one to tell you," he said. "Are you going to be all right?"

"All right? Sure." I smiled. "I hope you and Carolina have a wonderful life together."

"If you can sleep at night." Bink came out of his sulk in the corner long enough to snort his contempt. Mitch turned to him.

"I'm sorry, Binkman. It was just one of those things. It just happened. Part of me is sick over it. I—we—never intended—"

"You Judas!" Bink snarled, then charged for the door.

"Bink! Bink, wait!" Mitch cried, but Bink marched out and slammed the door behind him.

We both stared at the closed door for a full minute, then Mitch swung around to face me, the hurt shining in his eyes.

"He'll get over it, Mitch. Next time he needs something from you, he'll forget all about this. You'll see."

"I tried to talk her out of breaking it off with him, but Carolina told me she could never marry Bink. We talked about it a long time. She wanted to see him through these hard times, but she realized he wasn't for her."

I looked away and nodded.

"Ron? Are you going to be all right? I mean, *really*?"

I rose and put my hand on his shoulder. The shoulder I'd caressed so many times, the same shoulder I'd cried on when my parents died, the one I'd taken for granted and thought would always be there. "I'm fine, Mitch. Really. Now, go! Go spend time with your bride. Make your plans."

"Thanks, Ron." He kissed my cheek, beamed a thousand-watt smile at me, then vanished out the door.

"Congratulations," I said to the empty room around me. Then I dropped onto the sofa, put my head in my hands, and cried.

Gloria White's debut novel, *Murder on the Run*, which was nominated for an Anthony Award, introduced readers to private investigator Ronnie Ventana. Gloria White lives in San Francisco.

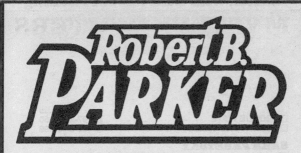

"The toughest, funniest, wisest private-eye in the field."*

☐ A CATSKILL EAGLE	11132-3	$4.99
☐ CEREMONY	10993-0	$4.99
☐ CRIMSON JOY	20343-0	$4.99
☐ EARLY AUTUMN	21387-8	$2.99
☐ GOD SAVE THE CHILD	12899-4	$4.99
☐ THE GODWULF MANUSCRIPT	12961-3	$4.99
☐ THE JUDAS GOAT	14196-6	$4.99
☐ LOOKING FOR RACHEL WALLACE	15316-6	$4.99
☐ LOVE AND GLORY	14629-1	$4.95
☐ MORTAL STAKES	15758-7	$4.99
☐ PROMISED LAND	17197-0	$4.99
☐ A SAVAGE PLACE	18095-3	$4.99
☐ TAMING A SEAHORSE	18841-5	$4.99
☐ VALEDICTION	19246-3	$4.99
☐ THE WIDENING GYRE	19535-7	$4.99
☐ WILDERNESS	19328-1	$4.99

*The Houston Post

At your local bookstore or use this handy page for ordering:

**DELL READERS SERVICE, DEPT. DRP
2451 S. Wolf Rd., Des Plaines, IL. 60018**

Please send me the above title(s). I am enclosing $_____.
(Please add $2.50 per order to cover shipping and handling.) Send
check or money order—no cash or C.O.D.s please.

Ms./Mrs./Mr._____

Address _____

City/State _____ Zip _____

DRP-3/93

Prices and availability subject to change without notice. Please allow four to six
weeks for delivery.